"ANY FINAL WORDS FOR POSTERITY?"
OSBORNE ASKS . . .

I nod.

"As a matter of fact . . . yeah. I got two."

"Only two?" He smiles. "Go on."

"Drop dead," I say, at the same time yanking on my right arm, which is when the wrist restraint rips free of the table.

I pop my claws and drive them into Osborne's chest.

They go in an inch and stop. The bastard's wearing Kevlar.

The impact is jarring. The pain is instant and excruciating—my nerves scream. I scream.

I struck hard enough to send Osborne flying across the room. He smashes into one of the soldiers. Both of them land on the ground.

I cut the restraint on my left wrist with the claws. I slash at the one on my right ankle and cut that, too.

I look up. Osborne's back on his feet. He charges, driving one of the machines right into me, which sends me and the bed and every machine in the room into a heap on the floor together. I get to my feet, dragging the bed with me, just in time to catch Osborne's fist across my jaw. I taste blood; I stagger. He kicks me in the gut; I go flying back and land on the floor, looking up.

He draws a gun and fires.

978.

~~Fivepointe~~
Highpointe
Circle,
Langhorne
PA 19047

- Fitness Quest -
Leg magic -

WOLVERINE®

THE NATURE OF THE BEAST

a novel by
Dave Stern

based on the
Marvel Comic Book

POCKET STAR BOOKS

NEW YORK   LONDON   TORONTO   SYDNEY

Pocket Star Books
A Division of Simon & Schuster, Inc.
1230 Avenue of the Americas
New York, NY 10020

This book is a work of fiction. Names, characters, places, and incidents are products of the author's imagination or are used fictitiously. Any resemblance to actual events or locales or persons, living or dead, is entirely coincidental.

First Pocket Star Books paperback edition May 2008

POCKET STAR BOOKS and colophon are registered trademarks of Simon & Schuster, Inc.

For information about special discounts for bulk purchases, please contact Simon & Schuster Special Sales at 1-800-456-6798 or business@simonandschuster.com

Cover by Bill Sienkiewicz

Manufactured in the United States of America

10 9 8 7 6 5 4 3 2 1

ISBN-13: 978-1-4165-1077-2
ISBN-10:   1-4165-1077-X

Author's Note

This novel takes place in the gap between Wolverine (Second Series) #76 and #77. Logan's body has been stripped of adamantium; his claws and skeleton are the bone he was born with. His mutant healing power has deserted him.

He is as God made him.

As close to human—and as spiritually lost—as he has ever been . . .

1

BLOOD ON THE ROCK SCRAMBLE AT THE BASE OF
the mountain, blood on the trail leading up.

Fresh blood, bright red blood. I'm two steps out
from behind a boulder at the base of the mountain
when I see it. I react instinctively, slip back behind
cover, and watch. And wait.

And frown—should've smelled that blood long before I saw it. More proof, if I needed it; my senses ain't
what they used to be. I ain't what I used to be. Cheery
thought. I set it aside, circle around the scramble so
that I'm upwind, and move closer.

Fifty feet away, I get my first whiff—blood, and the
body to go with it. A second later, I see the corpse,
obscured by the brush. A desert bighorn, a couple of
huge bites missing out of its hindquarters.

I freeze, wait a couple of minutes. Nothing. No
sound, no scent. Whatever killed the sheep is long

2 Dave Stern

gone. I move in to get a closer look at the kill, and that's when I notice something else is gone, too.

The sheep's head.

I find that ten feet away from the body, bit clean through at the neck. The bighorn—it's a ram, a big one, a couple hundred pounds, antlers four feet across—has a look of resignation on its face. Looks like a deer trapped in the headlights, seeing death coming straight at it and knowing there's nothing to be done.

No need to wonder what killed it; I find the evidence right next to the body. Animal tracks, cougar tracks. There's a good number of the big cats scattered throughout the DNR. I ran into one the first day I got here, a female stalking two bighorns, a mother and her lamb. The female saw me coming, growled, tried to warn me off her prey.

I growled back and stared her down. She slunk off into the forest, and disappeared.

That cat was maybe six feet long, a hundred eighty pounds. The one that made these tracks was a helluva lot bigger. A helluva lot more massive. Three hundred pounds, easy, judging from the depth of the spoor I'm looking at. A male, judging from the size of the pad. Maybe as much as eight, nine feet long.

I straighten up and frown.

The cougar that weighs three hundred pounds ain't been born yet.

The cougar that can take a sheep's head off with a single bite ain't been born yet, either.

Something strange going on here.

I feel a little tingle in the base of my spine: excitement. I ain't felt that in a while. I look toward the top of the mountain. The blood leads that way.

My feet are heading in that direction almost before I can stop them.

And then I remember.

I came here to get away from strange. To get away from everything that might remind me of the unusual—the uncanny, you might say—and the life I used to lead. Before that life was ripped away from me.

Three-hundred-pound cougars that can rip off a sheep's head in a single bite? I want no part of them.

I move off the trail, fade back into the pines.

Night finds me back at my campsite.

It's about five miles due north of where I found the dead sheep, high up in the rocks, a bedroll tucked under a boulder. I'm eating jackrabbit again; or I will be, once it gets dark, and I can risk a fire. The DNR rangers don't know I'm here, and that's the way I want to keep it. I want my privacy. I want my space.

I want to figure out what comes next.

I've been here a couple of weeks now. Left my bike in the brush outside the refuge, at the base of Tickapoo Mountain; left most of my possessions with it. Took a knife and a canteen and started hiking.

I've been here since, sometimes in the woods, sometimes in one of the mountain caves. Living off the land, keeping out of sight. This part of the DNR borders on Nellis Air Force Base. There's more traffic than you'd expect around. Some military, some rangers, some other campers as well. At a guess, I've seen a couple dozen people since I've been here.

Nobody's seen me. Nobody will, unless I want them to.

I skin the rabbit and grab up some brush to make a fire. Could've taken a few high-tech gadgets from the mansion, I guess, make this part a little easier, but that wouldn't be getting away from everything then, would it?

The sun goes down; reds and oranges fill the sky, casting shadows on the slopes around me, on the desert below. The colors remind me of Jeannie, a little bit. This part of the refuge reminds me of somethin' else, too: Canada. The wide-open spaces, the stark landscape . . . the past. People I've grown apart from, people I've let slide away from my life. People who lived, people who died.

The sun goes down; the stars come out. Eventually, I light the fire, and I eat.

When I'm done with that, I spread out the bedroll and lie down.

The sky is pitch-black, except for a faint glow near the horizon, way to the south. Las Vegas. The city's only about forty miles from here. Forty miles, and a world away. I'm in the middle of the biggest wildlife refuge on the continent, the DNR—Desert National

Refuge. A million or so acres of just about every kind of climate you could imagine, from pine forest to desert and everything in between, all wilderness, with just a bare handful of paved roads. One of the few places in the country that ain't choked with ATVs and RVs and people whose idea of roughing it is no electric toothbrushes.

It's a place of solitude, like I said. Which suits me fine at the moment.

I got some heavy thinking to do.

I lie back, focus on the stars again, and the night sky.

One minute I'm looking up at the Milky Way, and the next . . .

I'm right in the middle of it.

I'm flying. In a Blackbird SR-71, suited up for EVA, headed toward a space station. Flying off to save the world again, which back in the day was my job.

I'm dreaming, of course. Dreaming like I have every night for the last two weeks.

Dreaming of the day I died.

My name's Logan, by the way. Just one word. First, last, categorize it however you like; tell you the truth, I'm not sure which it is. I got a problem with my memory, you see: I don't have one. At least, not one that dates back to when I was a kid. Oh, I flash on images sometimes—a man, a woman, a girl with red hair—but I can't make heads or tails of them.

I got the government to thank for that.

The U.S. government, and what they did to me in pursuit of what you might call the perfect weapon. Who they thought might be yours truly—the old Canucklehead right here, talking to you.

My first coherent memories are from a couple dozen years ago, after I escaped from Uncle Sam's tender clutches and went north of the border, where I ended up working with the Canadians for a while. A special branch of the Canadian government, set up by a scientist named Jimmy Hudson, for special people like me, and Veronique Campion, and J. C. Perrault, and Stephen St. George. Special, as in blessed—cursed, if you like—with extraordinary powers. Something in our genetic makeup, our DNA. Something that made us a little more than human. Not *Homo sapiens. Homo superior.* Mutant.

After a while up north, I returned to the good old U.S. and joined up with another team of mutants. That's where the saving-the-world part of my life comes in.

In the dream—the dream where I'm in that space station, suited up for EVA, walkin' straight into the fight that's going to end with me dyin'—I'm surrounded by that other team, those other mutants. Along with us on the trip is our leader, a guy named Charles Xavier, Professor Xavier—who just happens to have the ability to read, and control, people's minds. A mutant himself, Xavier owns the mansion we operate out of; we live there, too. It's a refuge, not just for us but for a whole group of young mutants he's brought there, kids Xavier's taught how to cope with their powers, taught how to cope with the fearful, hostile, angry world that Earth can sometimes be. Xavier himself never gets angry, though; he's always calm, always trying to talk to the people—or the things—attacking us, always preaching negotiation, understanding.

Always, that is, except for this time. Except for this trip in the Blackbird, in my dream, which really isn't a dream at all but me reliving the past, reliving what happened two weeks back. In this dream, Xavier's jaw is set. So is his mind.

We're heading toward a space station parked around Earth called Avalon. We're heading for a showdown, and Xavier's already told us it's going to be kill or be killed.

As usual, he turns out to be right.

The part of the dream where I die—where who I am is literally ripped away from me, ripped out of me—wakes me up, like always. I lie in the bedroll, stunned, feeling the pain, the shock, all over again, seeing my friends' faces hovering above me, hearing them whisper to each other ("Is he all right?" "Is he goin' to live?") as if I'm not right there listening to every word they're saying.

After a while, the voices—and the pain—fade away.

I sense the sky around me beginning to lighten. A few birds chirp; branches rustle in the wind.

Something's watching me.

I can feel it—a presence, an intelligence nearby.

I get to my feet it in a slow, natural, Gosh-ain't-I-tired kind of way, as if I haven't got a care in the world. I do the necessaries, I stretch my muscles, I slip on my boots.

I set off down the mountain. A few hundred feet on, I make my move, ducking back into the scrub. I listen for the sounds of someone following me. I don't hear them. I double back toward my hideout, as close to silent as I can get.

I reconnoiter in a long, careful ellipse, circling the entire camp. I find nothing. No trace of anyone or anything. I do a second pass, a wider circle. Still nothing.

I'm about to head back to my bedroll and some breakfast when I see it. A lonely clump of grass in a patch of dirt, the blades splayed almost flat in all directions. It doesn't look natural to me. I move in closer and see my hunch is right. Someone stepped down hard on the grass, recently. Tromped on it, left the vaguest outlines of a print. I kneel down next to it.

It's not a human print.

It's animal.

It belongs, I realize, to the three-hundred-pound cougar from yesterday.

Huh.

Now that's interesting.

There's a boulder ten feet past the track. I climb to the top of it and look down.

And there, a couple dozen feet down the mountain, within easy jumping distance, is my bedroll.

I frown.

The cat could have reached me with a single leap across those rocks. It could've roared, and attacked, and I would've been pretty close to defenseless. For a few seconds, anyway. I ain't necessarily saying what would've happened after that, but still . . .

The thing had a good shot at making a meal out of me. Instead, it just sat there, starin'. Why? It didn't make any sense.

That little tingle I'd felt yesterday was back again. Something strange was going on.

Like I said, I wasn't in the mood to go chasin' after the uncanny. But now that the uncanny seemed to be chasin' after me . . .

Well, least I could do was figure out why.

I head back down to where the sheep was killed yesterday. There's maggots on the corpse already; it's a mess, picked down to the bone in some spots. But my concern ain't the sheep; it's the cougar's tracks. I follow them up the trail a little bit, goin' from scrub to scramble to rock. Big stride on the animal—huge stride. It went full-tilt down the mountain, full-tilt back up. Made the kill, took a couple bites, and ran like hell. Why? Somethin' must've spooked it, but what could spook a cat that big?

I'm tryin' to puzzle it out when I hear branches cracklin' behind me, the sound of pebbles bein' kicked on dirt.

Somebody's comin'; I decide to stick around and see who.

A few seconds later, a guy comes walkin' down from the rocks, headin' toward me. Big guy. Biceps like bowlin' balls stickin' out from his shirt, a camouflage number that goes with his camouflage shorts. He's wearin' mirror sunglasses and a park ranger hat. That's what he is, of course, a park ranger, comin' east out of the Corn Creek station, probably left his Jeep out on the old Mormon road, walked up this way. No surprise to see him here, but what is a surprise is the pistol on his belt, and the rifle he's carryin'.

Not standard park ranger equipment.

"Morning," I say.

He doesn't say anything. Behind those sunglasses, I know he's sizin' me up. Probably not too impressed with what he sees. My boots maybe get me to five-five. I got muscles, too, but not as many as he does. My guess, he goes 250 pounds. I used to get close to 200, but that was with metal added. Now, without . . . I guess I make 175.

None of which explains the vibe I'm gettin' off him. The way he's lookin' at me, the way his hand lingers

THE NATURE OF THE BEAST   11

near his gun as he gets closer. The smile he puts on his face—phony as a car salesman's handshake.

I don't get that he's glad to see me off that smile.

I get danger.

"Morning," he says. The name tag on his uniform reads "Osborne." He's got a goatee that isn't much more than stubble; it's reddish-blond, shading to gray. I put him somewhere between thirty-five and forty. I brace for a bunch of questions—who am I, what am I doin' in this part of the range, where's my campin' permit, that sort of thing. I brace myself for trouble, 'cause I don't have any of that.

Osborne surprises me.

He doesn't say a word.

He steps around me to take a look at the bighorn—what's left of it, anyway.

He gives it the once-over and then stands, a frown on his face. Before he can ask the question, I answer it.

"Head's right over there," I say, pointing.

He nods and goes to it. Comes back not ten seconds later.

"Helluva thing," he says. "What do you think happened?"

Innocent enough question; but the way he asks it, the way he's standing . . .

I get the feelin' my answer is very, very important.

I point to the tracks. "Take a look for yourself. The spoor there."

"Spoor," he repeats, sayin' the word as if he never

heard it before. Except spoor is just a fancy way of saying animal tracks. There ain't a park ranger alive who doesn't know that.

So maybe he's not a park ranger.

Handful of other things he could be: somebody who gets his jollies goin' around impersonating Ranger Rick, an incompetent who slipped through the cracks . . . Most likely thing he is, of course, is military. The DNR is huge, but it's just a drop in the bucket compared with the military sites around here. Nellis Air Force Base, Groom Lake Missile Range, Area 51—home to all sorts of military personnel and projects.

The question becomes, then, why is a military guy disguised as a park ranger?

"Got a dangerous animal here," he says. "Kill a sheep like that."

"Yeah," I say, restating the obvious.

"You better move along—move out of the area. While we handle the situation."

"I appreciate the warning. But I can handle myself."

The guy—Osborne—takes off his sunglasses then. Looks me up and down a second time, a closer look.

I've gone to more than a little trouble to disguise myself. Not that my face is the most recognizable on the planet, not that I expected to run into a lot of people out here in the middle of the desert, but still . . .

Better safe than sorry.

Hence the slicked-back hair, the full beard. Gives me the Elvis-meets-Jim Morrison look. Somethin' in Osborne's gaze makes me think he ain't buyin' it.

"I know you, don't I?" he asks.

"I don't think so."

"What's your name?"

I ain't in the habit of givin' that out to strangers, so I say the first thing that pops into my mind.

"Summers. Scott Summers."

It's a name out of my past, a guy I've known for what seems like forever. A guy with no sense of humor whatsoever; I'm making a joke.

Something flashes in Osborne's eyes for a split-second, gone almost before I can register it. But it was there, no doubt about it.

He recognizes the name.

He can't put me with it, though. Good thing.

"Well, Mister Summers, whether or not you can handle yourself, I'm asking you to move along. Could you do that for me, please, sir?"

It's phrased like a request, but it's spoken like an order. From a guy who's used to giving 'em.

I consider it, and the situation.

The three-hundred-pound cougar, the headless sheep. The "park ranger," and his command. The vibe I'm getting off Osborne, like if I don't move along voluntarily, he'll make me. Or try to, anyway.

Something strange indeed going on here.

I give him my best "yes sir" face and voice and smile, and then I do just like Park Ranger Osborne suggests.

I move on.

Fifteen minutes later, I double back.

Before long, I got Osborne—or his trail at least—in my sights. He, in turn, is following the cougar's trail up the mountain. Osborne's tracking skills are pretty mediocre—more proof that the ranger uniform he's wearing is a fake. He makes more noise than a semi goin' down a country road. He walks right past tracks a blind man could sniff out.

Thing is, for every trace he misses, the cat left a half-dozen more. It's almost as if the thing wanted to be followed.

The trail leads from the corpse up the mountain, into the rocks, into a cave, and then back out again, weaving in and out among the ledges and the dead-falls, up away from the desert floor and the scrub, into the higher elevations.

Farther up the mountain, I can see snow. Funny place, the DNR. Like I said, you got every kind of climate you can imagine here; you can go from desert to pine forest in an hour's hike.

Pine forest is exactly where I am now, in among a stand of bristlecones, clinging to the side of the mountain. These trees are just about the oldest, longest-living species on the planet. Thousands of years old, some of 'em. I put my hand on one as I walk past; the bark is rough and a little sticky with sap.

The tree smells like winter, like Canada. Like the past.

I take a deep breath and close my eyes.

Images flash through my mind: me and Jimmy Hudson and his wife Heather, ice-fishing out on Burns Lake; me and Jimmy in those stupid uniforms the bozos from Quebec made us wear, goin' toe-to-toe in those stupid drills they thought could teach us how to fight.

Me and Ronnie—Egret—dangling our feet off the dock, that last summer of her time with us. The summer before she lost her powers.

She shrank down right before my eyes after the accident; slid away from us, from me, and into her shell. I told her to keep her head up; who she was hadn't changed at all, just 'cause she couldn't do the things she used to. There was still a place for her with the team.

"You don't understand," she told me. "You can't understand."

I stop dead in my tracks then, in the middle of those Nevada bristlecones, and realize she was right. I had no idea what I was talking about then. None at all.

Now I do. Now I know exactly what she felt must have felt like, with everything that had defined who she was suddenly gone, stripped away. A third wheel, a useless appendage.

'Cause that's how I feel now.

That's why I'm out here in the middle of nowhere, instead of back in the mansion in Westchester, in the middle of it all. That's why . . .

I'm so busy thinking about Ronnie that I almost run right into Osborne.

He's coming back down the mountain at a jog. I hear him just in time; I duck behind a bristlecone as he passes. He's got the rifle slung over his shoulder and is talkin' into a cell phone as he goes. Barkin' into the phone is more like it; he's angry. I pick up enough of the conversation to figure out why.

He's lost the cougar's trail.

"—just ends, dammit. No. Back at the Ark," he says, and then he's past me, and gone.

I wait a minute before stepping out of hiding.

Ark, huh? Wonder if that's some kind of military acronym. Wonder where it is he's going. Wonder what the heck this is all about.

As I'm wondering, I'm walking, following the cougar's tracks up the mountain. Osborne's right; the trail just ends in the middle of a clearing. The tracks just stop, disappear entirely, which ain't possible—the cat had to go somewhere. I walk a few hundred yards in every direction. Nothing.

I backtrack, taking a closer look at the trail as I go. It takes me a minute before I realize somethin's botherin' me about the cougar's tracks. The cat's stride is too short—it either got very careful all of a sudden, or . . .

I pass a bare patch of ground, and the best impression yet of the cougar's pad. The heel—the back of the cougar's foot—is too deep, the front too shallow. Doesn't seem right to me. Why? What would cause that to happen?

I'm lookin' at that track when all at once, I get a crazy idea. An impossible idea, one I dismiss the second it pops into my head.

I straighten up. I realize I haven't eaten all day. I'm a little lightheaded; that's why my crazy notion of a second ago. I gotta get some food.

I turn back toward the trail . . .

And I get the exact same feeling I had this morning. The feeling I'm being watched.

I turn in a slow, careful circle. I look down the trail the way I came. I look into the forest. I look up the slope, toward the mountain face.

A pair of eyes is looking back.

Watchful eyes. Intelligent eyes. Hungry eyes. The animal they belong to is hidden in shadow.

I don't say a word, just meet its gaze. A minute passes.

Then it steps out from the darkness, from behind the rocks, and moves forward.

I blink once, twice, and then a third time. 'Cause I don't believe what I'm seeing.

It's the three-hundred-pound cougar; or, rather, it's the animal whose tracks made me think it was a three-hundred-pound cougar. But it ain't.

The animal I'm lookin' at is a tiger. A white tiger, to be precise. Native to the Asian continent, near extinct in the wild, the biggest and most dangerous of all the great cats. Ten feet long. Five hundred pounds, easy.

The question, of course, is what in the world is a white tiger doin' in the Desert National Refuge? My first thought is Siegfried and Roy—that the animal escaped from one of the shows down in Vegas and somehow made its way up into the hills.

Only that's not right, because you'd send Animal Control if a tiger got loose from a casino or someplace like that. You wouldn't send a guy like Osborne.

The tiger growls, low in its throat, then opens its mouth, showing fangs half a foot long.

It begins moving forward. Padding straight toward me.

I stand my ground.

Maybe my senses ain't what they used to be, but I think I can still tell when something means me harm. And this animal doesn't. Its measured stride is proof of that; so, though I know it sounds nuts, is the look in its eyes.

So is the fact that it stood over my campsite last night for a good chunk of time and didn't do anything.

"It's all right," I say, kneelin' down, tryin' to put eyes on a level. "Nobody here's gonna hurt you. I'm a friend—I'm friendly."

The words are less important than my tone, of course. Soothing. Calm.

I swear I can see the tiger relax as I'm talkin'. As if it can understand what I'm saying.

It stops five feet away from me and makes a low noise in its throat.

"Where you from, buddy?" I ask. "What are you doin' here?"

In response, it starts pawin' at the ground—over and over again with its right paw. With purpose. I don't get why, at first.

Then I look down. My eyes widen.

It's writing letters in the dirt. Four of them; they make a word.

HELP.

I read it out loud. I look the tiger in the eye.

It makes the same growling noise in its throat as before; only this time, I realize it's not really a growl.

The tiger is trying to talk.

2

I BLINK AGAIN. PINCH MYSELF. THE TIGER IS STILL there. The letters are still there: HELP.

Which is when I know that crazy idea I had about how its tracks could have possibly disappeared into thin air wasn't so crazy after all.

The cat was walking backward.

Retracing its own steps, walking slowly, carefully, back the way it had come. That was what made the back half of the pad deeper, the front shallower. That was why it had run pell-mell up the trail yesterday, not caring whether or not it would be easy to track. What it cared about was getting far enough ahead so that it could have time to double back and then the leave the trail altogether, jump up into a tree, or onto an overhang, and simply disappear.

A ten-foot white tiger that understands English and knows how to disguise its trail.

I'm beginning to understand why Osborne was so keen to find it. It's not a freak of nature.

It's man-made.

By somebody playin' God—playin' Dr. Frankenstein—yet again.

That sticks in my craw. That makes me feel for the tiger: I know what it's like to be the monster in the mad scientist's experiment.

"Help," I say again. "Okay. What kind of help do you need?"

I don't really expect an answer. But the animal responds to my words; it gets to its feet and takes a step toward me. It limps as it comes. There's something wrong with its right hind leg. The fur there is matted red with blood, fairly fresh blood.

It's injured.

I squat down and let it brush up against me. Its coat is rough and dirty and covered with leaves. Its ribs are showing through; the animal is not in good shape. It's hurting, and not just from the wound in its back leg. At a guess, it's starving as well.

That doesn't make sense; the size of this animal, the abundance of game in the refuge . . .

On the other hand, it jibes with what happened yesterday—the cat takin' two seconds on the kill and then running. Running from Osborne, probably—and others like him.

The tiger lies down and stretches out to give me a look at its wound. It's a cut, a slash, maybe from a fight of some kind? I lean in and take a look. The wound looks fresh; it looks clean. I bend down to take a closer look; there's a lump of some kind just under the skin. I press down lightly; the tiger whimpers.

"Easy," I say, and touch the lump again. It's hard as a rock—not a tumor, then. Some kind of bone spur? A knife blade that broke off in the wound?

As I'm thinking, the tiger touches a paw to its wound. It makes a quick slashing motion. Once, and then a second time, letting its claws come to rest right on top of the lump.

I look at the shape of the claw and the shape of the wound, and then I get it.

"You cut yourself," I say.

It makes a different growl then, one I could swear sounds like a yes.

"Why?"

In answer, it slashes at the lump again.

"This hurts?"

Different growl. A no.

"Then what?"

It puts its paw on the wound again and digs into the skin. Blood wells up. It digs again.

It's scratching at the lump.

I get it now.

"You want this thing out?"

Another yes growl.

"All right. We gotta get you someplace where—"

A loud roar—no—and then the tiger looks me in the eye. I nod and take a deep breath.

"All right, then. Hold on. This is going to hurt," I say, and hope the animal can understand me.

I take hold of the tiger's skin right near the wound and pull it back. What I'm doin' has to hurt like the dickens. Any other animal—hell, most people, for that matter—would react by striking out. The tiger doesn't.

It makes a kind of chuffing noise, a short exhalation of breath that starts the bones under my hands vibrating, and then turns its head away.

I bring mine closer, bending right down to the wound, to have a look at the lump underneath it.

Surprise number two of the morning.

It's something artificial, all right.

It's a black plastic disk, about the size and shape of a quarter.

I touch it, and the thing throbs under my finger. Pulsing with energy.

I know what it is right away.

You make something like a talking tiger in your lab, you're not gonna want to let it disappear on you. So you put a homing beacon on it, a tracking device. Usually on a collar, but in this case . . .

I realize right then the tiger knows about the homing beacon. Its behavior is evidence of that—the fact that it didn't want to stay in one place too long, that it ran back up the mountain after the kill. It might also explain why the animal was staying so close to the rocks. The stone might block the signal.

That explains Osborne showing up. It explains the animal's impatience as well. If it spends too much time out in the open, Osborne'll get a fix on it.

Which means we gotta do this quick.

"Right," I say, and then, from my belt, I very, very slowly pull out my hunting knife. The metal gleams in the sun. I show it to the tiger; I touch it to the wound.

Another growl. Which I take as "Go ahead—do what you gotta do."

I push down on the blade, and it slowly—slowly—enters the skin.

The next thirty or so seconds . . .

I'll spare you the details.

There was a lot of blood. There was a lot of noise; the tiger made the vast majority of it, but I did my fair share of cursing, too.

At the end of the process—call it an operation, if you like—the black disk is out and lying on the ground. The tiger is licking its wound, which is bleeding more than I would like. I rip off a strip of cloth from the sleeve of my shirt and make it a bandage.

Then I pick up the disk. It is surprisingly cool to the touch, considering where it came from; some kind of plastic composite, not metal.

I put it down on the ground and crush it under my boot. It makes a satisfying little crackle.

The tiger looks up and snarls; at the same instant, I become aware that the two of us are no longer alone in the little clearing.

Osborne is coming through the forest toward us. Half a dozen men are right behind him. All of them are holding weapons, wearing black jumpsuits with a little gold trim at the shoulders, black boots. Fashion-forward bad guys. Seven of them; no, make that eight. Nine.

Me and the tiger are surrounded.

Osborne steps forward, holding a pistol level with my gut. He's got a big smile on his face.

"Summers. I thought I told you to move along."

"Osborne." I step back and put a hand on the tiger. It growls again. I can feel its muscles bunching beneath the skin. I can sense its anger. "I got a better idea. How about you and your buddies be the ones to head on out of here?"

"Not likely." His men shift position, tighten up the circle around the tiger and myself. They're well trained; their movements are precise and definitive. Their hands don't move from their weapons; their eyes don't leave me for a second.

They're military; or at least, they got a military background.

"Whatever you plan on doin' here, I'd think twice about it," I say.

"Oh? And why's that?"

By way of an answer, I return his smile with one of my own.

"Because I wouldn't want to see you and yours get hurt."

"Don't worry about us. Whatever hurtin's goin' to be done around here"—he sends his eyes around the circle at his men—"we'll take care of it. Startin' with our property here. The tiger." His smile disappears then. "You're interfering with a U.S. government operation here."

"Is that so?"

"That's so. Now, step aside."

"I don't see any U.S. government uniforms here. I don't see any U.S. government insignia. I don't see any U.S. government authorization. Show me some of that, maybe I'll reconsider."

Osborne's expression doesn't change.

"Move," he says, motioning with the gun. "Last chance."

His weapon isn't the only one on me now. So are half a dozen others.

Decision time.

And really, there's very little thinking I need to do.

I don't like the twist of Osborne's mouth. I don't like the way he and his men snuck up on us. I don't think this is a U.S. government operation at all, and even if it is . . .

It clearly ain't somethin' on the books, it's black ops, and me and the black ops guys go back to the Weapon X days. No love lost there.

"I'm going to count to three," Osborne says. "And then—"

"Save your breath, buddy," I tell him. "You're gonna need it."

I draw my arms back, and then—for the first time in the two weeks since I left Westchester—I become the thing I was born to be.

The code name the Canadians gave me was Wolverine. Mostly because of the way I fought—no quarter asked, none given. Even in training exercises, I had a hard time toning it down.

But the name was also because of the claws.

Metal claws that popped out of the back of my hands, right along the knuckle line. And not just any kind of metal: adamantium. Hardest known substance on the planet. Slice through six-inch steel like a hot knife through butter. Hard enough to do a lot of other nasty things, too; use your imagination if you like.

Those claws made me pretty close to unstoppable—especially when you factored in my mutant healing power and a skeleton that was made of the same darned near invulnerable metal.

The metal was gone now, ripped away from me that day at Avalon.

The healing factor was gone, too.

What I had left were the weapons I was born with. Claws of bone—shorter than the metal ones, not as strong. Not as sharp.

But they'd do against Osborne and his guys.

That was my thinking, anyway.

I was bettin'—I was hoping—I was right.

Blood trickles down the back of my hands, where the claws punched through the skin. Pain shoots through my body. The price of my mutant "gift."

I take a step forward and snarl; my claws precede me.

Osborne's eyes widen at the sight of 'em—and then he smiles and shakes his head. "I knew you looked familiar."

"You'll have to tell me why," I say. "After I cut you up."

"Oh, I will," he says. "I'm sure we'll have plenty of time to talk."

I'm not waitin' for him to give the order to fire. Halfway through his reply, I'm in the air, headin' right for Osborne, claws out in front of me.

Problem is, his men aren't waitin' for orders, either.

I hear gunshots even as I crouch down to spring.

I hear the tiger snarl behind me.

Out of the corner of my eye, I see movement. Soldiers on my left movin' toward the tiger, those on the right jumpin' back. I see a flash of white.

Osborne's eyes widen, and he reaches for his gun.

As I slam into him, I feel something stick me in the leg. Once, twice.

He's quick, rolling out from underneath me even as I drive him down toward the ground. I get right back up and onto my feet again. That's the theory, anyway. In practice . . .

I barely make it onto my hands and knees. My head, all at once, is full of marshmallows.

I hear the tiger roar piteously. A boot catches me in the side, and down I go. A toe rolls me over.

Osborne is standing above me, and I can't move.

Why can't I move?

My leg.

I look down, expecting to see blood.

Instead, I see two darts, each the size of a Coke bottle, sticking into me. Tranquilizers.

My vision blurs. Osborne smiles.

"Nighty-night, Summers. Or should I say Wolverine?"

I snarl, and then everything goes black.

3

I DRIFT IN AND OUT OF SLEEP—MY BODY SWEATING, my mind in a million different places at once.

On Avalon, in one of the corridors, running as fast as I can. Running to meet my destiny, you could say, though I'm not sure I got the right to call what I do running, considering who's up ahead of me, standing stock-still, waiting for me to catch up, which I do a few seconds later, only to have the guy dart off ahead of me again, moving like quicksilver down the corridor, which is only appropriate, as that's what people call him, Quicksilver, though his real name is Pietro. Funny name, that. Pietro. Who the heck names their kid Pietro?

Oh, wait. Now I remember.

The corridor in front of me explodes, and there he is. Pietro's dad. Floating in midair. Raising his arms above his head.

"The curtain falls," he says. "The play is finished."

Crappy poetry. But he's right. For me, it's done. I'm done.

He waves his hand, and like Patsy Cline used to say, I fall to pieces.

The dream changes. I'm in the Blackbird, on the way back from Avalon. Lying in the medi unit, my friends leaning over me, talking like I'm not there, talking like I'm dead already. Jean, Xavier, Jubilee on the comm unit.

I'm in the Genesis tank, my mind falling apart as Uncle Sam's finest go about their business, sticking needles into every part of my body, bonding metal to the bone of my skin, trying to turn me into the ultimate weapon.

I'm pulling the tracking device out of the tiger's wound, leaping at Osborne, even as the tranquilizer darts slam into my leg, even as I fall, and everything goes black.

It comes to me then. I can't fight worth a lick.

I got too used to having the adamantium, too used to my healing factor, too used to being able to make mistakes and recover from them with no harm done. I couldn't even handle a half-dozen soldiers from some hack military unit. I couldn't save the tiger. I couldn't even save myself.

Back in the day, I was the best at what I did. The best man in a scrap, the best fighter on the planet. Now what am I? What am I good for?

The questions float all around my head.

They're still floating as I wake up.

Black gives way to white, to brilliant, dazzling, blinding light. For a minute, I imagine I'm back in the DNR, back in the desert—bakin' on a rock somewhere, the sun beatin' down on me full force. All that about the tiger and Osborne was just a dream.

Then I blink and open my eyes.

I'm lyin' on a steel slab, naked as the day I was born. White light shines down from above—way above, two stories above. I sit up, and right away, I'm nauseated. I stop moving for a second; that helps.

I look around. I'm in a room maybe twenty feet square. The slab I'm on is the only furniture. The ceiling is a sheet of white light. The walls—well, they're not really walls, they're light, too—curtains of yellow, all four of them, pulsing like a traffic signal. Pulsing like the tracking device, pulsing in time with the pounding in my head, with the almost subliminal, low-pitched humming I suddenly notice as well. The sound of energy, the sound of power.

I wait a couple minutes for the nausea to lessen and then put my feet on the floor. As I do, I notice a big black-and-blue mark on my right leg, the upper thigh where the tranquilizer shot went in. It's throbbing like a sonuvagun. Gotta be at least a couple hours since they shot me—if I was my old self, my normal self, that pain woulda been gone by now. I'm not used to pain that doesn't go away.

I push it aside for a moment. The floor under my feet is gray—feels like some kinda stone composite. Cold to the touch. The room itself is warm, though, a good thing considerin' my clothes, or lack thereof.

There's a pair of shorts slung over a chair next to the bed. I slide 'em on and walk over to one of the walls. I can feel heat comin' off it as I get close. Some kind of energy field. I put a hand out to touch it and get a gentle push back, like when you're trying to bring two magnets together. I push harder—so does the light. Not only does it push harder, it gets hotter. My palm heats up. My palm starts to burn.

"That's not a good idea."

The voice comes from behind me. I turn and see a vaguely humanoid shape on the other side of the wall o' light opposite. I walk across the room; as I get closer to the light, it gets easier to see through.

The vaguely humanoid shape turns into a vaguely humanoid monkey.

It's standing about five feet back from the light barrier between us. It's about five feet tall. It's wearing a white lab coat and sandals.

It smiles and starts talking again.

"The barrier works on a molecular attraction principle," the monkey says. "The more force you exert, the more energy is transmitted the barrier, and—"

"The hotter it gets—I got that, thanks." I shake my head. "You're a monkey."

The monkey laughs. "And you got that, too. Very well done. I am a monkey indeed, though that is a gross generalization, of course. I am a monkey as you are a *Homo sapien*—a man, which is a somewhat useful descriptor but hardly enough to completely describe us as individuals, *n'est-ce pas*?"

The monkey doesn't wait for an answer. It goes on talking.

"They call me Brinklow. And you, I understand, are Logan. No first name? Rather unusual. Or is that your first name? They were unclear—"

"Brinklow," I interrupt.

"Yes?"

"Where am I? What is this place?"

"This place?" The monkey frowns. "Why, this is the Ark, of course."

Osborne's words on the trail come back to me, and I nod.

"The Ark?" I ask. "What's that mean? As in Noah and the Ark? As in two of every creature kind of Ark, or . . . ?"

The monkey shakes its head. "I'm afraid I'm not completely certain as to the reasons for your presence here at this time. I have to plead ignorance, which is something I don't enjoy doing." Brinklow smiles, flashing a lot of very white teeth. "To quote the man, I just work here. I hope you understand."

"Yeah," I say. "I get the picture."

If I wasn't sure of it before, I am now.

He's on the other side.

I'm about to ask him a few more questions when the humming noise suddenly lessens in intensity.

I turn around in time to see the curtain of light—the yellow wall—disappear.

Osborne's standing there. Two guys are standing behind him.

"Wolverine," Osborne says. "Glad to see you're awake."

The soldiers have guns; they hold them on me as Osborne takes a step forward. Behind them, I see a wall of rock—sandstone, just like the rocks I've been campin' in, walkin' through, these last few weeks. This is a cave, an underground chamber. I'd bet money now—we're not far from the DNR. Still in Nevada, or near it.

Osborne and his men enter the room.

"Comfy?" he asks.

"Lights are a little bright, but . . ." I shrug. "I've been in worse places."

"You're getting acclimated. Good. I'm glad to hear it. You'll be here awhile."

"You want to tell me where here is?"

"The Ark." He smiles. "Like the monkey said."

I hear footsteps behind me. I turn and see the curtain of light between me and the monkey is gone, too.

"Mister Osborne." The monkey looks annoyed. "I

really would prefer it if you would call me by name, as opposed to—"

"I'll take it under consideration," Osborne says, and smiles. "Monkey."

The two men behind him smile, too.

Some tension there, between Brinklow and the others. Not hard to figure out why.

"The Ark," I say. "So, who does that make you, then? Noah?"

Osborne doesn't respond. He doesn't need to, though, 'cause I know the answer to that as soon as I ask it. He's a soldier. The brains behind this is a scientist. Not Brinklow. Who?

Osborne interrupts my train of thought. "You don't remember me."

"Should I?"

"Maybe. Ten years back—I was soldiering for a guy named Culver, arms dealer out of Montreal. You came through and busted things up. Busted up a couple buddies of mine pretty good, too. Remember now?"

"Vaguely." I do remember—not Osborne but the incident. It was before I joined up with Xavier, back when I was working for Department H, up in Canada. Just two of us on that op—me and Jimmy. No, three, if you count J.C., who was working liaison and pissed about it, pissed about being taken off active duty. I was angry at the time, too. Very, very angry. Took that anger out on Culver and his men.

If I'm remembering right, it was just after Ronnie's accident.

"Back then, you were different." He gestures toward my arms. "What happened to your claws? The metal?"

"None of your freakin' business what happened."

"Come on," he says, smiling. Baiting me. "I'm curious."

"Yeah, well . . . you know what they say about curiosity." I pop the claws.

Osborne can't help it; he flinches and takes a step back.

The soldiers snap to attention. The rifles go up.

"It's all right," Osborne says. "He won't hurt me."

"You sure about that?"

"Positive." He smiles again. "How's the leg?"

"The leg is fine," I say, though of course it's not.

"You sure about *that*?"

He reaches into his pocket then and pulls out a little something about the size and shape of a book of matches. It's black, plastic . . .

He holds it up in front of his chest and presses a little button on it.

The leg burns—the wound burns, as if it's on fire. Pulsing with pain.

My vision swims. I look down, and then, all at once, I get it.

"You sonuvabitch," I say.

"A little implant of your own," Osborne says. "A

precaution we took while you were unconscious. Multipurpose kind of device—a homing beacon, a little something to help calm you down. Right now, it's releasing a sedative into your system. You should—"

I'm leaping for him on the word "sedative"—my leap gets me all of two feet.

I get my arms out just in time to break my fall. I lie there mashed into the floor for a minute; then I feel somebody grabbin' my arms. Two somebodies. The soldiers. They drag me back to the steel slab.

The rest is blackness.

I wake to the monkey standing over me. Brinklow. My arms strapped to my side. A needle in one.

"What the hell?"

"Just relax," he says. "This won't hurt a bit."

He lifts up a test tube, filled with a dark purple liquid. Blood. My blood.

My eyes widen.

I curse a blue streak.

Brinklow takes a step back, startled.

"That kind of vulgarity is really not necessary."

"It is for me," I say, and give him a bunch more of it.

He picks up a second test tube and starts to fill it, too.

"You really should try to relax." Brinklow smiles down at me. "Close your eyes. Go back to sleep. This'll all be over soon."

That's just what I'm afraid of, of course.

A sudden weakness comes over me.

I try to pop my claws and can't even summon up the energy to do that. I try to scream, and send a little river of drool rolling down my chin.

A lab rat. I'm a goddamn lab rat again.

It goes on like that for a while.

I wake to Brinklow standing over me again, taking tissue samples this time. Scraping skin from the tip of my nose, from the inside of my cheek, from everywhere and anywhere he can reach, it seems. I'm awake for some of it, unconscious for most. I can feel all kinds of drugs pouring through my system—sedatives, painkillers, God knows what else. I can barely maintain a coherent thought. What are they doing to me? And why? And where's Osborne, so I can carve him a new one?

I sleep. I dream. Some of those dreams are more real than others. Some of them are so real they feel like they're happening in the here and now.

Avalon, of course. Pietro's dad—Magneto—ripping the adamantium outta my body, molecule by molecule. I feel it all over again: the metal leaching out of me, cuts in my skin everywhere, blood everywhere, my healing factor working overtime to keep up with the injuries and failing.

I feel myself getting weaker and weaker. I'm lying in the medi unit on the Blackbird, dying.

I'm lying in bed with Mariko, on our wedding night.

I'm lying in my cell, on the steel slab. Somebody sayin' my name. Brinklow.

". . . apologize again, Mister Logan. I suggest this all will go much quicker if you don't struggle. Struggling only . . ."

I close my eyes, and when I open them again, Ronnie's standing over me. She's exactly as I remember her. Not a wrinkle on her face. Unchanged, in what—eleven, twelve years?

She smiles. Her face morphs into Osborne's. He's smilin', too.

He's holdin' up the tiger's head.

"Had to shoot it," he says. "Nature of the beast."

I close my eyes. When I open them, Ronnie's back. She's wearin' a white lab coat, too. Underneath it, she's not wearing anything.

Her hair is jet black, her skin pale as ivory. We make love, just like I always—always—wanted to do, back in the day. It goes on for a good long while.

It's a nice dream. It doesn't last.

Next thing I know, a whole team of people—real people, honest-to-God humans—in lab coats are standing over me. One of those has an electric razor. He's takin' it to my head. He's shaving my head. I pull at the restraints; I twist on the table.

"He's got enough in his system to knock out an elephant," one of the lab coats says. "How is he still conscious?"

A second later, I'm not. More dreams; more Ronnie, more Mariko, more Pietro's dad, more me not carin' if I live or die. I've been through this kind of thing before, the Weapon X days. I never wanted to go through it again, and yet . . .

Here I am.

Helpless. Powerless. Alone.

Might as well be dead.

Finally, I stop dreaming and wake up. Which is when I look down at my body and realize that some of what I was dreamin' wasn't a dream at all. The bastards really shaved my head. And they didn't stop there.

They shaved every inch of me.

I got all sorts of electrodes and gizmos dangling off me. I got machines on every side of my body. My ribs are showing through; I flash on an image of myself as some sort of concentration camp survivor. I ain't that thin, of course, but they ain't actually been feedin' me, that's clear, too. I doubt I'd recognize myself if I looked in the mirror.

"Ah. You're back with us."

I roll my head to one side. Brinklow's standing there, hands clasped behind his back, smiling at me.

"How do you feel?"

I'm about to give him what for again when I realize that all things considered, I feel better than I have in days.

I turn my head. Everything looks exactly the same as it did last time I was conscious. Even the machines next to my bed, with the IV's still pumping away, just like before. Takes me a second to figure out what that means.

They didn't stop the drugs; they're just not working the way they used to.

I feel a little tingle in the base of my spine, a few goose bumps on my arms.

My healing factor's coming back.

"Well. You're doing wonderfully," Brinklow says. "I'll be back to check on you again very soon, I promise."

"Peachy," I say as he leaves.

Soon as he's gone, I lift off the bed, or try to, anyway. I got restraints holdin' me down. No surprise there; some kinda plastic bands, on my wrists and ankles. I take a deep breath and try again. I think—I'm pretty sure—I feel the one on my right wrist loosen a little.

That's a starting point, anyway. I focus on it.

As I'm doing that, one of the machines beeps softly. I turn my head, in time to see the numbers goin' up on its control panel. More drugs, triggered by my activity. I can feel them takin' effect; things go fuzzy again. I try to stay alert, awake . . . but I can't.

Next time I open my eyes, Osborne's standin' over me. He's fiddlin' with one of the machines next to my bed. He pulls a little silver disk out of it and puts it in a metal case about the size of a paperback book.

He turns back, sees I'm awake, and smiles.

"Good timing. Gives us a chance to say good-bye."

"Leavin' so soon? I was hopin' we could get to know each other better."

"Sorry." He sets the metal case down on top of one of the machines. "We're all done here."

"What's that mean?"

"The Ark has served its purpose. We're shutting it down."

I notice all at once that the humming noise—the sound of the energy fields that make up the walls of the cell—has stopped. I look past Osborne and see that behind him, the curtain of light is gone, too.

Two black jumpsuits are standin' in the room, lookin' at us.

"So what happens to me?" I ask.

"What do you think?"

He starts punchin' buttons on one of the machines—the one, I realize, that's been pumpin' me full of drugs this whole time.

I don't need to be a scientist to guess what comes next.

"Any final words for posterity?"

"As a matter of fact . . . yeah. I got two."

"Only two?" He smiles. "Go on."

I smile, too. "Drop dead," I say, at the same time yanking on my right arm, which is when the wrist restraint—which I was working on before my last blackout—rips free of the table.

I pop my claws and drive them into Osborne's chest.

They go in an inch and stop. The bastard's wearing Kevlar.

The impact is jarring. The pain is instant and excruciating—my nerves scream. I scream.

I struck hard enough to send Osborne flying across the room. He smashes into one of the soldiers. Both of them land on the ground. So does the metal case on top of the machine.

I cut the restraint on my left wrist with the claws. I slash at the one on my right ankle and cut that, too.

I look up. Osborne's back on his feet. He charges, driving one of the machines right into me, which sends me and the bed and every machine in the room into a heap on the floor together. I get to my feet, dragging the bed with me, just in time to catch Osborne's fist across my jaw. I taste blood; I stagger. He kicks me in the gut; I go flying back and land on the floor, looking up.

He draws a gun and fires.

I move at the last second. The bullet catches me in the shoulder.

I yank one of the machines along with me. It slams into Osborne, not hard enough to hurt but hard enough that he drops the gun.

He dives for it as I cut the last restraint.

We're on our feet at the same instant. He's got the drop on me.

I don't worry about it; I just charge.

He fires as I come—two shots—one misses, one hits, left shoulder again.

I'm past the point of feeling pain, so I ignore it.

I slash at him with my right hand. Osborne leans his head back out of the way just in time to avoid getting decapitated. I grab him with my left hand, break my momentum, and backhand him with my right, right across the face. Nasty cuts; blood wells up, he grunts, and he starts to raise the gun again.

I slash down with my left hand; the weapon falls to the ground.

Most of his index finger goes with it.

I backhand him again, this time with a closed fist, catching him right on the jaw. He follows the weapon to the ground and lies still.

The soldiers are comin' at me by that point. I pick up Osborne's gun and stop them dead in their tracks, so to speak.

Osborne's still out cold. I bend down and search his body. He's got keys in his pocket and an ID card hanging from a chain around his neck. I take both.

I take his pants, too. They hang like a fat man's pajamas around my waist.

I take a step toward the far door, when it opens, sliding up from the ground, revealing two more soldiers. They see me, they see Osborne on the ground, and they react. One draws a weapon. The other slaps a button on the wall. Sirens start sounding.

I scream and jump to meet them.

4

THERE'S A REASON ALL THOSE KUNG FU GUYS MAKE noise when they fight: it breaks the opponents' concentration. Throws them off their game. I do the same thing, only with me, it's not calculated. It's something I do naturally; the shock value is an added bonus.

The soldier who hit the alarm has his weapon out, too, now; he's a step behind his buddy. My scream makes both of them hesitate. I'm surprised. These are trained guys; they oughtta know better than to let a little yellin' faze them.

Though give 'em credit; maybe it's not just the yelling. Maybe it's the claws, too, and the half-naked bald guy coming at them.

I'm guessing that they're wearing Kevlar, like Osborne. So, instead of trying to go through them, I bring 'em along for the ride. Claws out to the side, a fist in the gut for each, legs churning as I go. I take the first one and then the second out through the door with me.

I slam them into the far wall of the corridor. I hear something to my left—the click of metal on metal—and react just in time.

I grab one of the soldiers I got hold of by the scruff of the neck and spin him around in front of me; the bullets hit him instead. He dances like a marionette in my hand.

A second later, he's dead weight. I shove him toward the shooter. I don't have the strength to get him all the way off the ground, but the body travels far enough out in front of me to be an obstacle.

I'm about to follow up when I hear a noise behind me. I drop to the floor and kick out. My foot catches bone; I spin to see I've gotten one of the soldiers in the knee. He's groaning. I windmill across the floor and chop his legs out from underneath him.

He hits the ground. I somersault over him and into the corridor beyond. I start running. Bullets hit the wall to my right; I hit the ground. I got Osborne's gun in my hand as I come back up; I fire blind. The shooter behind me drops, too, using one of the bodies on the floor for cover. He fires again; I return the shot.

Stalemate, for a second.

Stalemate doesn't favor me.

I look up. The corridor is stone, lined with doors like the one I came through. Blinking green lights next to each of them, a touchpad next to each of the lights.

I finger the ID card I took off Osborne. His picture on one side. A magnetic stripe on the other.

The shooter fires again. I do the same. This time, as I pull the trigger, I'm up on my feet. In two steps, I'm at the nearest door: I slap the card, magnetic stripe down, on the pad next to the blinking light.

The door opens.

Something roars and charges out at me.

I dodge out of the way just in time; the thing that came through the door doesn't.

Bullets from the soldier hit it, and it goes down.

It's a man—with the head of a wolf.

I stare down at the thing, wounded, twitching, its life blood oozing out on the floor, and a little bell goes off in the back of my head.

A picture flashes in front of my face. An image I saw a long time back.

Not a man with a wolf's head. A wolf, walking upright like a man.

I think about that picture, this creature, about Brinklow and the tiger, and all at once, I got a pretty good idea who's runnin' this show. Who Noah is. And he ain't with the government; not any government I ever heard of, anyway.

A bullet shatters the wall next to me, interrupting my train of thought, getting me moving again. I slap the card against every door I pass as I go. Some of them open; some of them don't. Other things—it'd be wrong to call them animals, 'cause they don't resemble

THE NATURE OF THE BEAST

any natural-born animal—come charging out. Some run off blindly; some attack the first thing they see; others mill around in confusion. All of it adds to the chaos.

In the meantime, I'm running as fast as I can, running for my life.

I ain't Pietro, but I do all right. I manage to reach the end of the corridor without getting hit again. I shove Osborne's ID in my pocket.

That corridor ends in a T. I look left, see a hall lined with more doors like the ones I just opened. I look right, and I see two more of Osborne's men coming for me.

There's a glass door behind them; through it, I can see a lot of video screens, a lot of electronic equipment.

That's where I wanna go. Too bad for the two guys coming toward me, who never know what hit 'em. By never, I mean just that: never.

They ain't wearing Kevlar.

The glass door is locked, and it ain't really glass, some kind of translucent plastic. It wobbles the first few times I kick it before finally shattering.

I punch through the rest of the plastic and step through. Another siren starts whooping.

I look the room over. There's a wall of cabinets in front of me, a blank wall to my left, a wall of video screens to my right, with a desk in front of them. The video screens are showing feed from the chaos

I just left behind. Escaped experiments, tangling with some of Osborne's soldiers, tangling with other experiments. Talkin' tigers, walkin' wolves, monkeys and men. Hard for me to tell who's on whose side and who's winning, if anyone, but that doesn't really matter. All I want is time, time to figure out a way out of this place.

I go right, to the screens and the desk. There's a big video console built into it. The console is dark. I retract my claws, look around for a keyboard, a mouse. I don't see anything. I touch the screen. It comes to life, three white words on a blue background with a blinking prompt: USER INPUT REQUIRED.

I curse.

Where the hell is the keyboard? I do a three-sixty, don't see anything. I get down on my hands and knees. No visible drawer. I don't see any sort of slide-out drawer or—

Voice input?

"Hello," I say.

The prompt keeps blinking.

"Hey!" I yell.

Still nothing.

I touch the screen again. It goes dark, and then comes back up: USER INPUT REQUIRED.

I barely keep myself from drawin' my claws and giving the screen a kind of input it'll never forget.

Think, Logan, think. Input. Okay. What kind of input . . .

I look up at the video screens again. The fighting is still going, but unless I miss my guess, there's more soldiers than before. A lot more.

I ain't got all day here.

I lean over the screen. A flash of red catches my eye as I bend down.

A laser. Laser scan. Fingerprints? Retina?

I grab one of the dead guys from the hall and drag him over to the console. I spread his hand and wave it front of the laser. Nothing. I grab him by the hair with one hand and pull his eyelids open with the other. First the right, then the left. Still nothing.

Maybe I'm not gettin' it at the right angle. I try the hand again I try the head again. Still nothing.

Tell me I'm gonna have to cut this guy's eyes out of his head to make it work.

The light from the video screens glints on a chain around the guy's neck. His ID card dangles from the chain.

Ah.

I drop the guy to the floor. I pull Osborne's ID out of my pocket and run it across the screen.

The blinking prompt disappears. I get a new screen with four options: Communications, Applications, Documents, System. I touch Documents; a bunch of folders pop up on-screen. I scan 'em, looking for references to the Ark. I don't see any. They got names like Project Shangri-La, E-Code, Mandate 12—interesting names but not what I'm looking for; nothing I got time to check. I want a map of this place. I wanna know where I am and how to get out.

I try System. I get a bunch of files with funny names and funnier extensions on 'em.

I try Communications. I get a list of e-mails. I scan the subject lines—nothin' much of help there.

I grit my teeth.

"Come on." I hit the button on the screen that says "Previous" as quickly as I can. "Come on come on come on . . ."

In Applications, I get an option called Control.

Under Control, I get an option called Security. Finally. Something useful.

I reach for the Security button, and the screen explodes.

The whole console explodes. Bullets flying everywhere. I dive and somersault and turn in one motion. The wall behind me is going up. Very quietly. There's another wall behind it, and an opening in that wall. Sliding steel doors, and coming through them, firing as he goes, is another one of Osborne's guys.

Another second-rate soldier. He's got no idea what an easy target he is standing there, framed in that doorway. His first—and last—mistake of the day.

That little somersault I did got me a gun of my own, the one that used to belong to one of the guards in here. I return fire; a second or two later, I'm walking past the dead guy and through the door he came in. Surprise—my first pleasant one of the last couple of weeks.

I'm standing in an elevator. Capacity 2500 pounds. It looks like any old passenger elevator, like the kind you'd find in your run-of-the-mill hotel/motel/office building. There's a key in the fire marshal lock; there's a half-dozen buttons on the panel to my right, none of them numbered. I slap the topmost one; up is the way I wanna go. Outta this cave, wherever we are, and up toward the outside world. The car starts movin'; it's a long ride. Much longer than I thought.

I tense up, crouch down, face the door. Gotta be ready for whatever's standing there when it opens. Whatever one of Noah's monsters, however many of Noah's soldiers. I take a few deep breaths, in and out.

I feel the implant in my leg tingling. I gotta get out and away before they can trigger it again.

The elevator slows. I drop my claws to my sides. I feel a scream building in my throat. I let it come.

The elevator stops.

The bell dings.

The door opens.

I'm staring at a bank of three other elevators opposite me, along a mirrored wall. Plants hanging down between the doors. A floor of polished marble.

A guy in a green tuxedo, holdin' a tray full of drinks, with his back to me.

He turns. He's wearin' a bad toupee and a nameplate that says "Sergio—Head Waiter" on it.

He sees me, screams, drops the tray, and runs.

I step out of the car, past the "Elevator Out of Service" sign, and look to my left.

Into a room the size of a basketball auditorium, filled with people in purple sweatsuits, sitting in front of row after row of one-armed bandits. Slot machines.

I guessed wrong. The Ark wasn't buried under a mountain.

It was buried under a casino.

5

THE PARADISE CASINO AND RESORT HOTEL, TO be exact—Vegas's Newest, Most Spectacular Gaming Destination, Featuring Authentic Native Dancers and the Fabulous Hidden Waterfalls of Tibet, according to the billboards plastered on the wall to my left. I note a "Construction completed by" date a few weeks from now. Either they got done early, or they finished the gaming room here first, and there's construction still goin' on elsewhere in the hotel. I vote for the latter, which probably has provided a pretty neat cover for what Osborne and Noah are up to underneath it.

All of which is only tangentially relevant to the mess I'm in at the moment.

The few hundred or so people sittin' in front of the Paradise's slot machines turn my way now. A large majority of them take one look and follow Sergio's lead.

In other words, they start screaming as well. They run for the exits.

Two big guys in dark suits, wearing sunglasses and earpieces, shove their way through the crowd straight toward me.

They both pull guns, point 'em at me.

"Hey," I say, holdin' up my hands. "Easy. My name is Logan, I'm a—"

The two guys fire.

Somethin' in my gut warns me just in the nick of time; I duck. Bullets ping off the wall behind me; plastic shatters. Somebody cries out in pain. I turn back to the elevator in time to see a woman stagger and fall to the floor, clutching her upper leg with both hands.

Blood pools up between her fingers.

She screams.

Another elevator car opens up, and Osborne steps out.

He's slipped a suit jacket over his coverall. He's got a phone pressed to his ear; he's got a big nasty slash along one side of his face, a bandage wrapped around one hand.

His eyes meet mine across the room.

Half a dozen more security guys stream out from behind him. They have earpieces and sunglasses, too. Which explains the hostile greeting a second ago: the security guys and Osborne, they're on the same team.

They all start heading toward me.

I start backing away; I change direction, head to my left.

Two more push their way toward me from that direction. They got guns out, too.

I'm surrounded.

Really, there's only one way out of this for me.

I take a deep breath.

I give in to the moment.

What it is is a berserker rage. From the old Icelandic, I found out a few years back, courtesy of one of Charlie Xavier's lectures. *Berserker* meaning "bear skin," *berserker* meaning "animal-like," *berserker* meaning "killing frenzy."

It's what happens to me, now and then, in the heat of battle. Helped me fight off the Hulk himself, once upon a time. Usually when I go into that rage, I lose myself in it entirely.

I can't afford to do that right now. Osborne and his guys, I don't give a rat's ass about them. But the innocent bystanders, the innocent security guards at the casino here (if there are any) . . . I can't be killing them indiscriminately.

So I keep what I can of my head about me.

I keep the blood to a minimum.

I keep my exit strategy—such as it is—firmly in mind.

I slash, and I punch, and I leap, and I kick, and I get cut, I get shot, I bleed, and I keep moving.

Osborne's face flashes in front of my eyes, and I strike out again, and again, and the next thing I know . . .

It's over.

I'm in an elevator, by myself. Not the one I came up out of the Ark in—another. Numbered buttons. All the way up to twenty-six. I hit the top one and slump back against the elevator wall.

Up we go. I imagine the cops are in the casino by now. I wouldn't be surprised if they call the army in for this, especially if they recognize me. Maybe even if they don't. I'm a mutant, clearly, and the mood the country's in about mutants these days . . .

They'll all be on Osborne's side, all with Osborne's guys—I realize I'm still thinking of them as Osborne's guys, even though I'm pretty sure now who the real brains behind this whole thing is—on their walkie-talkies, phones, whatever, climbing the stairs, climbing into the other elevators, watching my progress, calling in reinforcements, planning to be waiting for me wherever—whenever—I come back out.

Which is why I have no intention of following the elevator up.

I pop my claws—only then do I realize I've had them in the whole time—kneel down, and start punching at the side of the car. The car frame is metal, of course, but the panels are all wood. In ten seconds, I'm through, looking over at the cable assembly of the car next to me—and a rapidly increasing drop.

In the old days, the days before Avalon, I woulda

jumped without a second thought, grabbing onto the cable as I fell.

Now I take five more seconds to rip off one of my pant legs, wrap it around my hands, and squeeze myself out through the side of the car.

Then I leap.

I grab hold of the steel cable, the thin cloth of my pants protecting my hands from the wire, and start falling.

I get two seconds of pain-free descent, and then the pants cloth wears through. The metal rubs against the palm of my hands. The flesh starts burning. Starts shredding off.

I grit my teeth.

Lucky it only takes about two more seconds after that for me to hit bottom. A sub-basement, I'm sure. I get to my feet and pull myself up level with the elevator doors. Bits of bloodied pants fabric are stuck to my hands. I pop my claws again and pry open the doors.

Subbasement it is. Dark tunnels, steam pipes, electrical conduit. I run along one of those tunnels till I find an exit sign. I follow the arrow to a fire-alarmed door and kick it open without a second thought.

The sun hits me like an anvil.

It's midday, gotta be a hundred degrees. I shield my eyes and step out into the light, and the first fresh air I've tasted in weeks.

I'm in an alley ten feet across. Opposite me is a big blank brick wall. On my left is a Dumpster. I look past it, to the end of the alley, and see a cop car parked there, lights flashing. A mob milling around the car and in the street alongside it. Heads craned, looking in the same direction the cop car is pointed. Toward the front of the building, where the action is. Where I supposedly am.

That's not the way out.

I look to my right and see a giant concrete column. I follow the column up to what looks like an elevated railroad track. Except, of course, there are no elevated railroads in Las Vegas. So what is it?

As I'm lookin' at the column, I hear a whooshing noise comin' toward me, getting louder. Silver glints in the distance, moving closer. The ground starts to shake a little. I smile.

No elevated railroads in Vegas, but they did build a monorail.

That's my way out.

I dig myself handholds and make my way up the side of the column just in the nick of time.

The monorail slows to make the turn at the column. As it passes, I flip myself up onto the tracks and barely manage to get a hand on the bumper of the last car.

There's a window at the back of that car, a little kid is peering out of it. A girl, maybe eight years old, in a little purple sweatsuit, of course. I smile at her.

She points straight at me and opens her mouth and screams. I can't hear her, but I can read her lips, read the word she spits out like a curse.

"Mutant."

I realize then my claws are still out.

Too late to retract 'em; too late to do anything but take a deep breath and use the last of my strength to flip myself up, and over, and onto the roof of the car. I land with a big thud and flatten myself down. Flat enough, I hope, that no one can see me. I hope no one will believe the kid about what she saw.

We'll find out, I guess.

We pass right by the Paradise; I get a bird's-eye view of the casino and a big tower goin' up behind it. The hotel, I'm guessin'. There's a big pit next to that, with some kind of steel-framed structure risin' up from inside it. I wonder what it's gonna be. I wonder how the folks who're buildin' the Paradise are connected to Osborne and his people. To Noah.

I'm wonderin' that the entire monorail ride. I'm also wonderin' what the best way's gonna be to contact Westchester from here. Can't just walk into a police station now, not after what just happened. They're likely to shoot first, too, ask questions later.

Gotta let the situation cool down a bit, get myself out of these clothes, such as they are, and into some kind of disguise, before I do anything.

I jump the monorail as it pulls into the Bally's station, slither down the support beam to a V-shaped nook under the tracks. I wait a few seconds, make sure nobody's seen me, and wedge myself in good and tight.

I let out a long, slow breath, and wait for sleep to

come. Memory hits me instead. The DNR, the tiger, Osborne. Brinklow, the hallucinations, Mariko and Avalon, Jeannie and Xavier. Ronnie in her white lab coat, Ronnie and J.C. Jimmy and Heather. Dan Wilson, and all the other CIC suits. Department H.

The past.

I'm soaked through with sweat. The steel is slick against my back.

I close my eyes and drift away.

Fifteen years ago.

I'm on my hands and knees, crawlin' through a maintenance duct in the Athabasca Sands Power Plant. I'm three stories below the surface; it's gotta be a hundred degrees in here, humidity pushin' a hundred percent. My coverall is drenched with sweat; I'm startin' to stick to the tunnel.

Sweat drips down my forehead into my eyes. I wipe it away.

"Next grate." Jimmy's voice comes from behind me. He sounds a little out of breath. "That's the auxiliary control room. That's where they are."

We reach the grate in less than a minute. I peer out through it and squint into the semidarkness.

The room is the size of an old railroad car. There's two people in it, a man and a woman, with their backs to us, crouched down in front of the main door. The man is holdin' somethin' in his hands, a tube of some kind. No, a wire. Thick wire. A cable. My eyes adjust to the darkness. I trace the cable back along the floor to a control panel off to the right and curse under my breath.

"What?" Jimmy asks. "You see 'em?"

"I see 'em. They got the door electrified. Whoever touches it . . ."

"The SWAT team's five minutes off," Jimmy says. "If they charge that door, we got more dead cops on our hands. That won't be good at all."

No doubt about that. Right now, we got authorities with itchy fingers. Any more uniforms go down, they'll turn into a lynch mob.

"We have to call that SWAT team off, Logan. Tell them to stay back."

I shake my head. The cops aren't likely to listen to reason. They're angry, and they're scared. They hear about a booby trap, they're likely to escalate the situation, bring in even heavier artillery. The military.

We gotta get these two outta here. Now.

"The hell with that. I'm goin' in," I tell Jimmy.

"Logan, wait," he says. "Let's talk about this. We ought to—"

I slide my legs underneath me, brace myself against the tunnel wall, and kick the grate out.

Even as it's fallin', I'm pushin' myself through behind it.

I land on my feet, as the two of them turn to face me.

The guy is Jean-Claude Perrault. Boy genius—graduated from college at twelve years old. Parents put him on the local TV station, made a fortune off the kid. He sued to be free of them when he was fifteen. File had a picture of him comin' out of court after winning the case. He looked angry enough to take on the whole world then.

He looks even angrier now.

The girl looks mostly scared.

She's part native—high cheekbones, almond eyes. Her name is Veronique Campion—she was adopted by the Campions, also McMurray natives, when she was four years old. Real parents both died of radiation poisoning—the file implies, but doesn't say explicitly, that they were caught in some kind of weapons test.

"I'm here to help," I say.

"That's a lie." Jean-Claude's voice is flat, emotionless. "You're here to take us in. Ronnie?"

It's not a question; it's a command.

Before I can say a word, the girl changes.

Her arms morph into wings.

Her face lengthens, and stretches, and changes shape.

She lunges forward, razor-sharp bill thrusting directly at me.

I step aside and leap to the top of one of the panels.

"I know you didn't mean for anyone to get hurt," I say. "Believe me, I understand what you were feeling."

Jean-Claude shakes his head. "How could you possibly know what we were feeling?"

"Because," I say, "I'm just like you. A mutant."

I pop my claws.

"I'm here to take you someplace safe."

The girl—the creature that was the girl—who was circling the room, getting ready to attack again—lands on the ground next to Jean-Claude. He frowns and looks at her.

Her expression, such as it is, is unreadable.

"Logan!" That's Jimmy, at the grate above. "The SWAT team."

I hear them, too, now. Footsteps shuffling around. Takin' up positions around the door . . .

Only a matter of seconds now.

"Disconnect it," I say to Jean-Claude, nodding at the cable. "And let's go."

"Why should I?" he says. "They were going to kill us."

"They're bigots. Fools. No changing their minds. But if you hurt 'em, you'll change a lot of others. You'll make things a lot worse. For yourself. For me."

I hop down to the ground, so that the three of us are on a level.

"You two comin' or not?"

He hesitates. She doesn't. She changes back—bird to woman once more.

"We can't run forever, Jean-Claude." She puts a hand on his shoulder. "Remove the cable. Come."

"They were going to kill you," he says. "Because you were different."

"I'm all right now," she says, and looks me in the eye and smiles.

When I wake, it's dark out, or as dark as Vegas gets, anyway. Good a time as any for a little reconnaissance.

I slide out from my hiding place and climb back up to the monorail tracks. No train in sight. I crouch low and backtrack toward the Paradise. Soon enough, I got the construction site in view again.

Things have changed since this afternoon.

The place is ringed with police barricades, crowds pressin' up against them to get a look at what's happening. The casino's shut down, clearly; there's flashin' red lights everywhere. Cops. Firemen. Ambulances. Looks like a bomb hit the place. I see workers movin' to and fro, some shouting orders, some carrying furniture, some in forklifts, moving crates the size of refrigerators onto a line of waiting semis.

I didn't think I did that much damage, is my first thought.

Then I realize what's really going on.

They're moving everything out.

They're closing down the Ark, just like Osborne said.

Anybody shows up tomorrow looking for a subterranean laboratory, all they're gonna find is sand and rock.

I've been thinkin' about callin' in the X-Men, but I don't have time now.

I'm movin' before I even realize it. Climbing down the same concrete support I climbed up earlier to escape. My thought is, I'll hitch a ride on one of the trucks, find out where they're goin', and—

My leg starts throbbin' like a sonuvagun.

My head goes woozy. I'm ten feet off the ground. I almost lose my grip; I dangle out in space a second before righting myself.

The implant.

I forgot all about it. I musta been outta range before. Osborne's probably got the button on that little black triggering device taped down, probably hopin' I'll do somethin' stupid like show up and fall over unconscious.

Damn if he wasn't right, or pretty close to it.

I manage to drag myself back up on the tracks—

And of course, here comes the monorail.

I squeeze down in between the rails and lie face-down on the track bed. It's all I have time to do.

The train passes over me, so close that I'm glad, at that moment, that Osborne and his friends shaved my head.

I roll back over when it's passed and realize two things.

I gotta get the implant out.

And I gotta stop thinking of Osborne as the brains behind what happened to me.

I know who Noah is—or at least, I think I do.

Time to find out if I'm right.

6

VEGAS NEVER SLEEPS.

It does slow down a little, though. Sometime in those wee hours just before dawn, the streets empty out a bit, the cop cars cruise a little less frequently, the guys shilling for the casinos duck inside to give their vocal cords a rest . . .

The perfect time for me to get a little exercise, in other words.

I duck into a convenience-store rest room, clean up best as I can. Wipe off the grime, and the grease, and the sweat, and the dark red spots dried on my face. Slick back my hair with a little soap, and strip down to my shorts—Osborne's shorts, really—and head off down Flamingo at a jog.

I'm headin' east, away from the Strip. A mile or so on, I turn in at the entrance to the University of Las Vegas. Just another student, returnin' to the dorms after an early-morning run. That's what I hope people think, anyway.

I've been to UNLV once before, a few years back. Me and one of my X-buddies, name of Warren Worthington III, stopped in to check out the coeds on our way to check out the show girls. Hung out for a couple of hours. Warren showed off his convertible, and we moved on.

This time, I plan to stay a while longer.

I pass a couple of other runners out clearin' out the early-morning fog, give 'em the "How you doin'" nod, and move on. Doesn't take me long to find the gym. I grab a shower there, break into the equipment room, and grab a spare soccer uniform. New shorts, new shirt, new me.

The sun's up by then. I head over to the cafeteria, hang around the back entrance to the kitchen long enough to catch a break, a shift change that lets me duck into the walk-in fridge and fill my stomach. Midday finds me at the campus store, where I snag myself some cosmetics, painkillers, and a roll of bandages.

I find an empty bathroom on a deserted floor of a lecture hall and cut out the implant.

Takes me a few hours to recover from that, but by sunset, I'm ready to roll again.

What hair I got is dyed shoe-polish black. I'm wearing a big gold hoop through my left ear, and a tattoo that says "SHARK" on my right arm. Big, multicolored tattoo, courtesy of the art department painting supplies. Temporary, but it oughtta do the trick for now. Misdirection—drawing people's attention to everything about me but my face. A necessary precaution, considering that while I was in the campus store, I saw my picture on the front page of every Vegas paper, with appropriate headlines: "Mutant Psycho Sought in Casino Attack"; "X-Man Goes Rogue"; "Killer Mutant on the Strip." Etc.

The picture they're all using is a shot from a security camera, mounted in the lobby, near the elevator bank I came out of. Probably the only one that was released to the press. In the shot, I'm skin and bones—way too many bones, the claws most prominent among them, to look even remotely human. I got blood on my face; I got blood on every square inch of my body.

The headlines got it right: I do look like a psycho. Osborne's intent, no doubt. Get people to think I really am crazy, get the cops ready to shoot me on sight.

Wonder what Jeannie and the others think. I'm sure they've seen the paper by now. Sure the news has made its way back east. Maybe they think I've gone 'round the bend at last. That what happened up at Avalon unhinged me entirely. I oughtta call, disabuse them of that notion. Ask for help. I been thinkin' about doin' that all day.

Thing is . . .

I can't.

I don't wanna.

These guys have made it personal.

• • •

Dusk comes. I make my way across campus to the UNLV library and in through the front door. There's three middle-aged ladies workin' at the library's reference desk. I'm tryin' to decide which one of 'em to talk to when the one nearest me looks up. "Ms. Parrish," says the nameplate on her desk. Mousy brown hair, glasses, fifty pounds overweight, wearing a shapeless black dress. No wedding ring. Frown lines creased into her face. I give her my best smile.

She gives me her best frown right back.

"You want what?"

"To use a computer." I keep smiling. "One with access to the Internet. If you have one."

"Of course we do," she says.

"That's great," I say. "If I could—"

"They're for the students."

She points to the sign at the front of the desk, which, sure enough, says, "Computers for Student Use Only." I saw it when I walked in, of course.

"Well, I was hoping—"

"Are you a student here?"

"No, but—"

"Then I'm sorry. Can I help you with something else?"

I keep the smile frozen on my face and count to ten.

One of the other middle-aged ladies looks up.

A student—a girl with close-cropped red hair—passes by the desk and stares at me.

Last thing I need, a lot of people lookin' at my face.

I thank Ms. Parrish for her time. I exit the library. Okay. Plan B. The information I want is probably available—

I stop dead in my tracks, on the steps in front of the library building. Somebody's following me. I turn around.

It's the girl from downstairs. The redhead.

"You want somethin'?" I ask, with a little more bite than necessary.

She gulps. "I was just gonna say—I heard you talkin' to Miss Parrish." Her voice has a little quiver in it.

I nod. "So?"

She looks over my shoulder toward the front desk. "If you want to use the Internet, there's a terminal in the third-floor stacks. In the annex. Nobody ever goes there."

I don't say anything for a second.

"If you want," she says. "That's all. I just thought I'd offer, because—"

"No." I manage a faint smile. "I appreciate it. Thanks."

"You're welcome." She smiles, too.

Third-floor annex. I make my way to the elevator and find a map.

The kid wasn't lying. I find the computer easy enough, right in front of a long row of book stacks. Nobody around, just like she said.

I smile. Maybe there's hope for people—humans and mutants livin' together—yet.

I take a seat. The welcome screen's a library catalog, but it takes me all of two clicks to get outta that and onto the Internet proper.

It doesn't take me long to find what I'm looking for. An old magazine article, from a few years back. A feature and a bunch of pictures.

The first has three people in it. Well, really one person and two . . . experiments, for lack of a better word.

The experiments look exactly like some of the creatures I saw back at the Ark. Some of the ones I let out while I was trying to escape. Two men—with wolves' heads.

They flank a third figure between them. They're standing; he's seated in a tall, cushioned chair, at the head of a long wooden table.

The way it's posed, the guy at the head looks like a king. He's dressed for the part as well, wearin' what looks like a suit of armor and a knight's helm, although the helm in this case is more than a helm, it covers his whole face. On top of which, it's a purplish pink, which, though it does match his cloak and tunic, is not a color any self-respecting knight would be caught dead in.

But then, this guy is not a knight. He's a scientist. An Oxford geneticist by the name of Herbert Edgar Wyndham, according to the article. I didn't even know he had a name, tell you the truth.

I knew him as the High Evolutionary; right now, though, I'm thinkin' of him as Noah.

I read on.

The article has some general statements about the purpose of Wyndham's work: the evolution of other animal species to something resembling human intelligence. What he called his "New Men," though it seems they ended up having the same problems as the "Old" models—fighting among themselves, to the point of self-destruction.

There's a part of the article that focuses on the equipment he used, in particular, something called a "genetic accelerator." Supposedly, that let Wyndham mutate and evolve his creations far faster than the normal evolutionary process would. Grow an intelligent, humanoid-looking dog out of a puppy in minutes—which he apparently did with his own pet, a Dalmatian name of Dempsey. Turned it into kind of a Man Friday; the dog was shot and killed by hunters who mistook it for a monster.

There's even a picture of the guy back before he donned his High Evolutionary armor. Typical British scientist, tall thin guy in a white lab coat, bad teeth, worse hair. He looks harmless enough, but then don't they all, the mad-scientist types, the guys who start out with some noble enough kind of purpose and end up using that to justify the most monstrous kind of actions you can imagine.

Far as I'm concerned, this guy flashes warning signals from the get-go. Treating his own dog like a lab rat, for God's sake. Just a short hop, skip, and jump from that to experimenting on people—to experimenting on me.

Question I'm asking myself is what's he want with the old Canucklehead? I answer that easy enough: I'm a mutant. So now Wyndham's experimenting on mutants? Why? *Homo superior* as the next natural step in evolution? That's my guess; I find no evidence to support it in the article, though.

I run a few queries through Nevada State Archives, starting with info on the Paradise Hotel. Ownership documents, construction papers, that kind of thing. Wyndham's name doesn't show up anywhere. I cross-reference the guys who do show up as owners; they seem like legit businessmen. I make a note of the construction company. I run a search on Wyndham; nothing on his current whereabouts. I look for info on the genetic accelerator, on the lab he first built, in Wundagore. On one of the scientists he worked with, Jonathan Drew, though he hasn't worked with Drew in almost ten years, according to the articles I find. I draw a series of blanks.

Which is when I realize who he has worked with quite recently.

Osborne.

I pause, take my fingers off the keyboard for a second, trying to remember Osborne's exact words.

We met ten years ago . . .

He was standing over my bed.

A guy named Culver—arms dealer out of Montreal.

Doubtful I'll find anything on either of those guys with what I can get to here. What I really need is access to a law-enforcement database—a Canadian law-enforcement database, probably.

A face flashes before my eyes then, almost like a bolt of inspiration, out of the blue. A guy who'll most certainly have access to every Canadian law-enforcement database I can think of, and then some.

The question is whether or not he'll wanna share any of that information with me.

All at once, the hairs on the back of my neck stand up straight.

I turn and see the girl from downstairs again, peerin' out at me from behind one of the stacks.

"Hey," she says. "You found it."

"Yeah. I found it."

"Good." She manages a half-smile. "Good. I'm glad."

But she doesn't look glad. She looks nervous. "Listen, there's somethin' I need to tell you," she says.

And all at once, I got a bad feeling.

I get up from the computer.

"What?" I snap.

The girl backs off a step.

"I mean, I'm not sure, but . . ."

As she stumbles over her words, I notice a folded-up piece of paper sticking out of her front pocket. It's a

Xerox of a picture. Somebody's face. I see an eye, and a forehead—

I take a quick step forward and rip the paper out of her pocket.

"Hey!" she says.

I ignore her and unfold it.

It's a wanted poster. With my picture on it. And the words "$50,000 Reward" printed in bold.

So much for the future of mutant-human relations.

"Thanks for the help," I say. "Who did you talk to? The army? The police?"

"Nobody," she says. "I didn't talk to anybody. Ms. Parrish just got this down at the front desk, and I wanted to show you before—"

"Save it," I snap, and crumple the paper.

The girl puts a hand on my arm.

"I would never turn you in," she says. "Your friend saved my life. Saved my whole family. Nightcrawler, I mean. We were in Bosnia, and he—"

I pull away from her and shut down the computer. I gotta go. Now.

"I think you get a raw deal all the time," she calls after me. "You X-Men. That's why—"

"Freeze!"

A new voice. I turn to see two cops, two guns, twenty feet away.

Outside, sirens begin to howl.

7

"ON THE FLOOR," THE ONE CLOSER TO ME SAYS, motioning with his gun. "Now."

The second doesn't say anything.

I size them up.

The first guy, Hispanic, late thirties, pot belly, calm enough, holds the gun like he means business.

The other, Asian, late twenties, built like a weight-lifter, holds the gun like he wants to use it.

I hold my hands up and smile.

"Guys. Listen. You don't wanna mess with me," I say.

"Let's not play games," the older cop says. "On the floor. Now."

I shake my head. "I don't think so."

The younger cop moves closer. "Do it!"

He sounds a little tense. Good. I can work with that.

"You know who I am, right?" I ask, keeping my eyes focused on the younger cop.

"You're some kind of mutant freak is what you are," he says. "You killed a dozen people."

"Wrong," I say. "I'm an X-Man, bub. And I didn't kill anybody."

The older guy speaks up. "Then come peacefully. We'll straighten it all out."

I shake my head.

The girl steps forward.

"He's telling the truth," she says. "He is one of the X-Men, you know? He's Wolverine. He's a hero."

She says it with such conviction that I start to wonder if she wasn't tellin' the truth before, about ratting on me. Not that it matters, really, this second.

"We got twenty guys comin' behind us, buddy," the older cop says. "Now, unless you can dodge a bullet, I suggest you lie down—"

"Bullets can't hurt me," I say. "You can't hurt me."

The first flicker of doubt appears in the older guy's eyes.

The younger guy's hands twitch on the trigger of his weapon.

"Down!" he yells again. "Do it! Do it!"

I can see, right then, in my mind's eye, how the next few seconds are gonna unfold.

The younger guy is gonna make a move on me, try and scare me into goin' to the floor by comin' closer, by puttin' the gun to my head. When he moves, the older guy is going to turn and tell him to hold his position, to stay out of striking range.

Of course, I'll be movin' by then. The second the old guy's eyes are off me, I'm on him. I'll put him between me and the young guy, who'll hesitate, and then I'll be in close enough that the guns won't matter, and it won't take me more'n a few punches to knock them both cold, and then I'll be out of here, and on my way again.

It's gonna be perfect.

And then the girl messes it all up.

She takes a step forward and pulls out something from behind her back.

A book.

"Run, Wolverine!" she yells, and cocks her arm back to throw it. She's aiming for the younger cop. He turns his head, sees her ready to throw somethin' at him, and swings the gun around.

There's no good decision to make here.

He's panicking; he's going to shoot.

I leap toward him, try to get in between the gun and the girl.

The younger cop squeezes the trigger.

Half a dozen bullets in a row. I swear I can almost see them travelin' through the air. A helluva lot faster than I am.

One hits the book the girl's holdin', sends it flyin' out of her hand.

Three hit the wall.

One hits the girl, right in the shoulder. She spins and falls to the ground, screaming in pain.

I land on the ground, somersault, and turn.

The younger cop's gun is danglin' from his hand. He drops it to the ground.

His eyes are wide, glazed over in shock.

I feel myself losin' control, feel myself goin' into that berserker rage again.

'Cause seein' the girl lying on the ground there, I realize who she reminds me of. What she reminds me of.

Ronnie. That day at Dorval, when everything went bad.

Time seems to slow. I hear a voice comin' over the radio—no, over one of the cops' walkie-talkies. "Shots fired. Shots fired. We're on annex two, shots came from above." More voices than I can pay attention to.

My own voice.

My own scream.

I'm flyin' through the air at the young cop; my claws are out.

I come to myself just in time to pull them back in, to hit him with my fist instead of my claws. He staggers. The older guy fires at me. but his shot goes wide. He fires again. I swing the younger cop in front of me, and he can't fire a third time, and I drive the younger cop forward right into the older guy, even as he's reaching for his nightstick, and I slam 'em both backward into one of the big metal shelving units, one of the stacks, and that sways and bends, and books the size of encyclopedias start fallin' from the shelves like rain, and I step back as the cops are buried under an avalanche of 'em.

I look back at the girl on the floor and the cops in front of me, and I know that whatever hot water I was in before, it's been doubled—hell, tripled—now.

I run back to the computer and rip the power cord out of the wall, cover my tracks.

The older cop is emerging from underneath a pile of books. Behind him, at the end of the row of books, I see a window.

Flashing blue lights shinin' through it.

I run that way, pausing long enough to topple over a second stack on top of the older cop, burying him for a second time.

I reach the window and look outside.

The library annex—the building I'm in—is circular. Shaped like a doughnut, three rings high. The main building—the one I entered through—is behind it, to my left. There's a little plaza in the front, ringed by a row of fake-looking shrubs, a patch of lawn next to it.

When I entered, the plaza was empty.

It's jampacked now, full of cop cars and flashing lights and guys in uniforms and suits. I see students being escorted out of the building.

I see a cop talkin' to a woman whose silhouette resembles that of Ms. Parrish.

I see a chopper coming in for a landing. It sets down on the plaza, and a bunch of guys in camo jumpsuits jump out. Guys with awfully big guns. Army guys. How they hell did they get here so quickly?

Makes me think Osborne might not have been blowing smoke after all, that what was happening at the Ark really was some kind of government operation. I don't like that idea at all, but I ain't got time to dwell on it right now.

I gotta clear out. Of the library, the city, the state . . .

Maybe even the whole damn country.

The window is painted shut. I slice along the molding, peel off the old paint, and kick it open. Squeeze my head out and look down. It's forty feet to the ground.

I make twenty-five or so of 'em using a fire hose I find along the wall. The last fifteen I have to jump. I land just in time. The Army guys have been settin' up klieg lights on the ground; they go on as I land, illuminating the outside of the library. The glare reflects off the building, off the plaza, making the night bright as day for a second.

I duck low behind a trash barrel just as another cop car comes squealin' up the drive in front of the library.

I dash across the concrete and right up next to the copter. I put a hand on the passenger-side door and freeze.

The pilot's one of Osborne's soldiers.

He's from the Ark.

I freeze.

No doubt about it now—the Ark is a government operation.

As I'm absorbin' that bit of bad news, more comes my way.

The pilot turns and sees me.

He blinks, as if he can't quite process what he's lookin' at.

I unfreeze, yank the door open, and rip him out of the seat.

". . . right here, he's right here . . ." the guy says into the headset he's wearing, but that's all he has time for. I hurl him out of the copter and to the ground outside.

Two camo-suited soldiers turn and see him.

Then they see me and pull their guns out. Raise them.

I look around the copter. There's a lever on my left, a stick between my legs, two pedals on the floor in front of me.

Don't think, I tell myself. *Just go.*

I slam the lever forward, and the copter rises in the air.

I'm operating purely on instinct, muscle memory. Been a long, long time since I flew a chopper.

My feet work the pedals; my left hand's on the collective—that's what the lever is called—my right on the cyclic. The joystick.

I'm up over the trees in front of the library. I'm up over the campus almost before I can think. I can hear the bullets whistling by.

I slam the stick forward, and I'm out over Flamingo Road. Right over it; I can hear cars screeching and honking underneath me as I pass.

I gotta get higher.

The collective; the cyclic; the pedals.

I hear a voice comin' from the seat next to me: I turn and see the headset the pilot was wearing. Do I care what's comin' over the air?

I put on the headset.

". . . unidentified air vehicle, you are in restricted airspace, please proceed immediately to . . ."

It's the local control tower. I don't care what they're saying.

I rip the wire out of the control panel, and the noise stops.

I look out through the glass: there's the Strip, the MGM, the monorail. The steel frame of the Paradise's hotel tower. Interstate 15, heading south to LA, north to Salt Lake.

I check the fuel gauge: close to full. I do a little math in my head, a little thinking about the information I need and where I'm likely to find it. About how popular—or, rather, unpopular—I'm gonna be with the local authorities, local meaning not just Vegas but Nevada and beyond.

That same face that flashed in front of my eyes back at the library flashes in front of 'em again, and I make my decision.

I bank the chopper hard right. Takes me a minute

or two to clear the metropolis; then I shut the lights and bring the copter as low to the ground as I can get it. I keep the highway in sight, to my right.

I keep my final destination firmly in mind.

Half a year after they took him off the active roster, J.C. left Department H. "They" meaning the suits who financed the team, government guys like Wilson and Conway, not "they" meaning me and Jimmy Hudson, who were operational heads of the squad. We had nothin' to do with the decision—didn't stop J.C. from blamin' us, though, me in particular. Called me all sorts of names the afternoon we told him the news. Threw a few halfhearted punches. I didn't blame him, really. I even let a couple of 'em connect.

As Jimmy said to me, more than once, I'd been J.C.'s role model for a while, the first few months he was with us. A bit of a hero to him, for the way I stood up to those suits every now and then, the way I told Conway to leave the trainin' to us and to concentrate on his paperwork, the way I kept shooting down Wilson's stupid suggestions at every mission briefing.

We had more than our share of good times back then, me and Jimmy and J.C. And Ronnie, which was, when you get down to it, the real reason things between me and Jean-Claude went so sour so fast.

The copter dies sixty miles out of Helena, sputtering far enough in advance that I'm able to make a decent landing out in the middle of somebody's farm.

Somebody whose lights go on, whose voices I can hear yellin' behind me as I take off at a run in the general direction of the interstate. I don't make it all the way there; first road I hit, I find a gas station. Closed, but not to me. I break in, grab food—such as it is—out of the mini-mart, and hot-wire a motorcycle I find in the back. I leave a note with my apologies, tellin' the owner to bill me for the bike, c/o Charlie Xavier, Westchester.

By sunup, I'm seein' signs for Sweetgrass and the border. I pull off the road and grab some shut-eye. At twilight, I wake and cross into the last remnants of Her Majesty's Empire on the North American continent, headin' due north again. Midafternoon the next day, I'm pullin into Fort Mac, Fort McMurray.

It's a boomtown now; it was a boomtown ten years ago, the first time I saw it. Boomtown meaning a lot of migrant workers comin' in to work the refining plants, to help pull the oil out of the Athabasca sands. I drive down Franklin, the main drag, and get some dirty looks from the locals. Like they remember me. Remember what happened here a decade back.

Which is maybe not so crazy. 'Cause I remember. I can't hardly forget, after all.

Fort Mac's where it all started. For me, for Ronnie, for J.C.

Fort Mac, in a way, is where it all ended, too.

I take a little jog out of my way, for old times' sake, for Ronnie's sake, past the power plant and the church.

I pull up in front of her parents' house and almost—almost—ring the doorbell.

Then I shake off the past, concentrate on the here and now.

J.C.'s house—his compound—is northeast of the town. I put the pedal to the metal and head in that direction. Twenty minutes and a few turns later, the road ends. A trail continues off into the woods—two yellow slashes across the base of a pine marking where it starts. I ditch the bike and start walking. Soon enough, I come to a clearing.

J.C.'s house sits in the middle of it. Looks exactly the same as it did half a dozen years back, last time I was here, except the cinderblocks on the south side of the ground floor are painted a slightly different shade of red from the others. They mark the spot where J.C. put up a new wall, to replace the one we knocked down last time I came out here. During our little "get-reacquainted conversation."

I was comin' through Alberta, thought it was time to try and patch things up between us. Figured enough time had passed, figured I'd grown up a little, thanks to Xavier. Figured I owed J.C. an apology or two, and if he saw fit to send one my way for his behavior . . . that'd be fine, too.

I called him. He seemed surprised to hear from me. We met in Fort Mac. We had a drink at a bar there. It was awkward; he didn't seem comfortable, kept looking around like he was afraid people might recognize him. We made small talk. I told him things he probably already knew about my life, about the X-Men. He told me that Wilson had hired him back, to help design some new databases for the CIC.

An hour or so into the meal, he loosened up. I couldn't tell if it was the liquor or not. He had somethin' he wanted to tell me; no, he decided, somethin' he wanted to show me. Somethin' out at his place.

When we got out there, we opened a second bottle of wine—mistake number one.

Mistake number two: I brought up Ronnie. I tried to apologize. He told me to forgot about it; it didn't matter. It really didn't matter. What was done was done. Guess I took that the wrong way. "You still sayin' it was my fault?"

"You sayin' it wasn't," he asked.

It went downhill from there. I guess I wasn't in the mood to let him hit me that night. He ended up with a shiner; I woulda had one myself, only the healing factor was working strong back in those days. Which is to say that he gave as good as he got that night; I was impressed. He hadn't just been sittin' on his butt, tidyin' up the government's data. He'd been keepin' himself in shape.

Can't say we ended up settling things between us, but at least we got it all out in the open. Gave us something to build on, or at least I thought so at the time.

I wonder what kind of reception I'm gonna get now. Wonder if workin' for the government has made him a government man. I wonder for a few long minutes, in the gathering darkness, and then decide there's no point in wondering further.

I cross the clearing to the steel doors that serve as the house's main entrance. Doesn't look like anyone's home. I'd ring the bell, only there is no bell. Just an electronic keypad to the right of the door. A speaker above it—an intercom system, most likely. Probably a camera up there as well.

"Hey! J.C.!"

I wait a minute. No reply.

Under normal circumstances, I'd leave and come back later.

These aren't normal circumstances, though.

I turn to the keypad. Your standard twelve-digit type, like on a telephone, numbers and letters on each key. Punch in the right code, the door swings open. Punch in the wrong one . . .

Something bad happens.

I take a deep breath and punch in "Athabasca." The door swings open. Cool air comes with it, climate-controlled. I hear the steady hum of machinery in the background; I can almost sense the current. I sense somethin' else, too: danger.

I take a step forward; the floorboard creaks beneath my feet. I wait for a reaction, a sound. I take a second and then a third step. Still nothing. Then I'm all the way in. I let my eyes adjust to the darkness.

There's enough light comin' through the windows

that I can make out the layout of the house: looks exactly the same as it did six years ago. I'm in an entryway. Stairs right in front of me. A door to my left, a door to my right . . .

Sudden movement from that direction.

I get my hand up just in time to catch a wrist, a grunt of surprise, of pain. I take the wrist and twist it. The wrist was holdin' somethin'; it clatters to the floor.

A foot slams into my gut, slammin' me into the wall. My grip on the wrist loosens. I sense, rather than see, another fist flyin' for me, and I duck, and it slams into the wall, and then I kick out, leg-sweep, sending my attacker to the floor, and then I got one arm up, claws popped, ready to end it.

And the guy under me starts to laugh.

I blink, and the scene comes into focus.

"Look what we have here," he says. "America's most wanted."

I stop my hand in mid-strike, 'cause I recognize that voice.

It's J.C.

8

I GAVE HIM THE NICKNAME THE FIRST WEEK WE
met: J.C., short not for Jean-Claude but Jesus Christ,
'cause he was always such a know-it-all about everything. The first time I called him that, I thought he
was gonna explode. I guess it was also the first time
somebody actually dared to tease him, to treat him as
if he was normal. Took him a couple of weeks to get
over it.

Of course, by that time, he had another nickname
as well, one he liked a lot better. Daemon. His official
code name within the group. *Daemon* meaning the lit-
eral "ghost in the machine," the guy so deep inside the
computer system that he was part of it.

I never liked the name. I didn't think it was accurate. J.C.'s mutation was that he had a parallel processor for a brain; he could be arguing one side of a
complex problem with you and workin' on another

while he talked. Daemon didn't accurately describe that ability, far as I was concerned.

Another reason I didn't like the name, I suppose: Wilson came up with it.

I get up and extend a hand. J.C. gets to his feet.

"Logan," he says. "You look terrible."

"There's a reason for that."

"I know."

"You know."

He nods. "It's all over the news. Even up here. You're a person of interest."

He waves a hand at the wall, and the lights come on.

We're standing in the middle of a large, open space—table off to my left, like I said before, stairs in front of me. No other furniture. Bare wood floors, bare walls painted industrial white.

J.C.'s in jeans and a blue work shirt. What hair he has left is cut in a GI flat-top. He's lost weight—not that he needed to. Back in the day, he went six foot, one-sixty. Looks five pounds down from that now. Looks like one of those Hollywood actors—body of a fifteen-year-old kid, face of a forty-year-old guy.

He's wearing some kind of earpiece in his right ear, some kind of metallic bracelet on his right wrist.

We stare at each other a second.

"So I'm a person of interest?"

"That's right."

"You gonna call in the cavalry?"

"The government, you mean?"

"You know what I mean."

"Maybe I should. Call Hudson, put the decision in his lap."

He smiles. I don't.

"I didn't do any of it—what they're saying."

"Of course not. You're a Super Hero."

I shake my head. I don't know why I'm bothering.

"You ever hear of a guy named Wyndham? Herbert Edgar Wyndham?"

J.C. blinks.

I think it's the first time in my life I've ever seen him surprised. As if those words, comin' out of my mouth, were the last thing he expected to hear.

"Wyndham? The High Evolutionary?"

"One and the same," I say.

And then I give him the *Reader's Digest* version of my last couple of weeks. The tiger, Osborne, Brinklow, the wolf guys, the casino, the library. By the time I'm finished talking, he's smiling again, his usual cat-ate-the-canary smile, his I've-forgotten-more-than-you'll-ever-know smile that always drove me crazy. Still does.

I can't figure out why he's wearin' it now.

"So you think it was Wyndham experimenting on you?"

"I do."

He nods. "And why would he pick you for a test subject?"

"I don't think he planned it. I just happened to be

there. What he was doin' to me, though . . . that's what I want to find out."

"And you came to me for help." His smile broadens. "I'm touched. Why not call Xavier?"

I ignore the question. "You gonna help me, or not?"

"My guess is," he says, ignoring me the way I ignored him, "it's got somethin' to do with your claws. With why I see bone, not metal."

I glare.

"With why you were in Nevada in the first place. Trying to clear your head, I suspect. Deal with the fact that you're not quite as capable as you—"

"Enough!" I don't mean to yell, but I do. The guy gets under my skin. He always has.

"Sorry, Logan. I forgot how sensitive you were."

He smiles at his little victory.

I take a deep breath, calm down a second.

"So you want to find out where Wyndham and this other guy—"

"Osborne, yes. Where they went. What they might be up to."

He nods. "Well. I'm interested, too, now that I hear the story. I'll be glad to help."

"I appreciate it."

I hold out my hand. He reaches for it, we shake, and then he frowns.

"You could do somethin' for me, too," he says.

"Oh? What's that?"

"Shower."

He means it like a joke.

One thing J.C.'s never been, though, is funny.

I decide to take him up on the offer anyway. He turns to lead me up the stairs; the door to our right, the door he came through, clicks closed as we start up.

Somebody else is in the house, I realize. My senses ain't what they used to be, but all at once, I think I smell perfume. A woman.

J.C.'s a step ahead of me, a foot on the stairs already. He doesn't notice that I've noticed he's got company. I decide not to say anything. I smile anyway; part of me, the part that remembers how close the two of us used to be, feels good that he isn't spending all his time buildin' databases and playin' with test tubes, that he's got somethin' resembling a life goin' on now.

That he's moved on. That he's left Ronnie behind him, in the past, where she belongs.

Unlike me, who all of a sudden can't seem to stop thinking about her.

He leads me into the bathroom, hands me a set of spare clothes, and shuts the door behind him.

I start the water goin'; while I wait for it to get hot, I peel off my clothes and take a good look at myself in the mirror.

The little repair job I did back at UNLV has just about worn off.

My temporary tattoo is gone. The hair dye's gone

with it. I got bags under my bags; I got scrapes and bruises on every square inch of my body. I look like I just went fifteen rounds with Muhammad Ali in his prime; I look beat up. I look tired, washed out. Old.

Somethin' I've known for a long, long time—the healing factor slowed the aging process in my body. I mean, the last fifty years of my life, I've looked like a thirty-five-year-old man. Kinda lulled me into a false sense of security, lulled me into thinking I was immortal.

Wrong, of course; we're all livin' on borrowed time. Some of us just gotta pay it back sooner than others.

And again, I think about Ronnie.

I get dressed, come downstairs. J.C.'s standin' right where I left him, ear cocked to one side, like he's listenin' to somethin', which, of course, he is, the little doodad in his ear. An implant? A headset? Who knows?

I clear my throat. He looks up at me and nods.

"This way," he says. He leads me through the room with the table into the kitchen. Seein' his refrigerator, my stomach rumbles.

"You got any food?"

He smiles, shakes his head. "A mature digestive system doesn't benefit from food."

"Call me immature, then. You got anything?"

He opens a cupboard and pulls out a bottle of

vitamins. I see a dozen more just like it in the cabinet behind it.

"Concentrates," he says, offering it to me. "Full vitamin panel, glucosamine, coral calcium, magnesium, beta glusin—"

I take the bottle just to shut him up.

"This really is all you got?"

"All I got."

I open the bottle and pour out a handful.

"Two," he says.

I take six.

He shakes his head and puts the bottle back.

"Savin' up for a rainy day," I say.

He puts the bottle back, walks over to the microwave, and presses a series of buttons; *beep-beep, beep-beep, beep-beep.*

A low-pitched rumbling sound comes from underneath the floor, the sound of gears rumbling into place. Of big machines going to work.

The counter begins to slide away from me, moving toward the far wall. It travels about four feet and stops. Where it was, there's now a big dark opening in the floor. A light comes on a second later; there's a staircase leading down.

"Ooohhh," I say. "Real *Mission: Impossible* kind of stuff."

He smiles thinly. I can tell he's mad at me makin' fun of his toys.

"Don't be jealous," he says finally, and starts down

the stairs. "I cleared a path for a secure data trace while you were showering. We'll have ten minutes or so to search whatever databases you want before we start leaving footprints."

"Whatever you say," I tell him.

Downstairs is a warren of machines, with a space in the center. It's a raised platform, kind of like a throne. Surrounded by a circle of flat-screen monitors.

J.C. climbs the throne and sits.

He flexes his fingers. "Wyndham," he repeats.

"That's right."

He nods, smiles, and leans forward in his chair.

He taps on the screen in front of him, and a keyboard appears on it. He slides his fingers across the keyboard—looks as if he's just stroking the screen—but clearly he did something else, because the word "Wyndham" pops onto the display. J.C. touches the screen again, and a bunch of icons follow it.

"Databases," he says, and puts his hand on the screen again, right on the word "Wyndham," which he then physically drags over all the icons. "The clock starts now."

The other screens start filling with information. J.C. spins slowly in his chair.

There's nine screens total, countin' the one with the keyboard. I try to watch more than one of 'em but lose track pretty quickly.

J.C. keeps spinning slowly in his chair, watching them all.

"Here," he says, pointing to one. "A John Wyndham is part of the holding company that owns the land the casino is being built on. The Paradise."

"Could be him," I say.

"Doubtful," he says, and keeps turning. Every few seconds, he reaches out and touches one of the other screens, stopping the data flow.

"Newspaper article . . . no.

"Similar name, criminal database . . . no.

"Banking activity . . . no."

He goes on like that for a couple of minutes, swiveling this way and that, readin' data off the screens around him, then shakes his head.

"Nothing," he says. "No current information on Wyndham's whereabouts. Nothing at all."

I'm about to say you can't possibly know that when I remember who I'm talkin' to, and what his head can hold.

"Okay," I tell him. "Let's try Osborne."

"First name?"

"We didn't get around to discussing that. But he's connected to a weapons dealer named Culver."

"Culver." J.C. smiles again. "Of course. I remember him."

Of course he does, I realize. He was liaison on that op.

J.C. repeats the process; data start flowing across the screens, too fast for me to follow. J.C. sits back in his chair, takin' it all in.

Something on one of the screens catches my eye: movement.

I lean forward, and before J.C. can stop me, I touch the screen myself.

The display I put my fingers on has been playin' video—a piece of video, now frozen in mid-movement, that looks strangely familiar to me.

Takes me another second to figure out why.

"It's security-cam footage," I say. "From that night. From Culver's arrest."

I shake my head. I never saw this before. Never even knew it existed.

"I'd ask you," J.C. says, his voice tight, "not to do that again. To touch my equipment."

"Didn't know if you saw it," I said.

"I saw it." He touches the screen himself, and the figures on it start to move once more.

The video shows half a dozen guys in parkas and combat boots, standing by a warehouse docking bay. Each holdin' an automatic weapon, each scannin' the street and the dock behind them for unwanted company. The six guys form a rough circle around four others: two Chinese guys, two more in parkas. One of the guys in the circle I recognize. Seein' him refreshes my memory. Rodney Culver, skeezy little British guy, maybe a hundred-twenty pounds soaking wet. There's a crate open on the dock; one of the Chinese guys has out what looks like a rocket launcher. He's examining it closely.

Me and Jimmy appear out of nowhere, come down from above, screamin' to beat the band.

I'm leadin' the way, wearing my bright yellow uniform. I don't know whose brilliant idea that was—bright yellow uniform? Department H was supposed to be an under-the-radar operation. Yellow never made sense to me. Not that it mattered that night. We were in an isolated area; it didn't matter how much noise we made.

The first two guys make the mistake of trying to fight. I take them out in about five seconds. Don't even have to draw my claws.

While I'm handling the muscle, Jimmy's going for the brains of the operation. On the screen, he flies forward, and kayos one of the Chinese guys. The other picks up the rocket launcher and tries to use it like a club. Culver turns to run. His man draws a gun and steps forward, right into the camera's line of sight.

Sonuvagun.

I'm about to tap the screen again when I remember what J.C. said. I decide to be polite.

"Hey, freeze that, will you?"

J.C. taps the screen; the image holds.

I smile.

It's Osborne.

He's got a full head of hair—red hair, to my surprise—and fewer wrinkles. He's also got a scar runnin' down the side of his face, which I don't remember from the Ark, but that's beside the point.

"No doubt about it."

"Okay." J.C. slides his hand across the display; the security-cam video shrinks, moves to a corner of the screen, frozen on that shot of Osborne. Somethin' about the image bothers me, but I can't quite put a finger on it.

"Here we are," J.C. says.

I shift my gaze, and I'm lookin' at the rap sheet for one Riley P. Osborne, a.k.a. Richard O'Connell, a.k.a. Randall Oliver, a.k.a. Gerard Joubert. Impressive soldier-of-fortune statistics, if you go for that kind of thing. Born May 12, 1964, Montreal, high-school dropout, first arrest armed robbery at eighteen, five years in jail, arrested in South Africa by British Security Forces 1981, deported, arrested in Vancouver 1986 for arms smuggling, two years served . . .

I frown.

"The Culver thing—that was his second arrest for arms smuggling. He should've gone in for a good long while. Instead"—I point at the screen—"he's out after six months."

J.C.'s smiling. "He had a good lawyer, obviously."

I'm not amused. It ain't funny when a thug like Osborne gets caught red-handed and gets off with a slap on the wrist.

"So where's he now?"

"Checking that," J.C. says, his fingers already moving. He pulls the rap sheet to one side; it disappears off the edge of the screen. He taps a folder icon once, and then a second time, and a series of other icons spill out. He fans through them and drags one forward. It's a maple leaf.

He taps it again, and the leaf changes into a folder. There's writing on the front—"Department of Foreign Affairs"—and a flag. The Canadian flag. Osborne's name is on it as well.

The top sheet in the file is exactly what we're looking for: a record of Osborne's movements in and out of the country. A few trips to Europe, a few more to Asia, the most recent of which was more than two years ago.

"Dead end," J.C. says.

I shake my head. "Not so fast. Go back to his rap sheet."

J.C. does. I point to the top line—the list of Osborne's aliases.

"Let's check those names, too."

We find nothing on Oliver or Joubert, but under O'Connell, we strike paydirt.

Two dozen trips to Hong Kong in the last year, stays of a couple of weeks each time. Announced purpose of said visits: gathering zoological specimens.

"Wyndham's raw materials," I say, reading off a list of those specimens. "Chimpanzees. Multiple varieties of the Asian wolf. Shipped by V.C. Import/Export, 2440 Cotton Tree Lane, Hong Kong."

"Hong Kong," J.C. says. "That's a long way off."

"It sure is," I say, and clock him right across the jaw.

Down he goes—and out.

I feel bad about punchin' him out, for a second, but only a second. I just don't trust the guy. Somethin' about the way he kept smiling at me, like the cat that ate the canary . . .

I do a quick search of the house. I don't find any money upstairs or down.

The door to the right of the main entrance, the door I smelled the perfume comin' out from before, is locked. I decide not to force it.

I leave J.C. a note of thanks, and apology, and then I'm gone, out the door, down the trail, back on my bike, and back out on the highway, headin' west as fast as I can.

I use the back roads, navigating by the seat of my pants. I siphon off gas from a parked truck at an all-night diner. It gets me out of Alberta and into British Columbia, and from there I push north to Juneau, where I sell the bike and find an old buddy from the Corps who now works at the Marine Safety Office. He wants me to come in, turn myself over to him for safekeeping. Says it's not safe for me to travel, not because of Vegas but because of Avalon. Or, rather, what happened before Avalon, what prompted Xavier to schedule our little visit up to Magneto's home away from home in the first place. The so-called master of magnetism's disruption of the worldwide energy grid, which killed a few thousand people or so. My buddy tells me that ruffled quite a few feathers down in Washington, sparked up quite a bit of antimutant sentiment among the powers that be.

Things are in the works, he tells me, though he doesn't know what those things are. Things that are gonna make the world an awfully cold place for people like me. For mutants. Even colder than it usually is.

I tell my buddy thanks, but no thanks. It's been goin' on a week since I broke up Wyndham's party down in Vegas. Since Osborne said their work at the Ark was finished.

I don't know how soon whatever comes next is going to happen, but there's no sense in giving those guys too big a head start.

He gets me cash anyway, no questions asked. Enough for me to buy a fake passport and a ticket across the Pacific. I splurge, go first class, figurin' that after the last couple of weeks, I deserve a good night's rest.

Soon enough, I'm kickin' back in a fully reclining leather seat, with an airplane steak and a cold frosty one restin' comfortably in my stomach and a beautiful stewardess leanin' over me adjusting the pillow beneath my head.

I close my eyes and prepare for dreamland.

Of course, I can't sleep.

I end up spendin' the entire plane ride starin' out

the window. Thinkin' about the Ark, and the High Evolutionary, and Osborne. About Magneto, and Pietro, and Jean, and Xavier. J.C., Ronnie, Jimmy Hudson, and Heather. It's like my life is flashin' before my eyes.

That's not usually a good omen.

9

YOU SAY HONG KONG TO PEOPLE, THEY THINK
Berlin for some reason, Berlin from back in the Cold
War days, an island of democracy in the middle of a
Communist country. The island part is right—Hong
Kong is surrounded by water on all sides—but it's not
just one city. It's not even one island; Hong Kong territory includes a couple hundred islands south of the
Chinese mainland. There's Kowloon, Lantau, what
are called the New Territories, and Hong Kong Island
proper, the southernmost island, the beatin' heart—
economically, politically—of the entire region.

The north shore of Hong Kong Island is where
most of the people are, where most of the development is. The place is a crazy mix of Chinese and British culture, Chinese and British stores, Chinese and
British signs, mostly Chinese people. On the outskirts
of most of that development, 2440 Cotton Tree Lane is

a two-story brick building with a plate-glass storefront that's seen better days.

The cabby drops me by the entrance.

Seen through the glass, V.C. Import/Export looks like your standard flea-market kind of wholesaler, a couple of racks of Armani knockoffs, a wall full of unlocked cell phones, shelves of athletic sneakers, etc. There's a long glass counter along one wall; behind it is a kid—not much more than a teenager, really—sitting at a computer, oblivious to me standin' at the window, oblivious to just about everything except the screen in front of him and the plate of food at his elbow.

Talk about American kids bein' overweight . . . This kid has to be three hundred pounds. And growin'. Puttin' the fork to his face like there was no tomorrow.

I chide myself for uncharitable thoughts. Maybe it's somethin' genetic.

I push through the door; a little bell rings. The kid looks my way.

"No retail," he says, around a mouthful of noodles. "Wholesale only. Sorry."

He goes back to his game.

I clear my throat. "Who's in charge here?"

He looks at me again and shakes his head. "No retail, sorry."

He goes back to the game.

I move through the store, takin' a closer look at the displays. The clothes are six months out of style. So are the electronics.

I turn back to the counter.

"Hey, kid."

He puts the fork down at last. "Dude," he says, in a voice that tells me he's seen one too many American movies. "We are not a retail establishment. *Comprende?*"

The kids's got dark straight hair just over his ears and handsome features, if they weren't surrounded by so much blubber. He's wearing a blue silk shirt and black pants with creases so sharp you could cut your hand on 'em.

"I *comprende.* Now *comprende* this."

I take a step toward him. He shrinks back.

"This place is a front, sonny. And I know what for. So do us both a favor. Stop wastin' my time, and tell me where your boss is."

"Dude," he says again. "I don't know what you're talkin' about."

But he does. I can see it in his eyes.

I take another step.

He stands up, knocking over a stack of business cards next to the cash register in the process. They fan out across the counter.

"One more step, I call the police, okay?"

I shrug. "Okay."

He makes like he's reaching for the phone—

And then lunges out from behind the counter, moving toward the door. He moves quickly, a lot more quickly than I'd expect from someone his size.

But I'm quicker.

I grab the kid by the back of the shirt and spin him around so that our faces are almost touching. Takes some effort, considerin' the weight I'm pullin'.

"Forget your boss. You know a guy named Osborne?"

He shakes his head.

I remember the alias.

"What about O'Connell? Anybody named O'Connell?"

He shakes his head again—but I see the yes in his eyes.

"When's the last time you saw him?"

"Come on, man, give me a break," he says.

I do. I loosen up on my grip.

Mistake.

The kid's hand flashes under the counter. He comes up holdin' a gun.

"Dude," he says. "Now you leave the store. *Comprende?*"

I smack him across the face and grab the weapon out of his hands.

"Lesson one: Respect your elders." I tuck the gun into the waistband at the back of my pants. "Lesson two: Tell the truth. Understand?"

The kid glares and curses at me in Mandarin.

I repeat the lessons for him in the same language.

He glares again but nods his head slowly up and down.

"Good," I say, switchin' back to English. "'Cause if you tell me the truth, I won't need to go on to lesson three. And believe me, you don't want lesson three."

The kid nods some more. At the same time, his right hand sneaks under the counter.

Spunky little bastard.

I grab his wrist and lean over to take a look. This time, he's not reachin' for a weapon. He's reachin' for a button near the cash register.

I let his hand go. "Be my guest."

He presses the button. "You're gonna be sorry," he says. "Very sorry."

I smile back. I've been told that before.

A voice comes out of the air. A woman's voice, from a speaker under the counter.

"What is it, Freddy?"

"There's a guy down here."

"A guy."

"Name of Logan," I say, leaning forward. "I'm a friend of Mr. O'Connell's."

Silence. Then, "One minute."

I hear footsteps sound upstairs. Heavy footsteps, more than one set. Coming down toward us.

"Freddy," I say, lookin' at the kid. "You don't look like a Freddy."

"Frederick," he says. "My father was British. A diplomat."

"You could use a few lessons from him. In the art of diplomacy."

Freddy glares some more.

A door at the back of the store bursts open. Two men walk through; big guys. Enforcer types. A woman follows. The Shanghai Lil type.

Freddy points at me. "This is the guy. He was asking about Osborne."

The woman folds her arms across her chest. "And what did you tell him?"

"I didn't tell him anything."

"You called me." She shakes her head, walks up to him, and caresses the side of his face with one hand. "That told him something, didn't it? Freddy, Freddy, Freddy."

She slaps him hard, right across the face. Same side I just hit the kid on.

"Hey," he says. "What was that—"

She backhands him hard across the other side.

Freddy—all three hundred pounds of him—stumbles backward. The floor shakes a little. Lady's got some force to her punch; she knows how to hit.

"We'll discuss this later. At length."

The woman turns to me then. She's got good teeth. Very good teeth. A lot of other good points as well, visually speaking.

"Now. Mister . . . ?"

"Logan."

"Mister Logan. What is it exactly you want?"

"Information. Regarding O'Connell and a few recent purchases he made from you. Some animals. Zoological specimens."

The woman's gaze sharpens. "Mr. O'Connell made no such purchases here, I'm afraid."

She's lying. Probably they were illegal purchases. I don't care.

"Fine. Forget the animals. What I'm really interested in is O'Connell. Whatever information you got on him. Show me that, and I'm outta here. I won't bother you again."

She shakes her head. "Our customer records are confidential."

"I'll keep 'em that way. Between you and me."

"I don't think so, Mr. Logan."

I take one last shot.

"Listen, miss—"

"Ms. Siaow." She pronounces it "see-ow."

"Ms. Siaow." I spread my hands. "I don't know how much clearer I can make it. I got no interest in you, or Freddy, or Frick and Frack here." I nod at the two goons, who have taken up position on either side of her. "No interest in ratting you out to the authorities. No interest in investigating your little import/export scam, or—"

"I'm afraid you're wasting your time here, Mr. Logan. And mine." She snaps her fingers. The two goons step forward.

"My associates here will show you to the door."

I smile and take off my jacket. "We'll have to see about that, won't we?"

The two goons circle slowly, one on either side

of me. Their movements have a surprising kind of fluidity—a little more grace than I might've expected from a couple bruisers. Each of them has to be a couple inches over six feet, a few pounds on either side of the two hundred mark.

I don't want to use the claws, unless I have to. Point of professional pride. Another consideration: I don't want to alert Wyndham, or anyone associated with Wyndham, that I'm no longer in the States.

The guy on the right starts it.

He comes with a spinning leg kick; of course, it's just a feint, on the one hand for the hammer strike he's drawing back his right arm for or, on the other, for the pile-driver kick the guy on my left—now directly behind me—is launching.

I'm moving even as the leg kick flies past my head. I grab hold of that leg and move into his defense. He's too close for the hammer strike now; by the time he sees that, though, I'm even closer. Head butt; bloody nose.

The guy staggers.

I bring my arms back, clap them together over his ears. His eyes roll back in his head. He's down, I'm turning to absorb the pile-driver kick with my hip bone—

And I get a solid karate punch, right in the breadbasket. Knocks the wind out of me for a second. I stagger backward.

Ms. Siaow steps forward and smiles.

The lady not only knows how to hit, she's fast.

"I can see I will need to attend to this matter personally," she says.

Now it's her and goon number two, circling me. She's better trained than her errand boys; I can tell by the way she stands, the way her eyes dart back and forth, up and down, from my face to my feet, from my feet to my waist, and back up. Judging my intent, my center of gravity. When I'm in position to attack, when I'm prepared to defend.

I'm studying her, too. And the goon.

"You can show me those records now, if you want," I say.

She says nothing.

"Don't know how much Osborne paid you," I say, "but I can pretty much guarantee it's not worth it. Not worth taking the kind of beating he did."

I jerk my head in the direction of goon number one, still down on the ground, motionless.

They attack.

Must've been some kind of signal I missed. He comes from behind me, charging like a freight train. I got no choice but to react, to step aside. That's their plan.

She's waiting.

Thunder punch to the chest. I stagger. She delivers a second. And then a third, in rapid succession, too fast for me to follow her hands, or counter.

The big guy's back by then. He delivers a thunder

punch of his own. I go flying across the room and smack into the wall. I get to my feet, try to get my breath.

Ms. Siaow smiles.

She and goon number two charge again.

She launches herself straight at me, with a pile-driver kick of her own, boot heel first. Headed right for my forehead. I wait till the last possible second to lean out of the way. I catch her around the ankle. The smile on her face turns to a frown. She grimaces, try-ing to keep her balance.

Goon number two wades in, fists flying. One grazes my chin. I slide away, to my right, sweep kickin' at the same time. He goes down. I stomp his wrist. *Crunch.* He screams in pain. Heel to the forehead; he's out.

Mrs. Siaow spins out of my clutches. Spins back with a roundhouse kick. I lean back, lose my balance. She comes with a thunder punch again. Right into my gut. This time, I'm ready.

Her fist hits tensed muscle. She grimaces. I smile.

"Lucky for you I'm a gentleman," I say, and tap her on the jaw.

Well . . . not exactly a tap. Somewhere between that and a thunder punch. Her eyes roll back in her head, and down she goes.

I check the two goons; they're out, too. All three of them should be down for at least another hour. Plenty of time for me to find what I'm looking for. Especially considering I'm going to have help.

I glance around. The store looks empty. But I know it's not.

"Freddy!"

No response.

"Don't make me say it twice."

His head peeks out from under the counter.

"What do you say you and me have a look at those records, hey?"

He doesn't say anything. He just gulps.

I can hear him clear across the room.

There's a little office at the top of the stairs, with a little computer and a little filing cabinet. The filing cabinet is full of paperwork related to the building and the company—V.C.'s charter, corporation, government papers, all that sort of stuff. The computer's full of individual transaction records.

There is none on O'Connell. Or Osborne. Or Wyndham, for that matter.

"The names aren't in the system," Freddy says. He's sitting at the computer, typing. The system seems like a Tinker Toy compared with what J.C. had, but that's no excuse. Those names oughtta be in there. O'Connell's, at least. Doesn't make sense.

"Here."

I pull a folded-up piece of paper out of my back pocket—some notes I made back on the plane—and lay it in front of Freddy.

"What's this?"

"A list of the dates O'Connell was in Hong Kong. Try cross-referencing these against . . ."

"Our transaction list. Yeah, yeah. I got it." The kid is already typing, fat fingers flying across the keys. Ten seconds later, he's shaking his head.

"No matches."

"That's not possible."

He points to the screen. "Have a look for yourself."

I do. First transaction in the list is a big shipment—twenty cargo containers, construction equipment from Chungking to the Philippines. That rings a bell. A second later, I realize why and snort in disgust.

"Construction equipment, my ass. That's the same scam Osborne and Culver used up in Montreal. You guys are moving weapons, aren't you? That's how Osborne knew to come to you in the first place."

"Osborne?"

"O'Connell, I mean. Just an alias he uses."

"Oh. Listen, dude—I don't know anything about any weapons, okay?"

The kid's body language tells me he's lying—again. It tells me somethin' else, too. He's ashamed of himself.

That's a point in his favor.

I soften my tone just a little. "Hey, kid, how'd you get mixed up in all this?"

"Born into it."

"What does that mean?"

He smiles ruefully. "It's the family business."

"I thought your dad was a diplomat."

"He is. It's Mom I'm talking about."

"Mom."

"Ms. Siaow. Downstairs?"

My turn to stand there slack-jawed. I try to think of something smart—or at least something not too stupid—to say. I can't, so I decide instead to avoid the topic altogether.

I look back at the list of transactions on-screen. Electronics equipment, bound for San Francisco. Cultural artifacts, headed for Tokyo. No animals whatsoever.

"Told you," Freddy said.

"Yeah. The question is why. Why isn't he in your system? O'Connell?"

Freddy shakes his head. "I don't know. Why are you after him? What did he do?"

"Long story."

He looks up. We make eye contact.

"He's a bad guy, isn't he?"

"He sure is."

Freddy frowns a minute, thinking. "Hold on."

"What?"

"Maybe he didn't buy the animals here."

"I don't understand."

"We play middleman a lot of times. Somebody—some tourist, some small company—buys something out in the middle of nowhere, they use our shipping guys, our permits to send them back home."

"How do we find out if that's what happened?"

"We make a call." He swivels in his chair, picks up the phone, and dials. He speaks in rapid-fire Mandarin. I get part of it. He asks for somebody named Jackie, he makes a little small talk, he mentions O'Connell's name, and then he gives me a thumbs up.

He starts reading transaction dates off the paper, askin' for the point of origin on each. After the first few, he says thanks and good-bye and hangs up.

"That's how it was," he says, turning to me. "We were just middlemen."

"So where'd the animals come from?"

"Wubeng. A little village to the northwest. Yunnan Province.

"Wubeng. Yunnan Province. Got it." I take the paper and turn toward the door. "Thanks for the help, kid."

"You have to go through Zhongdian."

"What?"

"To get to Wubeng. You gotta go through Zhongdian. Actually, you have to go from Hong Kong to Kunming and then Zhongdian."

"Okay. Thanks. I know where the airport is."

"No flights till tomorrow. To Zhongdian."

I raise an eyebrow.

"They only go twice a day. And the last one left an hour ago."

"Pretty familiar with the schedule, aren't you?"

"It's my job. It's what I do."

"They ever fly off schedule?" I ask.

He shrugs. "Sometimes. You gotta make it worth their while."

"Bribe 'em, you mean?"

"That's right."

"Anyone in particular I should ask for?"

"Depends, really. On who's flyin', what other runs they gotta make . . . it's a complicated thing."

I nod to show I understand. "Right. You really gotta know the players."

"Dude." He smiles. "Exactly."

I smile back.

"What?" he asks.

"Dude," I say. "I could use a hand."

"Huh?"

I grab him by the arm, lift him to his feet.

"You're comin' with me."

He protests, but most of what he says is lost in the sound of traffic as we step out onto the street, and I hail a cab.

10

GETTING OUT OF HONG KONG—GETTING TO
Kunming—that leg of the trip is no problem. Two
hours in the hold of an old cargo plane, backs pressed
up against cold steel, forty degrees, engines roaring . . .
seems like old times to me. Freddy's got his fingers in
his ears. I sleep like a baby. No dreams, even.

Getting to Zhongdian, though, turns out to be a
problem.

Seems there's bad weather rollin' in from the west.
Big storm.

We're in a little office about the size of the one
over V.C. Import/Export, and three times as crowded.
Freddy's arguing with a skinny guy with a droopy Fu
Manchu mustache and a dirty blue T-shirt, who's
chain-smokin' as he talks. He's the flight supervisor
for all cargo shipments goin' in and out of Kunming.

There's a map of China pinned to one of the walls;

as he's talkin', the skinny guy stabs at the map. Storm here, he says, jabbing a finger at a spot to the west of where we are. He tracks its path south and east as he talks. I take a look at the map.

Yunnan Province is in southeast China, bordering Vietnam and Laos to the south, Burma and Tibet to the west. The storm he's up in arms about is comin' from Tibet. Zhongdian, he says, is right in its path. It's gonna be a monster; they're canceling flights already.

He turns away from Freddy and starts pullin' slips of paper off the desk. He barks at someone outside the door to come in and hands the slips to him. He picks up the phone and starts yellin' into it.

This won't do.

I walk up to his desk and stand in front of him until I catch his eye. I stare until he hangs up.

"What?" he barks.

I pull out a wad of cash—a good chunk of what my buddy gave me, converted from U.S. dollars to multicolored yuan—and flash a handful of pink Maos at him.

"Zhongdian."

His eyes glitter at the sight of that money. But still, he shakes his head.

"No flights. Airport closed."

"That's all right."

He frowns. I smile and explain what I have in mind.

Freddy turns white.

The skinny guy looks at the cash in my hand again. I can see the drool forming at the corners of his mouth. I can hear the wheels spinning in his head.

He smiles and gets to his feet.

"Okay," he says. "Deal."

He holds out his hand. I put the cash in it.

Ten minutes later, we're up in the air.

Dai—the skinny guy, who turns out to be an old Chinese Army sergeant—is behind the controls himself. He's all smiles. He's got a daughter at USC, turns out, and the Maos I gave him are gonna pay for his kid to go to graduate school. He passes me her picture; good-looking girl. Freddy perks up a little after he sees it, starts asking questions about her. Dai knows Freddy comes from money; he perks up, too.

So does the storm.

Dai has to turn his full attention to flying. He earns every yuan of the cash I gave him; the storm is every bit the bear he was telling Freddy. We have to go higher than he likes; a couple times the plane stalls out. A few nervous moments. I glance over at Freddy. He's white as a ghost.

"Relax," I tell him. "I've done this hundreds of times. It's like fallin' off a log."

He shakes his head. "It's a very long fall."

Finally, we're in sight of the Zhongdian airport. We got a cover story of a medical emergency goin' to justify our bein' in the airspace. No sense in panicking the powers that be. They refuse us landing, of course, direct Dai south to Lijiang, but by then, we're circling the airfield. It's barely visible through the clouds; a lot of good, flat level land, fallin' off to a lot of sharp, rocky cliffs all around. I see it from the copilot's seat; Freddy sees it from right behind me.

"Time," Dai says.

Freddy and I move to the cargo door. He grabs onto my back. We tighten the straps. I slide my goggles down on my face and turn back over my shoulder.

"Ready?"

Freddy shakes his head. "Dude. Is this completely necessary, that I come, because—"

I pop the release lever.

The cold hits me like a punch in the face. Ice crystals slap at my cheeks.

The wind whips right through my coat, right through every pore of my body.

Déjà vu.

I stand there a moment and remember.

Montreal. Ten years ago. Ten miles outside the city.

The International Airport, a cordon of army tanks around it. All flights canceled, all terminals evacuated. Nobody in or out.

A light snow fallin' as the four of us climb out of the half-track that brought us from our headquarters downtown.

Me, Jimmy, J.C., and Ronnie. I'm in my stupid yellow uniform; the other three have matching red-and-white ones. Jimmy's idea, to make me different. Like it was his idea to make me leader of the group.

I raise a hand, shield my eyes from the snow. A man in a dark overcoat detaches himself from a group of other men in uniforms and steps toward us.

His name's Dan Wilson. He's H's liaison with CIC. I don't like him. He doesn't like me. I don't think he likes mutants, period.

It's not a good working relationship.

He hands me a folder.

"Listen up, people. Here's what we know. His—"

"I can read, thanks."

We shoot daggers at each other.

Jimmy steps forward. "Thank you, sir. We'll take it from here."

Wilson isn't accepting apologies. "The minister said to give you thirty minutes. The clock starts now."

He turns and walks back to the soldiers.

Jimmy gives me a look of his own. "Smooth, Logan."

"His name's Maxwell Dillon," I say, reading off the top sheet of paper. "American. Worked for the electric company, got caught in a lightning storm; only instead of dying, the guy turns into a living capacitor."

"Mutagenic change," J.C. says. "He's one of us."

"He's a nut case," I say. "Calls himself Electro now."

"We've got code names, too," Ronnie puts in. "What does that make us?"

"Government-sponsored nut cases," I say.

She smiles. I smile back.

"So how do we do this?" Jimmy asks.

"Break off into pairs," I say, and look up at Ronnie.

Her hair blows in the wind. Jet-black. Her skin is like ivory.

"You're with me," I say to her.

The wind howls. In the distance, lightning flashes. The snow begins falling harder.

I jump.

Freddy clings to me like a baby koala holdin' to its father. Correction: like a three-hundred-pound baby koala clingin' to its father. In midair, all that weight is hard to feel, of course.

Comin' down, it's gonna be a different story.

We're in the middle of a storm cloud; it's like bein' in the middle of a hailstorm. These aren't just crystals peltin' us; they're like little golfballs. Freddy is cursin' like a truck driver. I'm tellin' him to keep still, to stop moving around so I can see the ground comin'. That's the real danger here; that's why nobody ever jumps in a storm, a little fact I didn't bother sharing with Freddy. Most anybody who tries it ends up splattered on the ground.

Luck is with us.

We come out of the cloud high enough up for me to get the lay of the land. The wind makes steerin' a bitch, but I'm able to guide us down on the plateau, to brace myself enough so that the impact of hittin' the ground is more like a one-story fall than a ten-story one.

Freddy lands just right, too, as far as I'm concerned. His weight on the ground, not me. He gets the wind knocked out of him, lies on the snow, gasping. I stand and cut the chute free; the wind whips it high into the air, and then it disappears into the distance.

"Good God," Freddy says. "Good God."

I look around. In the distance, I can see lights.

"Shelter," Freddy says, standing.

I shake my head. "Transportation."

We use another chunk of Maos to rent a four-wheel-drive. And buy a map. Freddy wasn't kiddin' about Wubeng bein' out in the sticks. The map shows it on the border with Tibet; it takes us another fourteen hours to get there. Ten by car, two by donkey, two on foot. I don't doubt it's a scenic journey; all we see on the way, though, is snow.

It's well into the wee hours by the time we hit the village. I'm practically carrying Freddy by that point, which is no easy task. A string of prayer flags blowing from a low-hanging branch lets me know we've arrived. I've seen some of them in Madripoor before. It's a Tibetan custom, not Chinese. Considerin' how close we are to the border, odds are this village is as much one as the other.

We hike past a few smaller woodframe dwellings and come to a larger one. I bang on the door till it opens. An old guy with a long braided goatee glares at me and starts shouting. I can't understand a word he's saying. Doesn't matter.

I flash a wad of multicolored Maos at him; a minute later, he's all smiles and leadin' Freddy and me into a room about the size of broom closet with a single bed about as wide as a broom handle in it.

Looks like the Sheraton Grand to me.

I toss Freddy down onto one side of the bed and take the other myself.

The rest is blackness.

I wake to somebody pokin' me in the stomach. Freddy, trying to hog the bed.

"Kid, you're about to lose that elbow," I mumble.

"Up."

That's not Freddy's voice.

I sit up in bed, to find myself staring down the barrel of a half-dozen rifles, held by a half-dozen tribesmen in fur coats. Two more hold Freddy up by his elbows next to the bed.

I get to my feet. These guys are speakin' English, so I do the same.

"What's the problem?"

"You. We don't want you here." The speaker's the oldest of those present, skinny guy, clean-shaven with dark hair. He's gotta be all of fifteen years old. He's got shiny black track pants to go with the fur coat. The evils of capitalism.

He motions toward our things with his gun. "Get your coats. Go."

Strange welcome.

I nod at Freddy, grab up my shoes and coat, and start puttin' em on. Freddy does the same.

"Listen." I shoulder my backpack. "I don't want any problems. I'm looking—"

"No talking." The guy motions me toward the door.

"I'm lookin' for somebody," I continue. "Westerner. Tall guy. Goes by the name of O'Connell. Or Osborne. I think he might've—"

The rifle butt comes at me so fast I barely have time to duck. As it is, I get hit with a glancing blow across the forehead. I feel a little drop of blood tricklin' down my face.

Temper, I think. *Temper, temper, temper.*

"O'Connell." Another one of the guys is speakin' now; he turns to the leader, who's eyeing me even more suspiciously, which I didn't think was possible. The two of them start arguing; I don't understand the language. It's not Mandarin, it's not Kham . . . some other kind of Tibetan dialect? I recognize some of the words: *balance, gods, monster.*

I'm trying to puzzle out what's being said, when all at once, the two guys stop arguing. The one who told me to get my coat is back in charge; he jabbers at the others in the same dialect. They take me and Freddy by the arm and hustle us outside. The old guy who let us in last night holds the door. I tell him thanks for the room and the wake-up call. He avoids my gaze.

Outside, it's a winter wonderland. Sickeningly picturesque. Trees outlined in snow, snow-capped mountains in the distance. The village is on a single, steep road winding through a forest, though the only way you can tell it's a road is by the lack of stumps.

The sun's high up in the sky; I figure it's around midday. The snow's stopped fallin'; the air is clean and crystal-clear. Like in the DNR. Like in Canada. This is no time to start reminiscing, though. Gotta focus on the here and now.

Our escorts take Freddy and me up the road about a quarter-mile, through a carpet of snow at least a foot thick. We don't pass a single person along the way; we do pass a number of huts, a handful of which have doors standing wide open. I can see snowdrifts inside.

Somethin' strange goin' on here.

We turn off the road toward another hut. This one's surrounded by prayer flags, rope after rope of 'em. We're shoved past and on through the front door.

Inside, there's a fire burnin'. The smell of incense. An old guy sittin' on the floor, head bowed, reading—chanting—off a scroll spread before him. He's wearing a red silk robe, patterned with orange and gold animals. He's got a long white goatee, just like the guy who gave us a bed last night, and an elaborate hat, with decorated panels that rise half a foot above his head.

THE NATURE OF THE BEAST

There's a good dozen other people in the room. Most seated on the floor, some standing against the far wall. Some are chanting along with the old guy. Some are just rocking in place. My guess is they're grateful to be someplace warm.

My question is, why aren't they in their own huts?

A woman in a Mao-style uniform enters from another room. She's carrying a kettle. Most of the people in the room are holding mugs. The woman goes around and starts refilling them.

Actually, it's a religious ceremony. The old guy, it turns out, is the village *dongba*—priest, shaman, spiritual leader, whatever—there's no exact Western equivalent. His name is Biquan. He's Naxi—ethnic Chinese. So is the village. So is their language. No wonder I had trouble understanding it.

The ceremony, near as I can follow along, has somethin' to do with restoring balance in the village. From the looks on people's faces as the praying goes on, though, I can tell it's a lot more serious than that.

It looks like life and death.

The praying stops; music begins. A guy my age takes out a stringed instrument that looks like an overweight balalaika and starts plucking; a young girl pulls out a flute and plays along.

Her instrument sounds like a *shakahuchi*—a Japanese flute. Hearin' it makes me smile; Mariko played one, too.

The old guy catches my smile and returns it with

one of his own. He waves over the woman with the tea kettle; she brings us cups.

The tea is strong and hot, like China black. Ginseng and caffeine in it. Perks me right up. Makes me realize how hungry I am. But food's gonna have to wait till we get this sorted out.

The music ends; the musicians put away their instruments.

The guys with rifles prod us forward, toward the old man. We're introduced; he switches to Mandarin when he sees I have trouble with the Naxi.

"You are friends of Mister O'Connell, I understand."

I shake my head. "No."

"But you are looking for him. Why?"

"Because he's done bad things. To me, and my friends. I want to stop him from doing anything more."

Biquan nods. "He has done bad things here as well."

"Then we have a common interest."

"So it would seem." He looks over my shoulder, at the guys who dragged Freddy and me up here. "Shailo?"

The kid who slammed me in the forehead with the rifle steps forward.

"We have nothing in common with these men, Grandfather. Send them away."

"Tell me where Osborne is," I say. "And I'll be happy to go."

"Osborne?" Biquan frowns.

"That's his real name. O'Connell's just an alias he uses."

"Tell them nothing, Grandfather. It will only make things worse," the kid—Shailo—says.

Biquan shakes his head. "I do not know how much worse things could get, Shailo. We have lost twenty since the storms began. We must do something. These men are Westerners—perhaps they—"

"Excuse me." I break in because I want to make sure of what I'm hearing. "You say you've lost twenty— twenty people dead? Is that what you mean? Osborne killed twenty people here?"

"Twenty people gone," Biquan says. "Six last night. Eighty left in the village."

"And Osborne did this?" I'm trying to put the time-table together in my head; he leaves the Ark two days ago, and—

"He is responsible!" Shailo is practically shouting. "He is the one who has disturbed the balance. Un-leashed the wrath of the gods—brought the *nien* down on us."

I raise an eyebrow. The *nien*'s a mythological crea-ture, a man-eater that appears at the start of every New Year, terrorizes people. Everybody knows it's just a story.

Except Shailo's not kidding. He means exactly what he says; I can see it in his eyes.

"Tell me about this *nien*," I say.

The two men exchange glances.

"We have never seen it," Biquan says. "It comes in the night. Steals babes from their mothers' arms. Wives from their husbands' beds. It roams the mountains during the day; we cannot walk the trails alone, or let pack animals from our sight, lest they vanish as well."

I nod.

I'm beginning to get an inkling of what's goin' on here.

"And Osborne brought it with him," I say.

"No." Biquan shakes his head. "It is a punishment from the gods. For what he did."

"Which was what?"

Biquan holds up a hand. Shailo helps him rise from the floor.

"Come," the old man says. "I will show you."

He leads us outside and onto the road.

Biquan has a walking stick; he plants it firmly in the ground and starts off uphill, away from the village. Shailo hangs on his elbow, ready to offer help if the old man needs it.

"O'Connell—Osborne—first came here two years ago," Biquan says as he trods slowly through the snow. "He brought men, and money, and treasures the likes of which our village had never seen. In return, he asked for our cooperation. Our help. Some were anxious to give it." Biquan shakes his head. "I tried to warn them. They should have known better."

"What did he want?"

Biquan stops in the middle of the road and points up toward the mountains in the distance. The sun breaks through at that moment, silhouetting the whitecaps with the colors of the morning. Red and reddish-gold, which lands on the tallest peak among the spires, making it look like something out of a painting. A picture postcard.

Making it look, all at once, familiar to me.

"Kawagebo," Biquan says.

"That's Kawagebo?" Freddy steps forward. "I've heard of it."

"It is the dwelling place of the gods. Or was." Biquan shakes his head.

I've heard of it, too, I realize. Tallest unclimbed peak in this part of the world. I remember reading about it in the news a few years back. A group of Japanese climbers were trying to be the first ones to reach the summit. About two dozen or so of them, if memory serves. A few days out, all contact was lost.

A few years later, their bodies were found clear on the other side of the mountain. Rumor was the gods threw them down for their arrogance.

Kawagebo was sacred ground, not meant to be trod by man.

"Osborne went up there," I say.

Biquan sighs. "Yes. And drove the gods away. They sent the *nien* to us then, as a punishment."

I stare up at the peak; the sunlight vanishes then, as does Kawagebo's golden crown. The sky above us is no longer blue; it's gray, and filled with ominous-looking clouds.

That storm that came through last night isn't done yet.

"When was the last time you saw him?" I ask. "Osborne?"

"Weeks ago," Shailo answers. "He passed through here, on his way from Zhongdian. He is up there. I am sure of it."

I'm not. He can't be two places in one time, and he was in Vegas just about a week or so ago. On the other hand, if they've had a lab up there for the last couple of years, there may be more than one way up and down the mountain.

There's really only one way to find out for sure. Looks like a long trek. So the earlier I get started . . .

"If he's up there, I'll find him," I say.

Biquan nods.

I clear my throat. "I haven't eaten since yesterday afternoon. If you have food you can spare . . ."

"The *nien* has not left us much," Biquan says. "But we will share what we have."

"I appreciate it."

I turn to go. Freddy's still standin' there, starin' up at the mountain.

"Come on, kid. No time to play tourist now. Let's eat."

"Tourist." Freddy snaps his fingers. "That's it—now I know why the name sounded familiar. Kawagebo."

"Uh-huh," I say, takin' his arm. "On the way to breakfast, you can tell me."

"It's Shangri-La," Freddy says.

My fingers slide off his coat sleeve. "What?"

"Shangri-La. Not the real one, of course. It's a big PR campaign," he goes on, oblivious to the look on my face. "Tryin' to make this whole part of the country more appealing to Westerners. Tourist dollars. And that"—he points toward the peak—"that's the centerpiece. It's on all the postcards, the travel brochures."

Now he does turn and look at me. And frown. "What?"

I shake my head.

Project Shangri-La.

I think I'm a step or two closer to finding out exactly what it means.

11

OF COURSE, I CAN'T TAKE FREDDY WITH ME.

I realize that even as we're turnin' back down the trail toward the village, even as Freddy and I are treated to what no doubt passes for a feast in Wubeng these days. Skydiving through a snowstorm is one thing; facing a stone-cold killer—much less an entire platoon of laboratory-created monsters—is something else entirely.

He doesn't take the news well when I tell him. Freddy's gotten into the whole spirit of things. Sees himself as my sidekick, my comrade in adventuring arms. I've had this problem before. Rogue. Jubilee. Ronnie.

Best to cut it off cold, before something bad happens.

"No," I tell him. "And that's my final word."

It's been my final word for the last fifteen minutes,

ever since we started up the mountain from Wubeng. "We" meaning me, him, and Shailo, who's leadin' the way. I'm in the middle; Freddy's bringing up the rear. The trail we're on now is the main pilgrimage route around the mountain. Come spring, people by the thousands will arrive here from all over the province, to pray, to bend a knee within sight of the gods above.

It's an easy route that time of year; it's a lot more hazardous now. Ice in some spots, a thousand-foot drop down a rocky slope in others. It's the first leg of my journey up the mountain. Shailo's goin' to take me to the spot where the pilgrimage trail intersects the path up the mountain. Two hours, more or less, till we get there. That's where the trek up will change from a walk to a climb. That's where things'll get hairy.

That's where the Japanese climbers disappeared.

The straps of my pack dig into my shoulders; it's full of every conceivable kind of climbing gear you could want, happily supplied by the good citizens of Wubeng to assist me in my mission. Killin' the *nien,* bringing the gods back home . . . I'm like the knight in those old fairy tales, headed off to slay the dragon.

Thinkin' about knights puts me in mind of Wyndham; I've been tryin' to put myself in his shoes while I walk. Think about his plans, old and new, about where I might fit into them. How I might help bring them to a premature ending.

The files say he started out wantin' to create a whole new civilization—a better world, free of bigotry and greed. He went down the evolutionary tree to people that world, made his New Men out of animals, with supposedly "nobler" instincts. That didn't work.

So now—at least, as it seems to me—he's decided to go up that tree, to go from *Homo sapiens* to *Homo superior,* mix a little mutant into his New Men mix, and see if he couldn't do better. The Ark, a.k.a. Project Shangri-La. A paradise on Earth, just like in the book.

I'm getting a bad feeling about this.

Usually, when nut jobs like Wyndham decide to create a paradise, it involves clearin' way for the new residents. Except that Wyndham could make New Men—Newer Men, if you want to call 'em that—all day long for a hundred years, and he wouldn't have enough to populate Rhode Island. Some of the pieces here don't quite fit. I need more information.

One thing's clear, though: I stumbled into his operation at exactly the right place, at exactly the right time, to play lab rat.

"In case you've forgotten," Freddy says, interrupting my train of thought, "I helped get us this far. Remember?"

"I'm savin' your life, kid. If you knew what was really goin' on here . . ."

"So tell me."

I shake my head. There's no need to open that can of worms with Freddy. He thinks the *nien* is Osborne—sorry, O'Connell—and his guys. Or some of those animals that Osborne was bringing in from here, to V.C. Tell the truth, I don't know exactly what he thinks. Doesn't really matter at this second, either.

"How much farther?" I yell out.

"Halfway," Shailo says. "Another hour."

We're on an easy part of the trail, the downhill grade of a hill Shailo called by the name of Yaytan. Funny name for a hill. Still a sheer dropoff to our left, but nowhere near as steep, or as far to fall. At the bottom of the downhill is a little clearing; a few hundred feet up ahead, the forest thickens again.

As we reach the clearing, I squint up into the sun to see if I can spot Kawagebo above us, but the mountain blocks my view. The sky is clear again, though. Shouldn't have any trouble finding the peak once I start the climb toward the summit.

I lower my gaze and almost run right into Shailo, who's stopped to study something on the ground.

"Snow leopard," he says, bent over the trail directly in front of him. "Big one."

I look down as well. He's lookin' at a set of animal tracks in the snow; they definitely belong to a big cat, he's right about that.

But it ain't no snow leopard.

The pad is a good half-dozen inches across. The track is sunk through the snow, into the ground below. The cat that made these tracks is three hundred pounds, easy. As much as eight, nine feet long.

I curse and let my pack slide off my shoulders. It hits the ground with a muffled thump.

Freddy's got a puzzled expression on his face. "What—?"

"More tracks here," Shailo says, walking off to his right. "I think . . ."

"Get behind me, you two," I say.

A hundred yards up the trail, a tiger walks out of the forest. A white tiger.

Two others follow, flanking it.

"Ah . . ." Freddy says. "Logan?"

Shailo says something, too, low and under his breath. I can't hear all of it, but I do pick up the word *nien* in there somewhere.

He's wrong about that, of course. There's nothin' supernatural goin' on here, even though there's little doubt in my mind that these animals are the ones responsible for all the dead villagers. More of Wyndham's creations.

I flash on Osborne, holding up the tiger's head, back at the Ark.

"Bad gene pool," he said.

I got a bad feeling I know exactly what he meant.

"Shailo, you got any weapons?"

"A rifle. A knife."

"Get the gun out. Do not fire until I tell you to."

The tigers are trotting toward us, one straight on, the other two on either side of the trail. I risk a glance behind me; there's a rock wall about two hundred yards behind us. I wouldn't mind havin' it at my back as I fight, but I'm not sure we could all reach it in time.

"Are they, uh, man-eaters?" Freddy asks.

"Wouldn't surprise me. You got any weapons?"

"Ah . . ."

"Take this." I pull a hunting blade off my belt that one of the villagers gave me. "Keep it at your side. Short stabbing motions—quick motions. Don't try throwin' it or slashing. Punch forward, okay? You understand?"

"Uh."

The tigers are coming faster now, the one in the middle taking the lead, the others falling back.

The middle one roars; the sound splits the valley.

"Are we going to die?" Freddy asks.

"Not today Shailo. Aim for the tiger on the right. Fire on my count. Yes?"

"Yes."

"Freddy? You got that knife out?"

No response.

I risk a glance over my left shoulder at him.

He's got the knife at his side, all right, but the look in his eyes . . .

He's scared to death. Terrified. Frozen with fear.

I flash back ten years again. Back to the airport at Montreal.

Back to the day everything went wrong.

Six months of training, and Ronnie can fly like a hawk. A hundred-twenty-pound hawk, with a ten-foot wingspan.

Six months of training, and she's strong enough to carry me underneath, hanging from a specially made harness.

We come in that way, snowstorm be damned, come in from the west side of the main terminal, heading for the control tower. A handful of people got out before Dillon got in; we don't know about the rest. Forty or so staffers, by best count. The hope is they're still alive. Those forty people aren't our main concern, though.

Our main concern is the four or five thousand up in the air, in airplanes circling above the storm, trying to get down. Which they can't do as long as Dillon's got control of the tower. The situation gets worse with each minute that passes. They get a minute shorter on fuel. A minute closer to a crash landing.

Same thing's goin' on all across the East Coast, the U.S. and Canada. A coordinated attack, multiple towers taken hostage. Ransom money in the billions bein' asked.

There's some kind of coordinated response goin' on, too. It's being run out of New York by a guy named Reed Richards, a.k.a. Mr. Fantastic. Of the Fantastic Four. First time I heard those code names, I had Richards and his team pegged for head cases. Swelled head cases. Naming yourself Fantastic . . .

Talking to him on the way down here, though, changed my mind.

Fantastic is about right, at least for him. He's some kind of savant—not a mutant, but as smart as anyone

I've ever met, and that includes Jean-Claude Perrault. Richards seems to have a mind that works the same way as our resident genius—always thinking, always planning. Focused on staying one step ahead of the opposition. Focused on the endgame. I'm focused on that, too, right now, as the tower comes into sight. Focused on the guy inside it, a million volts or so of bad news.

Ronnie banks and swoops low, so I can get a quick glimpse through the tower windows. I see people— maybe a dozen, maybe more—huddled on the floor, backs pressed against the far wall. No sign of Dillon.

Then we're past the window and rising. A second later, my feet touch the roof. I land as lightly as I can and unsnap the harness. Ronnie circles one time in the air above and then lands next to me herself. She changes.

"Logan." Jimmy's voice comes in my ear.

"Right here."

"We're in position."

"We are, too. Let's go at"—I glance at my watch, which is counting down the time remaining till the bad guys' deadline expires—"eighteen minutes exactly."

"Roger that. Out."

Twenty seconds from now. I pop the claws on my right hand and use my left to wipe the snow off the tower roof. Gettin' ready to slice off the metal and peel it back like an onion. See what I find underneath.

"Logan."

I look up. Ronnie's smiling at me. Tryin' to smile.

"I'm scared," she says.

"You're prepared. Six months of training. Whatever happens, you can handle it."

She nods, but the look in her eyes doesn't change.

Ten seconds.

"Are you scared?"

"Guy's a walking power plant, and I'm a natural conductor. Of course I'm scared." Though the truth is, I'm not. I'm only beginning to grasp the true nature of my healing factor—how powerful it is, how badly hurt I could get and still live.

"So how do you—"

"Five," I say, cutting her off. I hold up the thumb on my left hand. Then the forefinger. "Four." The middle finger. A last reassuring smile for Ronnie. "Three."

That's as far as I get. Out of the corner of my eye, I see green and gold. I'm movin' even as the air around me sizzles, as the fallin' snow suddenly vanishes in a ball of heat and light and fire.

A train hits me in the side of the chest.

One second I'm on the roof, the next I'm hangin' from it by one hand.

Dillon hovers twenty feet over me, floating on a bridge of static electricity.

"I see him, we're on our way. Hang on." That's Jimmy's voice in my ear. I don't bother respondin'.

I look over at Ronnie. She's frozen in place. Eyes wide. *Scared* is an understatement.

Three seconds have passed.

"The tower's mine, Yellow Boy. Or whatever your name is. Hands off." The air around his body shimmers; he's getting ready to strike again.

"How about claws?" I say, and slice a piece of metal about the size of a pie plate with my free hand, and fling it through the air toward him. He zaps it; I pull myself back up onto the roof while he's distracted.

"Ronnie!"

I want her to change. I want her to move.

She doesn't.

"She's not ready, Logan." That's Jimmy's voice; not in my ear, in my mind, a memory from a week ago, after a training session. "I'm not sure he is, either." "He" meanin' J.C. "She thinks too much. Doesn't react. He's got no sense of proportion—"

"Throw 'em in the fire," I said. "They'll learn. Like we did."

But maybe I was wrong.

The roof in front of me explodes. I stumble. Ronnie staggers and falls to her knees. Dillon laughs.

"You guys are Canadian, all right. Second-raters, through and through."

Ronnie looks up, and something in her eyes changes.

It's the first time I've ever seen her mad.

"You're the second-rater here," she says, and then changes. Faster than I've ever seen her do it before.

One second she's on her knees on the roof, the next

she's flying straight through the air, straight toward Dillon. Fast as a guided missile.

Lightning, of course, is a lot faster than that.

She screams.

She falls.

"Forget it," I say. "Get back to the village."

"What?" Shailo says.

"What?" Freddy asks.

The tigers are thirty feet away. I don't get the same thing off them that I got off the one in the DNR. No watchful intelligence here. I get predator. I get danger.

I get hungry.

"I said get back to the village." I don't know what I was thinking when I let them come even this far. I knew there was danger out here. What else could the *nien* be but one of Wyndham's experiments?

"Dude, you're crazy," Freddy says. "How do you expect to stop those things by yourself? I mean, fightin's one thing, but this—"

I pop my claws.

"Ah," Freddy says. "I get it."

He's got a funny look on his face. Considerin' the circumstances.

He's smiling.

"What's so funny?" I ask.

"X-dudes," he says. "I should've known it. I thought you looked familiar, but . . ."

"Keep it under your hat—*comprende?*"

He nods, suddenly serious. "*Comprende,* dude."

I turn to Shailo.

He's not smiling. He's lookin' at me as if I'm the *nien.*

He says something unintelligible under his breath.

Then he drops the rifle, eyes wide, turns and runs.

It's only then that I see the other tigers. Three more, comin' down the trail off of Yaytan behind us. Quiet as housecats on a shag carpet.

Shailo sees them then, too. They're the last thing he sees, in fact.

One takes him low, the other high. Blood spurts, splatters the snow for a good ten feet in every direction.

They leave the body and keep coming.

"Dude." Freddy sounds sick to his stomach. "Wolverine. I think I'm gonna—"

He does.

I yank him back from the puddle of puke. I shove the rifle into his hand.

"Buck up, kid. This is gonna get hairy."

12

IF I WAS ALONE, I'D TAKE THE FIGHT TO THEM. As
it is . . . I have to wait. I figure a few seconds, tops.
Two of 'em will charge then, from opposite directions.
Three, maybe. They can't all come at me at once—
they'd get in each other's way. Comforting thought.
So two will go for me, and while I'm occupied, another couple'll take Freddy.

Except none of the tigers is moving at all.

They've all stopped dead in their tracks and are eyeing me strangely. Eyeing my claws. Being careful.

"You ever fired a gun?" I ask Freddy.

"In a video game."

Not good.

"Good," I say. No sense in telling the truth; that'd
only depress him. I take the rifle out of his hands,
make sure the trigger's cocked, and hand it back. "Just
like a video game. Point and shoot. Not till I say."

"Not till you say. Got it."

As I'm talking, the tiger that came out of the forest first, the one in the center in the trail ahead of us, takes a few slow steps forward. It makes a low rumbling noise in its throat.

It speaks.

"Experiment."

"Oh, no." Freddy shakes his head and looks at me. "Tell me that tiger didn't just—"

"Keep it together, kid."

"Experiment." The tiger again. "How did you come down the mountain?"

Freddy's right, of course, the thing is talking to me, and it don't take a parallel processor for a brain to realize why. It thinks I'm one of Wyndham's lab creations. Down the mountain, down from Wyndham's lab. My guess, these animals are his guard dogs, stationed here to prevent intruders from getting back up. More developed—more evolved—versions of the tiger I saw back in the DNR.

No. Not more evolved. The way they killed Shailo—the fact that they're killing all the villagers—that's about as primal as you can get. Wyndham seems to have moved on from creating New Men; he's back to making savages. That doesn't make sense.

"I got down. I'm goin' back up. Does it matter how?" I make eye contact with the animal. What I see now confirms my early judgment. Intelligence, but not

intelligence looking for understanding. Intelligence
looking for food.

The tiger growls. "Tell us, experiment," it says, padding toward us as it speaks, coming off the trail, circling slightly to my right. I circle with it, to keep eye
contact. "What was your path?"

Out of the corner of my eye, I see the other two
tigers from the forest start circling around us the other
way, to my left.

The three that came down the mountain are moving, too.

I got a fifteen-foot perimeter marked in my mind; any
closer than that, the tigers are a single, standing leap away.
Any closer than that, and I do have to force the action.

I nod in the direction of Shailo's corpse.

"My path doesn't matter. What matters is you killin' that guy—which Wyndham's not gonna be happy
about."

"Wind-ham," the tiger says, drawing out the syl-
lables. "Wind-ham." It says the word as if it's never
heard it before. "Why do I care about Wind-ham?"

I frown.

The tiger's eyes shift almost imperceptibly. It growls
low in its throat.

Then it roars, and leaps.

Freddy fires.

I'd be mad at him for not waitin' for my order, but
there's no time.

The first tiger is on me. I get my hands—my claws—up in the air just as it reaches me, slams into me, sends me flying backward into Freddy. I barely manage to stay upright; the tiger's hissin' and spittin' and bleedin'—it's impaled itself on my claws.

"Experiment," it says, and then its body shudders, and it roars and dies. I yell, "Down, Freddy!" just as I rip out my claws from the tiger's body and whip my right arm around behind me, leading with the claws, a backhand slash that hits the tiger comin' at me from behind, hard enough that it falls back, but there's another one comin' right behind it. I slash at that one, too, but a weaker slash, and though the animal falls back, it stays focused on me, ready to jump again, but another tiger comes in on my left first and slams into me. The claws on my left hand are still trapped in the first tiger's body. I stumble, and almost trip on Freddy, who's crouching low, holding the knife I gave him down at his side, just like I told him to.

"Don't—" *be a hero,* I'm about to say, when he screams, raises the knife over his head with both hands, and brings it down through the skull of the tiger I got with my second backhand. Blood is spurting, the tiger is roaring in agony, Freddy is still screaming, and meanwhile, the tiger that slammed into me from the left now has its jaws clamped on my left shoulder. Most of what it's got is the big down jacket I'm wearing, but it's got flesh, too, and before it can get more, get at my neck, I retract the claws on my left hand and jab my bare fist into the tiger's gut.

I lean into the tiger and pop my claws again, rake them up and down and back and forth inside it, and even as blood and guts and the foulest smell I've smelled in a good long while spew out in my general direction, I'm fallin' backward, taking the tiger carcass with me, and the tiger charging me from behind ends up getting a face full of dead fur. By the time it's recovered its footing, I'm back on my feet, too.

It roars and backs away.

Freddy and I are standing side by side.

There's four dead tigers lying on the ground around us.

Two live ones are facing us. One is wounded—a slash across its face that's still bleeding. I growl low in my throat, and they back off some more.

"What the hell are those things?" Freddy stands next to me, breathing heavy.

"Experiments." I reconstruct the fight in my mind and realize that he killed two of these animals. One with the knife, one with the rifle. I find the shot tiger on the ground—bullet hole right between the eyes—and smile.

"Nice work, kid. Nice shooting."

"Thanks."

"Video games, huh?"

Freddy manages a slight smile, which disappears as he looks me over. "You're bleeding."

I put a hand to my shoulder. Hurts like hell, but I can feel the skin knitting together already. "I've had worse."

"Experiment." That from one of the live tigers, the one that's bleeding. Not as good a speaker as the other.

Get lost, I'm about to tell the animal, when I look behind it, toward the forest.

Another half-dozen tigers are emerging from it.

My turn for a string of curse words.

"What do we do?" Freddy asks.

I shake my head. There's nothin' else we can do.

"Run," I tell him.

I let Freddy take the lead. I tell him not to look back. By the time he hits the base of the trail leading up Yaytan, the new tigers have joined up with the two we left alive. I counted wrong before; there are ten altogether.

And now they're coming at full speed.

What I have to do is get Freddy someplace safe. Someplace where I don't have to worry about him, someplace where I got room to operate and keep my back safe. I'm trying to recall the trek on the way in, and I can't. I was too busy thinking about Wyndham, what he might be up to.

Wyndham.

Wind-ham.

"Why do I care about Wyndham?"

"Logan! Come on!"

Freddy's a few hundred feet in front of me now. And he's stopped to wait.

"Go!" I yell, and start up the trail after him. He starts moving again, and I look back, and not only are the tigers closer . . .

I realize I've made a bad mistake.

I've forgotten somethin' I did see on the way in, that the dropoff on the trail coming down Yaytan is not all that steep. Too steep for people to climb, yes, but tigers . . .

They're bounding straight up the slope, straight up the mountain. Bypassing the trail entirely. They're going to cut us off. I open my mouth to call for Freddy but realize it's already too late.

The fastest of 'em leaps right in front of me—right between me and Freddy. Who has no rifle now, no knife.

Another one jumps up alongside the first, but by that point, I'm already on the attack. I pop my claws and slash, and the two tigers both back off up the trail.

Another one jumps up behind me. And then another.

I turn and slash, but they keep their distance. Circle. Some stay between me and Freddy. Some stay behind me.

What we got here, I realize, is a new strategy. They're going to take their time. They're going to jump in, slash, and jump out. Wear me down.

There's no need for that kind of strategy with Freddy, of course. No need for any strategy at all.

They're just going to hunt him down and have lunch.

The damn fool kid is makin' it easy for 'em, too. Not only has he stopped running, he's actually coming back down the trail toward me. He's got a rock in his hand.

I admire the intent, but . . .

"Run, you idiot!" I yell at him.

Another tiger hops onto the trail ahead of all of us. It turns left, looks at me, turns right, looks at Freddy, and starts after him.

Freddy drops the rock and starts running again.

I growl and start forward. Two tigers close ranks to block me.

One charges from behind. I slash backward, catch some skin. It hisses and backs off.

The cut's barely deep enough to draw blood.

"Logan!"

I look up and see that somehow, Freddy's managed to switch positions with the tiger; he's running down the trail toward me, it's chasing along behind. Not that it makes that much of a difference.

Only one thing I can see to do now.

"Jump!" I tell him, and at the same time as I'm shouting, I'm moving, taking a leap off the side of the trail. I hit with my bad shoulder and start rolling, trying to shift as I go so that the impact falls mainly on my right side. I hear the tigers coming after me; I land, Freddy lands ten feet away, and right off, I can see he's hurt. He comes up holdin' his right shoulder.

We're back where we started. Fifty feet behind us is Shailo's corpse.

Another fifty beyond that are the four dead tigers.

I help him to his feet.

The tigers are coming down the mountain after us, not bothering with the trail, not even bothering to run. Loping down to the clearing like they got all day, which they do.

We, unfortunately, don't.

"Last stand." I'm about to apologize to Freddy for dragging him into all this—actually, for not shoving him out earlier when I should have—when all at once, in the distance, I hear a soft thrumming sound. Takes me a second to place the noise: machinery. Comin' from above me. I look up in the sky and see it. A black dot, getting bigger by the second. Headin' this way. Comin' fast and low. And quiet.

"It's an airplane," Freddy says.

I squint and shake my head. "Helicopter."

The tigers start growling. They pick up the pace down Yaytan, start bounding toward us as if they were being chased by somethin' themselves. As if they're afraid we're goin' to get away. Makes me think they know somethin' we don't about who's in the copter.

"Is it the good guys?" Freddy asks.

I turn to study the machine as it heads toward us.

It's not your standard-issue two-rotor job—there's some kind of circular propulsion engine on the tail. The craft is painted a dull black. It's high-tech gear.

Could be Wyndham. Could be J.C. or Xavier. Could be the Chinese army, out on patrol.

"No way of knowin'." Plan for the worst, hope for the best.

The tigers are at the base of the mountain. I step in front of Freddy, put myself between him and them. They're not operating with any kind of strategy now; they're just comin' full steam right for us.

A shadow passes overhead; the copter's directly above.

The tigers are fifty feet away when whoever it is above us starts firing. The snow dances. One of the tigers howls in pain, and they all stop. Hold position. More firing; they retreat but don't run.

Freddy taps me on the shoulder. He points behind us. I turn and see whoever's in the copter above is lowering a rope. Two ropes—each with a harness on the end.

I look up and squint into the sun. I can make out a guy in full trekking gear—parka, snow goggles, big gloves—leaning out the open chopper door. I got no idea who he is.

I turn and see the tigers, prowling, howling, angry. Tryin' to get at us.

The devil you know versus the devil you don't.

I grab the first harness and shove it toward Freddy.

"Put it on," I tell him. He fumbles around for a few seconds before I see he can't—his shoulder. I help him into it, then climb into the second myself. I give him the thumbs up; he nods, makes a signal himself, and all at once we're rising through the air.

I look over at Freddy and smile. He nods and smiles back . . . weakly. Kid did all right down there. Saved my life, maybe; definitely saved his own.

We draw close to the copter. It's bigger than it looked from below. No markings on the outside, two men visible as we reach the opening. One leans out, grabs my hand, and helps me inside. The other pulls Freddy up by the harness, none too gently, and deposits him on the aircraft deck.

I'm about to tell him to take it easy when I notice the guy standing behind them. A big guy, wearing goggles and a hooded parka, just like the other two. The guy from the copilot's seat. Even before he pulls back his hood, my instincts are screaming *danger.*

Then he takes his goggles off, too, and smiles, and I feel like screaming myself.

It's another devil I know.

Osborne.

"Took you long enough," he says.

13

I POP MY CLAWS.

The two other guys who helped us aboard have already drawn guns.

Osborne shoots me with a taser.

I hit the deck, twitching. Helpless.

I hear Osborne again. "Him we don't need."

Then I hear Freddy scream.

I've landed facedown on the floor. I get a good view of Freddy as he falls backward out the open copter door, eyes wide, arms wheeling madly, into the white beyond.

In real life, his scream lasts only a second before being swallowed by the wind.

In my mind, it goes on forever and melds with the sounds of the past.

Ronnie screams.

We can all hear her through the swinging doors

that lead into the surgical suite. It's a hoarse, guttural scream that doesn't sound entirely human. Of course, she herself isn't entirely human at this point.

She's stuck, halfway between bird form and her human self.

Me and Jimmy and Heather are in the waiting room outside the surgical suite.

It's two weeks after the thing at the airport. Ten days after Ronnie regained consciousness. Ten days since she started screaming.

Jimmy and Heather are holding hands. They both smile up at me. Trying to look encouraging.

I don't smile back. What's there to smile about?

The door from the main corridor bursts open, and J.C. walks through.

He's not smiling either.

"Where's Hobie?" he asks. He's talking about Rick Hobie, the lead geneticist on Ronnie's case. The one who's devised the shock treatment to try to return her to normal, if not get Ronnie her powers back.

"In the operating theater," Jimmy says. "Why?"

"Because we have to stop him, that's why." J.C. walks by me without looking once in my direction. We haven't exchanged a civil word since the airport. I think we've exchanged maybe a dozen words altogether. I've tried a couple times to talk to him; he's tried as hard as he can to pretend I don't exist.

Jimmy bounces up from his seat and goes after J.C., catching up to him just as he reaches the door to the surgical suite. He puts a hand on J.C.'s shoulder.

"Slow down," he says. "Tell me what this is about."

J.C. pauses. Jimmy is the only guy he does that for—the only guy he'll stop and explain himself to, at least once in a while. Less often now than his first year with Department H, but still . . .

"It's about Hobie not knowing his ass from his elbow," J.C. says. "About him being entirely incompetent."

I have to weigh in after that outburst. Rick Hobie's a good guy—maybe not an intellect on J.C.'s level, but . . .

"Hobie's made a career out of studying mutation," I say.

"He's making a mistake," J.C. says, still ignoring me, talking right past me to J.C. "Ronnie's neural pathways are already traumatized. Rest is what she needs. More voltage is only going to make things worse. Scramble her wiring so bad we'll never be able to reconstruct it. We have to stop him."

Jimmy looks J.C. in the eye a moment and then looks over at me.

Hobie's idea is to stimulate the neural pathways that enabled her to control the transformation, the pathways that Electro's attack shorted out. It's like some fancy kind of brain surgery; they're also using a fancy kind of technique while they operate, one that allows her to be awake. Which they need, because they're asking her to try to initiate the transformation as they selectively stimulate each of a few dozen or so pathways in return.

By selectively stimulate, I mean run a few thousand volts through her.

She won't stop screaming.

It's not a scream of pain; I can sense that intuitively, from what I hear. I'll learn later that I'm right.

What it is is a scream of frustration. Anger. Rage, at her inability to change form.

It's hard to listen to without wantin' to do somethin'. What, I have no idea. All I can do is pace the floor.

J.C. tries to do more.

He bursts through the door into the suite, me and Jimmy and Heather a step behind. He reaches the operating theater and charges at Hobie. Yells at him to stop.

"I've been doing this a little longer than you, Perrault," Hobie says.

J.C.'s hand clenches into a fist. For the first time in a while, I feel for him. I feel what he feels, but clockin' the doctor in charge of Ronnie's treatment isn't going to do anybody any good at this point.

I get him in a full Nelson. He goes crazy. Jimmy tries to talk sense to him; it's no use.

"You want to mess up your whole career, Jean-Claude?" Jimmy says.

He doesn't respond.

"Look at me," Jimmy commands. "Dammit, J.C., look at me!"

He doesn't. He looks past us, to the surgical suite beyond.

Ronnie starts to scream once more.

"Look at me."

That's Osborne's voice now. I ignore it for a minute and watch the snow outside as it starts to fall. A carpet of white.

I picture Freddy's arms wheelin' in space.

I picture him standing in that little office, at the top of the stairs, back in Hong Kong.

"Look at me, I said."

I count to ten, then manage to roll over onto my back. Osborne's got his finger on the taser trigger.

"You're not letting a little thing like fifty thousand volts get the better of you, are you?"

He's smiling.

"You better kill me now," I tell him. "Because when I get loose again—when I get my hands on you—"

"Oh, I'll be quite happy to kill you," Osborne says. "Soon. I promise. But right now, you still have something we need."

"What's that?"

He doesn't answer. He hands the taser to one of his guys. "A little shock every five minutes. Just to keep him in a cooperative mood."

"Five minutes starting when?" the guy asks.

"Now," Osborne says, and squeezes the trigger.

I try to concentrate on keepin' my head still; naturally, I can't. My skull slams into the deck again, and again.

I take it as a well-deserved punishment. For dragging Freddy—and Shailo, come to think of it—into this mess. For getting 'em both killed.

I should've been ready for those tigers on the trail from Wubeng. Should have been ready for somethin' to go wrong in the copter. I should've known something was gonna go wrong. But my senses ain't what they used to be. I ain't what I used to be.

Maybe Ronnie had the right idea after all.

Time passes.

The copter lands.

Somebody drags me to my feet. I focus, and I'm lookin' Osborne in the face again.

His parka's off; he's wearing a plain black jumpsuit now, along with an earpiece. He looks like hell, frankly, like he's lost ten pounds since Vegas. Maybe twenty, even. I like to think I had somethin' to do with that, my kickin' the crap out of him back in the Ark. Maybe he had to spend a little time strapped to an operating table, had to have a little surgery of his own. He definitely had some work done on his face, 'cause the scars—the ones I gave him when I was escaping—are completely gone.

He catches me looking at him and smiles. A nasty smile.

"Welcome to Shangri-La," he says, and then his guys drag me outside, into a hail of snow and ice, into an atmosphere so thin it hurts to breathe. We're up on top of Kawagebo, all right, and the sky has gone from gray and threatening to complete white-out, that storm I saw coming is here, but luckily, I don't have to experience it for more than a few seconds before I'm marched through an open door in the side of the mountain and down a corridor of prefab steel—a round tunnel, a big pipe dropped into place, segments welded together, another underground chamber. They plop me into the back of what looks like a golf cart, and off we go.

I try to get my body back under control, get my thoughts in order.

Question number one: Why am I still alive? Osborne was gonna kill me back at the Ark; he was gonna kill me at the casino. Why not just kill me now?

"You still have something we need," he said. What? They finished testing me back at the Ark, didn't they? So what do they need from me now? They want to run some more experiments? To what end? What are they trying to do? What is Project Shangri-La?

I traveled halfway around the world, and I'm no closer to an answer now than I was when I left Vegas.

"Stay with us, Mister Logan," Osborne says. "Just a little bit longer now."

"Mister Logan." I look up, manage a smile. The little golf cart has two bench seats, facing each other.

Osborne is opposite me, one soldier seated to his right, another to my left. "Why so formal, Mister Osborne?"

He smiles back, a cat-who-swallowed-the-canary kind of smile.

"I'm Osborne in Vegas. Up here, better if you call me O'Connell."

"Whatever. Mind tellin' me where we're headed? What's goin' on now? Or is that some kinda big secret?"

"Patience, Mister Logan. You'll find out soon enough."

The cart rounds a corner; we're goin' downhill now, down in a spiral path into the heart of the mountain. Another tunnel intersects the one we're on, goes up to my left, downhill to my right, with another intersection visible off in that direction. It's like a beehive in here. Tunnel after tunnel after tunnel.

We keep goin' down.

He came here two years ago, the old guy in the village said. He meaning Osborne, O'Connell, whatever. That's at least two years this work has been goin' on, maybe even longer. Project Shangri-La. What's the connection between this place and the Ark, between the experiments they were doin' down there and whatever it is that's happening here? What's Wyndham after? What's he up to?

I frown. The pieces of this puzzle still ain't fittin' together for me.

There's somethin' I'm missin'. Somethin' big.

The cart slows and halts with a sudden jerk. In front of us, the tunnel ends, in a big pair of gun-metal-gray doors twenty feet high. Rusted rivets, worn-looking steel, and standin' directly in front of 'em, two guys in white lab coats.

Correction. One guy, one of Wyndham's New Men. Half man, half monkey.

Brinklow.

"Mister Logan," he says, stepping forward and smiling. "I must admit, I didn't expect to see you here. I would have thought—"

"Shut up, monkey," I snap.

Osborne laughs.

I look at the guys standin' in front of me, Osborne and his soldiers, and Brinklow, of course. I feel the thrum of energy, the noise of machinery comin' from behind those big doors, and I know what it is they want from me now.

They want to make me their lab rat again.

And suddenly, I ain't tired anymore.

A red haze passes in front of my eyes, like a curtain of blood coming down on the scene, almost like a little taste of what's to come. I can feel the rage building.

"Last stop," Osborne/O'Connell says, climbing off the cart. He sounds a long way off to me.

The soldiers climb off, too, but I don't move a muscle, except for the neurons firin' in my skull, evaluatin' my situation.

Osborne is six feet away, standing between the cart and the guys in the white lab coats.

The soldiers flank me, one on either side.

The one on the left is too close. I can get to him, get his gun before he can fire.

Osborne sighs. "Mister Logan, please don't make this any harder than it has to be."

Instead of responding, I pop my claws.

Brinklow and Osborne both take an involuntary step back. The soldiers raise their guns.

I snarl.

"You don't want to do this," Osborne says.

"Shut up," I tell him.

"You don't want to do this," he continues, "because you'll miss seeing her. And I think you'd want to see her, one last time. Before it all ended."

I shake my head. "I have no idea what you're talkin' about."

Osborne opens his mouth and then smiles instead. "Here she comes now."

I hear somethin', too, now. A noise behind me. Somethin' comin'. Motorized. I turn and see another cart. Four more soldiers, and sittin' in between the two on the rear seat . . .

A third person, in a drab green coverall. A woman. Dark hair pinned back on her head, a confused look on her face. Pale skin.

Ivory skin.

I blink, and the red haze is gone, the anger's gone,

all at once, and my brain is on overload. I can't process what I'm seeing, because it makes absolutely no sense, and I stand there like an idiot with my arms down at my sides, and my mouth wide open, and somebody could step up to me right now and slap my face and pull down my pants, and I wouldn't have the where-withal to say boo or even try to stop them. Or care to stop them.

The cart stops. The two guards in the rear seat climb out and pull the woman with them.

She stands in front of me, not three feet away.

Impossible.

"Ronnie?" I say, in a whisper that doesn't sound like my own voice at all.

She looks at me, no less confused than I am. She doesn't say a word.

She doesn't have to, though.

It's her. Except, of course, it can't be.

Ronnie's dead.

14

TEN YEARS AGO, A LITTLE PATCH OF FOREST IN VIC-
toria Park, Ontario, a few miles from the U.S.-Canada
border.

I'm squatting down next to a runt of a pine tree.
There's a little piece of white cloth hangin' off one of
the branches, just barely visible in the predawn haze.

It's a little before six A.M., June 3. Three weeks after
J.C. got Hobie removed from Ronnie's case. One
week after the last of her operations. Two days after
she and I sat up talking in her room till three in the
morning, her sounding as depressed as any human
being I ever met in my life.

Ten hours after she broke out of the hospital in St.
Catherine's and went missing.

I've been tracking her nonstop since then. Started
out half a day behind her, because the Department
was out in Vancouver, doing a dog-and-pony show

for some U.S. general with white hair and a big fuzzy mustache. Blowhard. Guy name of Ross. Seemed more interested in making pronouncements about how untrustworthy Super Hero types were than in finding out our capabilities as a team. Sent us out on an all-day tracking mission out west, out into the middle of the Ojibwe reserve. Iron Lake tribe. The whole way out there, I had a bad feeling in my gut. Instinct. Something was wrong.

I broke quarantine and phoned in to the genetics lab, which was when they told me Ronnie was missing. J.C. was already out looking, they said. Jimmy and I—and the new guy, older guy out of Nova Scotia named Michael Two Youngman, code name Shaman on account of his particular abilities—cut the drill short and came back to help.

We're just behind her now. I can sense it.

I stand up and hold out the little piece of cloth for them to see. J.C. snatches it out of my hand.

"Linen," he says, fingering it gently. "Hospital gown."

"More'n likely," I agree. "Especially considering those."

I point to the muddy ground in front of us. And the small footprints in it. Leading straight ahead, deeper into the park. Cuttin' across landscaped lawns, children's zoo, and then out of the park and back onto the streets. Across a four-lane highway and then into another patch of greenery. Thick shrubs.

Which is when I hear the roaring. Takes everybody else another couple of seconds to tune in to the noise.

"What is that?" J.C. asks. Wet leaves slap my skin. I'm already soaking wet.

I don't blame him for not knowing—we came most of the way via back road, late at night, and then went off-road when we hit the edge of the forest and found the car Ronnie stole out of the lab parking lot. The focus wasn't on where we were but on catching up to her. We weren't looking at road signs—though I did mention how close we were getting to the border at one point, which made all of us pick up the pace more than a little; nobody wanted a situation where we had to cross the border to pick up Ronnie.

I tell J.C. what the noise is, and a look of absolute horror crosses his face.

I was pushin' the group on before, leading the way. Now J.C. breaks into a jog, and it's the rest of us followin' behind.

Two minutes on, we break through the brush and come face-to-face with the great-great-great-grand-daddy of all white noise makers.

Niagara Falls.

We cross from wet ground to paved tourist path. Ronnie's footprints—mud, and maybe a little bit of blood, though I don't stop to check—dirty the cement walkway. Ahead of us is the tourist lodge, not yet open for business. There's one of the guides, visible through the glass walls, headphones on, hips swayin' to music as he straightens out a display of brochures, oblivious to the outside world.

And maybe a hundred feet ahead of us is Ronnie—barefoot, her hospital gown half off, half a dozen holes in it, scratched and bleeding, standing on top of one of the guardrails at the edge of the falls.

Her back is to us. Her hair blows in the wind, strands of black—jet-black—in the white and blue spray from the falls before her.

She spreads her arms wide, as if to take it all in.

I move slowly. Forty feet away. Thirty-five.

J.C. pushes past me and shouts her name.

She turns and smiles.

"No!" J.C. yells, exactly the wrong thing to do, and I knew he was gonna do it even before he opened his mouth, so I'm movin' the second he appears at my shoulder, runnin' toward her, fast as I can, arms out, hands stretching to stop her . . .

But I ain't Quicksilver.

She stretches out her arms to the sky and jumps.

We never found the body. We had the funeral without it.

Looks like I know why now.

I take a step toward her.

"Ronnie?"

Osborne motions the two soldiers behind me. They cuff my hands and drag me forward. I barely pay attention.

"Ronnie?" I say again.

She doesn't answer.

Brinklow jabs a hypo into my arm. Deep in my arm. Stings like a sonuvagun.

I blink. "What the hell . . ."

"Forgive me," he says, and then does the same thing to Ronnie. She slaps at her arm as if she's been shot and then starts to cry.

She looks completely, totally lost. As if she doesn't know where she is or who any of us are.

There's something wrong with her, I realize. Something wrong with her brain.

". . . stuck in Hong Kong," the soldier is saying. "Because of the storm."

"What about Petrie?" Osborne asks.

"He's not coming, either."

"Then we'll wait." Osborne nods toward me and Ronnie. "Put them back in the cells."

"Together?" the soldier asks.

"Sure." Osborne smiles. "Together. Why not? Just like old times. We'll make sure Mister Logan here behaves himself. Right, Mister Logan?"

"Sure, Mister Osborne," I say through gritted teeth. "Whatever you say."

"That's right, Mister Logan. Whatever I say." He smiles again.

He smacks me across the face with the butt of his rifle.

I blink. The world spins a second. When it stops, the red haze is back again.

This time, it comes with actual blood. My own. Dripping down my forehead.

"As I said, the name here is O'Connell. Try to remember that."

The soldiers drag me back onto a cart. I don't try to wipe the blood away. I don't lift my eyes from Osborne's face.

I ain't a telepath like Xavier or Jeannie. I can't broadcast my thoughts into somebody else's mind the way they can, but I'm sure that my message is gettin' through to Osborne/O'Connell right now, that my glare is deliverin' it loud and clear.

I'll remember his name, all right.

I'll remember a whole bunch of things.

They bring us back up the tunnels and dump us into a cell—low-tech this time, no curtain of yellow light, just a bare room with a single cot, a pot in one corner, and a steel door with a slot for the hall light to come through.

They shut the door and leave us there.

I take Ronnie by the hand and sit her down on the cot, on the far edge, as far away from the pot and the smell comin' off it as I can.

I sit down next to her. She tries to back off, lookin' at me with a mixture of fear and apprehension.

"Jesus, kid," I say. "What the hell did they do to you?"

She shakes her head.

"Can you speak? Can you understand me?"

Blank, uncomprehending eyes.

"Do you remember me? Logan. Right? I'm Logan." I touch my chest. "You're Ronnie. Veronique— Veronique Campion. Department H. Fort Mac. Fort MacMurray. Remember?"

Still nothing.

"Athabasca Sands. The power plant. Jimmy Hudson and me. You and J.C.—"

Her eyes brighten a second.

"J.C.," she says, slowly, two distinct words. *Jay. Cee.*

"That's right. J.C. Jean-Claude Perrault. He was from Fort Mac, too."

She nods. "J.C."

"That's right. And I'm Logan."

"Logan." The beginnings of a smile cross her face. "Logan."

The words are thick and slow on her tongue. As if she hasn't spoken for a while.

No sense in trying to get her to remember events of ten years past, I realize. Who knows what's happened to her brain, her memory, if the damage is recent, or if it's from that jump she made a decade back? Better off tryin' to establish common ground in the here and now.

"Ronnie," I say again, and I look at her face, smooth and unlined, looking exactly like it did that day at Dorval, before the accident, before the operations, and I wonder how long these bastards have been experimenting on her, how many tries it took them to get her looking this way again. And I guess it can't be all bad, because she does look like that business with Electro never happened, and while I'm lookin' and thinkin'—

She leans forward and kisses me on the lips.

That done, she sits back and smiles.

"Logan," she says again.

I swear I feel myself blush a little bit.

"No time for that," I say, maybe a little too harshly, and she draws back from me, looking scared again, so I take her hand gently and smile myself.

"Sorry," I say. "I didn't mean to snap. I just . . ."

My voice trails off then, because in taking her hand, I see now what I missed before, a little green and gold leaf tattoo on the back of her hand, the same tattoo I remember from my hallucination back at the Ark, back when Ronnie and I made love, that hallucination that was, obviously, not a hallucination at all, and my mind, for the second time today, goes completely, utterly blank. Shock.

And then it starts workin' again.

I start thinkin' about the tests they ran on me at the Ark, and about Ronnie, in my cell, and what she might've been doin' there, the samples Brinklow took from me then, scrapin' my nose, swabbin' my cheek, and a little chill runs up my spine, down the back of my neck, makes the hairs—the very, very short hairs on my arm, just beginning to grow back now—stand up straight. The chill runs into my stomach, where it translates into nausea, and from there, it travels up into my brain, where the blank feeling I had changes into a touch of vertigo.

I think about Wyndham, and the genetic accelerator, and his brave New Men, and I realize I'm beginnin' to get an idea about just what sort of nastiness is goin' on here.

15

I GET NO SLEEP THAT NIGHT.

Ronnie lays her head down in my lap after we eat the swill they bring us for dinner, and she goes out in fifteen minutes. Stays out the whole night long, in a peaceful, easy slumber, takin' peaceful, easy breaths.

I stay awake, addin' the bits and pieces of information I've picked up over the last few hours to the bits of information I had before, tryin' to plan out what to do next.

While part of me's plannin' for the future, part of me's regrettin' the past. Ronnie—things I said to her ten years ago, things I did and didn't do. I try not to do too much of that woulda, shoulda, coulda stuff, but some of it I can't help.

Dorval.

That night in her hospital room.

The day she jumped.

Some of my regrets are more recent. Freddie, for one. Me not trustin' my instincts, for another.

This whole time, since I left the Ark, those Department H days have been on my mind way more than they should've been. And there was a reason, it turns out, because Ronnie wasn't just part of the past, she was part of the here and now, what happened to me in Vegas, what is happenin' here at Kawagebo. Project Shangri-La—whatever it is.

Right about the time I'm thinkin' it's morning, the cell door slams open. A soldier walks in, drops a couple of bowls of the same swill we had last night by the door, and leaves. Ronnie wakes at his entrance; we eat. She with abandon, me reluctantly. The swill is some kind of stew, with some kind of meat in it. *Tough* don't even begin to describe it. Might be tiger, for all I know.

Thinkin' about tigers gets me thinkin' about Freddy again, the attack on the way up Kawagebo. Osborne rescuin' us—or me, at least. Shootin' at the tigers to do so.

Those two ain't on the same side anymore, clearly. I was thinking about the tigers as watchdogs for whatever's happenin' up here, but that ain't right. They're feral. Wild animals again. Nature of the beast, as it were. Can't breed that out of them, which, as I recall, was a problem Wyndham had overall with his New Men: gettin' them to abandon their animal instincts. He tried awful hard to do that, if I'm remembering right, which I think I am. He cared about the creatures he created, which is another thing buggin' me about this situation, I realize.

Nobody around here—or at the Ark, for that matter—seems to care about these creatures at all. They treat 'em more like experimental subjects—lab rats—than intelligent creatures. Even the monkey man.

Food for thought. And speakin' of food . . .

I reach down for my bowl and find Ronnie's eyes on mine. She smiles.

I see she's finished with her grub already.

I hand her my bowl, and she grabs it eagerly and starts chowin' down like a dog that ain't eaten in a week.

I want to laugh.

I want to cry.

"When you finish, I wanna talk to you for a second, okay?"

She looks up.

"Can you understand what I'm saying?"

She smiles and keeps eating.

"We have to make a plan," I tell her. "You and me." I point to her on the word "you," to myself, when I say "me."

"You," she says, puttin' down the bowl, finished at last. "Logan."

"That's right. I'm Logan. And you're Ronnie. Veronique."

"Ronnie."

I hesitate. "Sometimes we called you Egret."

Her face changes. "Egret?"

"That's right. Like the bird."

"Bird." She points up toward the ceiling of the cell. Toward the sky beyond. She makes an up-and-down motion with one hand.

"Fly," she says.

"That's right. Birds fly." I point to her. "You, too. A long time ago."

She frowns at that, shakes her head. "No."

"Yes," I say. "Egret. You can fly."

She looks puzzled.

Someone knocks on the cell door. Before I can answer, the door swings open. Two soldiers this time. One points a gun at Ronnie.

"Time," he says.

She looks at me. I nod, and she gets to her feet, and then I do, too. The soldiers march us out of the cell and put us in a little cart and send us back down the tunnels to the big steel doors. This time, they swing open at our approach.

We drive on in, into a giant cave, a chamber that, unlike the tunnels, looks as if it was carved out of the rock, out of Kawagebo itself. It's the size of a basketball court, maybe a couple hundred feet high. The back half, farthest from the doors, is taken up by what looks to me to be a generator of some kind, thick cables running off it, metal shielding surrounding it. There's a particular sheen to that metal, a kind of shine I recognize right away.

It ain't steel or iron.

It's adamantium.

Not a lot of people can afford adamantium as a construction material. Stuff is twice as expensive as diamond, harder to work with than platinum.

There's a railing about ten feet above us, running in a U shape all around the chamber, except for the back, by the generator. Soldiers are stationed behind that railing every fifteen feet or so, guys in unmarked black coveralls, automatic weapons at the ready, keeping watch.

The cart comes to a stop in the center of the chamber, right near a circle of guys in suits.

One of 'em's Osborne; one of 'em's a gray-haired guy, his back to me. He's in the middle of talking.

". . . after Avalon," he says. "We pushed forward on Shangri-La. Over the past few months, we've sunk millions of dollars into both locations. And when we sink that kind of money in so quickly, we expect to see results. Replicable results. So this complication you talk about—"

"Has been handled. In fact," Osborne says, looking in my direction and smiling, "the complication—and our test subject—have both just arrived."

Everybody turns toward us then.

Gray-haired guy sees me, and his eyes widen.

I frown, 'cause he looks vaguely familiar.

"Bring her," Osborne says, motioning to Ronnie

and the soldiers on the cart. They climb off and wave their rifles at Ronnie to do the same.

She rises. So do I.

One of the soldiers jabs his rifle in my gut, sitting me back down.

My guess was they'd try to separate us. Wasn't sure it'd happen so quickly, though.

I shove his rifle aside, stand up, and take Ronnie's arm. The two of us stand together for a second, facing the circle of suits, soldiers behind us, soldiers above.

The gray-haired guy steps forward and shakes his head.

"Are you ever not a pain in the ass, Logan?" He's looking right at me, and now he looks more than vaguely familiar.

I know this guy.

I take the gray out of his hair, take off fifteen pounds and fifteen years, and then I have it.

The airport at Dorval, for starters.

Countless other meetings in Montreal, and H's headquarters, and a ton of phone calls, and video conferences after that, right up till the very end.

"Dan Wilson," I say. "A little out of your territory, aren't ya?"

Wilson's eyes narrow.

"I could say the same about you." Wilson's gaze goes to Osborne. "He's your complication?"

"Was." Osborne corrects him. "He's here now. And we have the samples."

"And how long was he out? Who did he talk to? Besides—"

"No one," Osborne interrupts. "We're certain."

"You'd better be."

"There's been no indication of anything. No chatter on Echelon or any of the security networks. Nothing."

Wilson doesn't look convinced. They talk some more, along the same lines, while I try to figure out what in the Sam Hill he's doin' here.

Ten years ago, Wilson worked for CSIS—Canadian Security Intelligence Service. He was liaison between H and the PM's office. Our watchdog, after Dorval. A role that fit him to a T.

He was a government man, through and through. A lifer. Which meant that maybe I was right about the government bein' involved in Wyndham's project, only maybe I was wrong about which government it was. Except that the Ark was in U.S. territory.

So maybe there's more than one government involved here. A joint U.S.-Canada kind of thing.

Just like Weapon X.

"Do we even need him anymore?" Wilson snaps, pointing right at me.

The monkey man steps out from behind the soldiers and speaks. "I would recommend against termination at this particular point, at least until we complete the procedure, when we can accurately sample the viability of—"

"All right, all right," Wilson interrupts, giving the monkey man the same look he gave me at the airport ten years ago.

Freak.

"Then, if we're ready," Wilson says, and Osborne nods, and the two soldiers who came with me and Ronnie on the cart step forward. I can tell they're gonna try to separate us again, and even though this ain't necessarily the best time for me to make a stand . . .

Well, sometimes you gotta play the hand you're dealt, no matter how crappy it is.

I pop the claws.

"Come on, Osborne," I say. "Let's see what you got."

He shakes his head. "Look around. You can see what I've got."

I don't need to look. But I risk a glance anyway.

Every soldier in the place has his weapon trained on me.

There's no way out. But like I said . . .

Sometimes you gotta play the hand you're dealt.

The suits are the key. If I can get to one of them, use him as a hostage . . .

"You really want to die today, Logan?" Osborne asks. "We'll be happy to oblige."

"I got no interest in dyin'." I relax my stance a little, take a subtle step forward and to the left. Bringin' me nearer the suits.

I figure on grabbin' one of 'em, using him as a hostage. Question is, of course, which one? Who's important, and who isn't? Choose the wrong guy, and they'll kill him and me, no doubt.

Safest course of action: Grab Wilson.

"But let me tell you this," I say, moving again, to my right a little, in his direction, just a step, but it's somethin'. "If I have to choose between dyin' and playin' lab rat again—"

"What about your friend there?" Wilson says, nodding at Ronnie. "Doesn't she get a vote?"

I snort. "That's funny. After what you did to her."

"We didn't do a damn thing," Osborne says.

I spin left a little, toward him, only instead of taking a step forward to do it, I step back with my right foot, puttin' me even closer to Wilson.

"Neither of us is gonna be part of your experiment," I say. "Hope that's clear enough."

"Little late for that, don't you think?" Wilson says.

"What's that supposed to mean?" I ask before I can stop myself, a mistake, because I wanted to keep everyone's attention on me and Osborne, keep the conflict there, keep the soldiers from lookin' in Wilson's direction.

"You did your part already, Logan. As I understand it," Wilson says. "You gave at the office."

Osborne laughs. "Yeah. Now it's time to see how you did," he says, and jerks his head in Wilson's direction, and there goes my whole plan, Wilson steps back, the rest of the suits step with him, stepping aside, opening up the circle, revealing a machine that looks like nothing so much as an oversized pop gun, with the barrel—about six inches thick, maybe two feet long—pointed straight at what looks like a La-Z-Boy recliner, except that said recliner, rather than being the traditional brown leather job, is coated with aluminum foil and has strategically located wrist and ankle cuffs.

It, too, looks vaguely familiar to me.

"Move," Osborne says, and he gestures toward the machine.

Now I recognize what this contraption is, and my frown turns into a curse.

A La-Z-Boy it is not.

It's Hubert Edgar Wyndham's genetic accelerator.

I stare at it a second.

Ronnie's the subject, Osborne said. They intend to use this on her.

I gave at the office, Wilson said. And Osborne laughed.

The tattoo on Ronnie's hand.

The cell back at the Ark.

"Tell me what this is all about," I say, though in my heart of hearts, I know already. I've known since last night.

Wilson shakes his head and turns back to the suits.

"Tell me!" I shout.

No one pays the slightest bit of attention to me.

"Put her here," Osborne says, indicating the chair attached to the machine, and the soldiers from the cart step forward and reach for Ronnie . . .

And I step forward and block them . . .

And then somethin' grabs me by the neck and starts shakin', and the next thing I know, I'm down on the ground twitching like one of the Stooges with his fingers caught in an electrical socket.

Osborne's taser.

"Jesus, why don't you just shoot him already?" I hear Wilson say.

"Like the monkey said. Not just yet. Besides," Osborne goes on, "you can see he's not what he used to be."

And then Ronnie starts screaming.

I manage to turn my head to the side, just a little, cheek pressed down onto the smooth gray concrete floor, eyes up just enough to see Ronnie struggling as they strap her into the chair.

"Six feet is the recommended safe distance," Brinklow says, from behind the barrel of the accelerator, which, with him in position, almost looks like one of those old WWII Navy guns, one of those babies they used in the Pacific to shoot down the kamikaze fighters, only now that long barrel is pointed not at the sky but right at Ronnie.

"Stop," I try to say, and it comes out like a long nonsensical stutter.

Brinklow pulls the switch.

A blue ray hits Ronnie square in the stomach. She screams even louder.

I groan and try to get to my feet.

I can't.

All I can do is watch. The blue ray, workin' on Ronnie.

It's changing her. The shape of her body. Not in an entirely unfamiliar way . . .

"Incredible," Wilson says, staring at Ronnie, as everyone else is starin' at Ronnie, or, rather, Ronnie's belly, which is really the part of her that they're all interested in.

Her belly. And what's growin' inside it.

Our kid.

16

THE GENETIC ACCELERATOR.

It allowed Wyndham to mutate the DNA of living creatures at an accelerated rate, allowed him, in essence, to evolve his dog up to a new kind of animal in a couple of minutes, as opposed to a couple million years. I never got the science, exactly; what I did get was that the machine, in essence, accelerated the speed at which preprogrammed genetic instructions were carried out. Sped up time.

That's what they're doin' with Ronnie now.

With her, and the baby inside.

Clearly, it's not a painless process. Ronnie is still screaming. I feel for her.

I feel for the kid, too.

My kid.

Our kid.

I can't quite get my mind around that yet.

What I can manage to piece together, in between the twitchin' the taser's makin' my body do, and Ronnie's screams, and the low buzz of energy comin' off the genetic accelerator, is that what's happenin' now is the whole reason I'm still alive.

The point of me bein' at the Ark, the point of me bein' here now, is this experiment. Is this kid, about to be born. Somethin' about it is gonna give them information, and considerin' who they are—Wilson, for starters—that information can mean nothin' good for mutants.

I try to listen to what Wilson's saying to the other suits; it comes to me in bits and pieces.

". . . that's the scientists' area of expertise," he's saying. "But I can assure you that there will be no more extreme cases like the ones you're used to seeing on the news."

"Define *extreme*," another voice says.

"We allow for a certain variance from the baseline DNA model, of course," a third voice interrupts. It sounds like the monkey man. "That, of course, is necessary for genetic diversity. To ensure the continued viability of the gene pool. To enforce complete variance—"

"Brave New World," a third voice says, and there's the sound of laughter. It fades away.

Ronnie's screamin' comes back. The sound turns into a long, slow groan that echoes throughout the chamber and bounces off the adamantium generator shield and the cave wall high above, straight into my skull like a dentist's drill. Worse than that, though, 'cause this pain ain't mine, ain't somethin' I can grin and bear.

The sound around me changes. Takes me a second to figure out why.

The genetic accelerator—I don't hear it anymore.

I lift my head and look toward Ronnie.

The blue ray's off. There's all sorts of figures crowding around her, obscuring her from view. Brinklow's givin' directions. They lay Ronnie down flat. She keeps screaming.

And then I hear another sound.

A baby's cry.

"Male." I hear Brinklow. "We'll begin the testing immediately."

"It looks completely human," another voice says.

"Don't they all?" a third adds.

Next thing I know, I don't know how I'm doin' it, but I'm on my feet. I got fifty thousand volts shootin' through me, and I still, somehow, am on my feet, screamin' and headin' toward Ronnie and the kid.

Only Osborne's in the way.

"Don't make a scene, Logan," he says. "Don't be stupid. Stay where you are, and—"

I make a noise that sounds more animal than human, even to my ears, and keep coming.

A soldier steps in my way, and I gut him.

I hear Ronnie screamin' my name. I hear my son crying.

My son.

All at once, fire shoots through my body, a hundred times worse than before. It's the worst pain I ever felt in my life—apart from Avalon, of course. It knocks me to my knees again.

I look up and see Osborne, his finger movin' on the taser.

I spit out his name, along with my three favorite curse words.

He shakes his head and smiles.

"When are you going to learn? I'm O'Connell here," he says, and then he says something else, but it's lost in the haze of power shootin' through my body. I can't focus on anything. It's like when Electro burned me on top of the control tower at Dorval; I got a vague sense of heat, of power, goin' through my arm, I got the smell of somethin' burnin' in my mouth . . .

The room spins, and spins, and spins. I go with it.

And then I'm gone.

I'm lyin' on cold, hard cement, staring up at the ceiling.

Half a dozen soldiers, same jet-black uniforms, gold piping along the arms and legs, are starin' down at me, weapons drawn.

I blink. That's about all I can manage. My muscles are jelly; my brain ain't much more.

Time has passed; how much, I got no idea.

I don't hear Ronnie screaming. I don't hear my son.

"Sir," one of the soldiers calls out, and I hear footsteps, and a new face joins theirs. Osborne's.

"Where are they?" I ask, or think I do, at any rate; I can't quite tell if I manage to speak, but in any case, he ignores me.

Wilson's face appears next to his.

"So what do you want us to do with him?" Osborne asks. "He's technically one of yours."

"We got what we needed, right? The kid?"

"That's right."

"So get rid of him," Wilson says, lookin' down at me. "And do it right."

"What's that supposed to mean?"

"It means don't forget who you're dealin' with here. What sort of powers he has." Wilson points a finger at Osborne. "There was a report on his healing factor, our guy at H did. Ran a whole series of tests designed to measure his recuperative powers. Try to quantify just how powerful it was."

"Our guy at H." I remember that report. What I remember, though, was J.C. doin' it. Bein' a pain in my butt about it, too. Takin' his own sweet time hurtin' me.

Wilson goes on. "He scored off the charts. In a way that had some people thinking that he couldn't be killed, unless you burned him up. That he was as close to immortal as you could get. No cellular deterioration whatsoever. Regeneration of any lost tissue."

"He's not what he used to be," Osborne said. "As you can see."

"But the potential is still in there. Way deep inside. Who knows what it'll take to trigger it."

"Your point being?"

"Don't take any chances. Burn the body. Cut off the head. Throw him off the mountain, a piece on either side."

"Sounds like overkill."

"Overkill's what I want."

"It'll be a pleasure."

"Good. Then get to it." Wilson turns his back then, and he's gone.

"Bring him," Osborne says to the soldiers, and they drag to me to my feet and out of the chamber and throw me onto the floor of one of the carts. It starts up with a jerk, starts moving back the way we came, up toward the surface.

There's two soldiers lookin' down at me, sittin' on the back rail of the cart. Osborne's in another cart in front of us; I know it's him only 'cause I can hear his voice.

". . . don't care about haplotypes, whatever they are. All we care about is whether or not it worked. When you finish running the tests, when you know that, get back to me."

A couple seconds of silence, after which Osborne says "Christ" in an entirely different voice, and then "God-damn freak," at which somebody up ahead laughs.

I can only assume they've been talkin' to Brinklow.

I can only assume they're talkin' about whatever test it is they're runnin' on the kid.

My kid.

"I wanna see him," I manage to say.

"Shut up." One of the soldiers slams a rifle butt into my stomach. I don't feel it at all.

I take stock of my situation. Not good.

The soldiers are focused on me. Weapons drawn, pointed right at my brain.

Gotta change that.

"Osborne," I say.

"Shut up." Another rifle butt to the gut; I still don't feel it, but I decide not to let these guys in on that particular piece of information just yet, so I let out what I hope is a pitiful-sounding groan. It bounces off the tunnel walls.

"What's goin' on back there?" Osborne calls back.

"Prisoner's awake, sir. Asking to see the test subjects."

"You had your chance before, Logan. You misbehaved."

"Let me see 'em," I shout back.

He doesn't respond. The soldiers are still starin' right at me.

I shift on the floor of the cart. The soldiers move their weapons to track me.

"Can I sit up at least?"

The same soldier who told me to shut up speaks again. "Sir, the prisoner wants—"

"I heard. Keep him on his back. Keep your weapons on him."

I shrug. "Fine," I say, though of course it's not fine, hard to make a move of any kind lyin' flat on your back.

The cart wheels roll over the cement floor. I'm about a foot and a half off that floor myself.

Just about the length of my claws.

"Here's my question," I say. "What's this all about?"

"Logan, Logan, Logan," Osborne says. "This isn't some James Bond movie, you know, where I tell you exactly what we plan to do and how we plan to do it."

I keep talkin'.

"It's got nothin' to do with Wyndham, obviously. You have his technology. His machines. But whatever it is you're doin' with it, it's a government thing."

Osborne doesn't respond.

That's fine. I'm talkin' just as much to change the dynamic of the situation as I am to try to get a response from him, to work out what's goin' on in my own head.

"A government thing that's got something to do with Avalon," I continue. "That's what Wilson said."

Avalon meaning not what happened to me, in this case. Avalon meaning what Magneto did from there in the first place. Avalon meaning murder—the few thousand or so people who died when Magneto messed with the worldwide power grid.

The few thousand or so humans killed by a single mutant. And what would a human government's response be to that?

Like I said . . .

Nothin' good.

"You wanted to know what happened to me before? Why my claws are bone now, not metal? Why I'm not what I was? I'll tell you what happened. Magneto happened."

"I wanted to know what? What are you talking about?"

I just barely keep myself from smilin'.

I got his interest now.

I take the liberty of sittin' up. One of the soldiers raises his rifle; I hold up both hands, palms facin' front, to show I don't mean any harm. A total lie, of course, but I keep talkin' to Osborne as I do it, figurin' they won't want to tread on their boss's conversation.

I sit on the seat; I turn to face Osborne, who's in the cart in front of us.

"What you asked back at the Ark—what happened to my claws?"

A light comes on in his eyes. "Right. Back at the Ark. Of course."

"It's when we went up to Avalon—Xavier and the

rest of us. We went there to take care of Magneto before he could hurt anybody else."

Osborne shakes his head. "I'm supposed to believe that."

"It's the truth. It's why the adamantium's gone. In the fight, Magneto ripped it out of me. Almost killed me in the process."

My voice catches suddenly.

Osborne smiles. "I guess it is the truth, at that."

I go on as if I never stopped.

"Xavier wiped his mind," I say. "Magneto's done. So whatever it is you're planning—"

"It's not necessary, that's what you're going to say?" Osborne smiles.

"That's right."

"Better minds than yours disagree."

"Better minds like Wilson?" I shake my head.

As I do, I notice a curve in the tunnel a few hundred feet ahead of us.

"Let me tell you some things about Wilson you may not know. First of all—"

"Shut up," Osborne says suddenly, and turns back around in his seat.

"Back on the floor," one of the soldiers says, just as quickly, and I turn and see he's got the rifle trained right on me still, and so does his partner, and that's fine, but as I go to sit, I put my hands down facing up on the cart floor.

I hold the soldiers' gaze as the cart takes the curve.

Entirely focused on me, they jostle each other just a bit, nowhere near enough to lose their balance but just enough that their trigger fingers loosen . . .

I pop the claws on my right hand. They go through the metal floor of the golf cart and hit cement.

They stick.

The car jerks to a sudden stop. The soldiers are already squeezing off a round, but they're flying through the air as they do, and so their aim is off, by a lot, and they curse as they fall forward, off the back of one seat and right into the seatback opposite them.

Somebody screams.

The driver, hit by a stray bullet.

I hear a screech; Osborne's cart stopping. He's shouting something. I pop the claws on my left hand, too, and pull my right hand up out of the floor, and as I try to rise, one of the soldiers gets his balance and aims at me. I kick him square in the gut, and he flies off the cart, and the other one is swingin' his gun around, and I swing my right arm, claws out, right at groin level. His eyes widen, he makes a noise and falls backward onto the cement floor, right on his butt, and starts firing. But I used the energy from my swing at him to push up and out of the cart, so his shells hit only air, and I hit the cement and roll, right under the cart, which I grab hold of and flip over, as if I'm goin' to use it as a shield, but even as bullets from the soldier on the floor and the guys in Osborne's cart hit it,

I'm movin' back down the tunnel, toward the curve we came around.

And here comes another cart, four more soldiers, and they start firing, too, and this is not gonna work. I look back up the tunnel, and the soldiers from Osborne's cart are off and moving as well. I look left, tunnel wall; I look right, tunnel wall; and I look up—

Cable pinned to the ceiling. Thick black cable, running next to a pipe about the same width.

I crouch, and I jump, and I slash and cut that cable, and there's a little jolt and a big spark, and the lights go out as I hit the ground again.

The tunnel is pitch-black.

I move again, in the darkness.

The emergency lights kick on.

A strip of fluourescent lights along one side of the tunnel, waist-high.

The soldiers riddle the floor where I was standing, only I'm not there anymore.

"Hold your fire!" Osborne yells. "Dammit, hold your fire!"

They do. Immediately—well-trained bastards that they are.

I'm hanging on the ceiling, one hand around the dangling cable, the other on one of the brackets holding the cable up.

Gonna take Osborne all of two seconds to spot me.

Take the fight to him.

I slash through the bracket but hang on to the cable.

I swing down right into the midst of Osborne's soldiers, screamin' as I come, just like a hairy little Tarzan, holdin' the sparkin' cable out in front of me.

I've felt my share of current these last couple days. This line's got plenty to spare.

I slam into Osborne, miss him with the cable, but he goes to the ground anyway, and as I planned, the soldiers hold their fire for a second, because I'm right next to the guy they're takin' orders from. I loosen my grip on the cable just enough to let it out a bit and swing it like a garden hose, around in a circle, and it sparks and hits one of Osborne's soldiers just right, and he goes flying backward as if he was shot out of a cannon, slams into the wall, and lies still. And it happens again; this time, the guy hits into one of his buddies, and both of them hit the floor.

I drop the cable and dive for Osborne and drag him back up against the tunnel wall. I put my right hand, claws out, right up against his throat.

He spits out a curse.

"You know the drill," I tell him.

He glares.

"Do it," I say.

"Hold your fire," he tells his men.

"Good. Now tell them to back away."

He does.

"Farther," I tell him. "Down the corridor. Out of sight."

They obey without asking.

"You bought yourself an extra minute, at the most," Osborne says when they're gone. "Wilson'll tell them to kill us both."

I ignore him. "Tell me where they are."

"One of the labs. I really don't know."

"How do I get to them?"

"Gee. Let me think. Oh, wait—you can just use the transporter. Like on *Star Trek*."

"Very funny." I yank on his ear with one hand, pullin' him back slightly, so that the whole neck is exposed. I press the claws against his neck; droplets of blood appear.

"Where are they?" I say again.

He's about to respond when somethin' metal groans above us.

I look up and see the pipe running along the ceiling sagging down a bit.

The bracket I ripped off held it up, too, I realize.

The groaning sound is another bracket, one fifty feet down the tunnel, about to give as well.

Osborne spits out a curse, and before I can respond—

The bracket snaps.

The pipe drops a couple of feet from the ceiling, and then it snaps, too.

Liquid starts spewing out.

Gas. I can smell it.

Osborne strains against my grip.

"Let me go, dammit! We have to get out of here."

"Where . . . are . . . they?" I say again, slowly, as if I got all the time in the world.

Osborne strains again. Curses a third time, and then a fourth.

I don't budge.

"There's a second set of cells near the labs. They're in there."

"Is there another way out? Besides the entrance we came through?"

"No. Up is the only way. When we built the place—"

Bullets riddle the floor around us.

I look up and see a handful of rifle barrels poking around the tunnel bend.

Osborne uses the distraction to break free.

He runs toward the soldiers, waving his arms, hollering at the top of his lungs.

"Hold your fire! Hold your fire! There's a gas—"

I think his next word was gonna be *leak*.

That's when the explosion comes.

I see it, a flare of light and heat that materializes in the tunnel out of nowhere, like one of those *Star Trek* characters materializing in a transporter beam. I don't know if it was a bullet that caused it or sparks from the cable I cut, and it doesn't matter, because there's nothing I can do.

There's nothin' Osborne can do, either; he goes up in flames even as I turn to run, to get away from the blast, to head on up the tunnel, up toward the surface.

I almost finish my first step.

Then something lifts me into the air, and for a second I'm flyin' like a free, free bird. Just like Ronnie used to fly. I can smell fresh air. I can see the clouds.

Then the ground rises up and smacks me, once, twice, a third time.

Then all I see is black.

17

AFTER I DIED . . .

After Magneto peeled the adamantium from my skeleton and sucked it out of my flesh . . .

After Avalon, on the way down to Earth, in the medi unit in the Blackbird . . .

I felt Xavier and Jeannie in my mind. Usin' their mutant powers to reach deep into my psyche, to try to keep me together—physically, mentally. Trying to keep me with 'em here on planet Earth, keep me away from the light, and the voices callin' me to join them on the other side. The voices of those who died. It took some doin'; there was a part of me that didn't want to live anymore, after what had happened. I was ready to go. Ready to walk up to the edge of that cliff and jump off.

I ain't ready this time.

This time, I want to live. I need to live. I need to

find Ronnie, and the kid. I need to get them some-place safe, and then I need to take care of Osborne, and Wilson, and whoever else is involved in this thing. Project Shangri-La.

Brave New World. A certain degree of genetic variance. No more extreme cases.

The answer's hoverin' there, somewhere in the back of my mind.

Somethin' else is hoverin' there, too. A realization. I don't need to worry about Osborne anymore. Or O'Connell, or whatever he calls himself. He's already taken care of. The explosion in the tunnel.

Thing is, I got a bad feelin' that blast might've taken care of me, too.

There's snow fallin' on my face. Thick, wet flakes that I can barely feel, my skin is so frozen. Frostbite for sure, on my hands, my arms, my legs. I can smell burned flesh, and I know it's mine. The blast blew off my coat; I think it blew off a big chunk of my right leg, too.

Blew me clear out the side of the mountain, left me lyin' here, flat on my back, watchin' the sky rain down little chunks of white on me.

The thought crosses my mind that maybe this is how those missin' Japanese mountain climbers felt, the ones who thought they'd be the first up Kawagebo. One second they're on top of the world, or just about, and the next . . .

They're buried under it.

Most of 'em probably went painlessly, though; that's what freezin' to death is like. Probably they knew what had happened, what was going to happen, probably they said a little prayer to their ancestors, to their gods, to take care of them in the afterlife, in the whatever was to come next.

Not like I got a strong relationship with the Almighty goin' on, but I do a little prayin' myself. I figure that whatever kind of Supreme Being/Beings are out there, the closest we get to touchin' 'em's at the moment we're about to pass on. Only, like I said, I ain't ready to go beyond that veil just yet. So if you're out there, God . . .

Pick me back up, will ya?

The snow just keeps on fallin'.

I move my head just enough to see a little drift begin to cover the lower half of my body. I start to wonder if this is how I'm goin' to check out. Buried under a soft cushion of fluffy white powder. Nibbled to death by ducks. The great Weapon X, goin' out not with a bang but a whimper.

I manage to smile at the irony.

Time passes.

The sun rises; the sun sets. It happens a second time, and then a third.

I'm starving by then, my stomach howling as loud as the wind. My mouth is as dry as the desert sand. My vision swims; the mountain seems to swim with it. The rocks go fluid. The snow dazzles with buried diamonds and shimmers like the desert blacktop on a hundred-degree day.

Freddy leans over me, lookin' none the worse for wear after his thousand-foot jump out into empty space, and smiles.

Here come, obviously, the hallucinations.

"Mister Logan. Dude. I thought you were dead there a minute."

Talking hallucinations. That's nice.

I play along.

"Soon enough," I say. "Stick around awhile."

The hallucination looks worried. One arm disappears from sight for a second and then reappears holding a canteen.

It reaches out with one hand and leans my head forward. "Here. Have some tea," it says.

The hand behind my head feels solid enough. So does the canteen against my lips.

So does the tea going down my throat.

I blink as I swallow.

"Better?" the Freddy hallucination asks.

I sit all the way up. Hurts like the dickens. I grab the hallucination's wrist. That feels real enough, too.

"No," I say. "It can't be."

Freddy smiles.

"It is."

"You fell," I say. "Out of a plane. A thousand feet up."

Freddy nods. "I fell," he says, and smiles again. "I bounced."

• • •

He's got a pack full of food. Some goat cheese, to go along with the tea. While I eat, while I try to get some warmth back into my body, some feeling back into my hands and arms and legs and face, he tells me the story of what happened when he fell. When he bounced, though from the sound of it he didn't so much bounce as manage to disperse the kinetic energy his body had absorbed before he hit the ground.

I don't really need the details, though. I've already gleaned the most important thing of all just from his presence here. From the simple fact that he's here— that he's alive.

He's a mutant, too.

That makes Mama's—Ms. Siaow's—speed and strength a little more understandable. Fightin' her, I wasn't fightin' somebody human. I was fightin' one of my own. A mutant.

Freddy's power also might explain how he got away from the tigers on the trail before—some unconscious use of his power, his body doin' reflexively what needed to be done without his mind bein' aware of it. Wouldn't be the first time somethin' like that happened; I remember the elf telling me somethin' similar went on with him. *Bamf!* when he wasn't expectin' it. Somethin' about a girls' locker room.

I smile and take another gulp of the tea; I must have a half-gallon sloshing around in my belly by now.

Freddy's talkin' about what happened when he got back to Wubeng.

"I managed to convince them that what was happening—what'd they call it, the *nien* . . . ?"

"Yeah. *Nien*."

"That it wasn't really anything supernatural. That Osborne was behind it, and that you were going to take care of him and all those tigers when you got up to the top of Kawagebo."

"You said that?"

"Uh-huh."

"After they pushed you out of the copter? After Osborne pulled the taser on me?"

"Yeah."

He shrugs. I smile.

"You had a lot of confidence in me."

"I know who you are," he says, lookin' away for a second. "I know about the X-Men. What they do."

Those words put a smile on my face. "I don't know what to say to that, except thanks."

I drink some more tea. Chew a little more cheese. Frown. "You didn't run into any of those tigers on the trail?"

Freddy shakes his head. "Didn't see a one. I guess the guys on the copter got 'em all."

I nod, but that's not the way I remember it. A bunch were shot. A bunch survived, too. At least, I thought so. But if they had . . . I don't see Freddy, bouncin' power or not, gettin' by them a second time.

"Guess so," I say. "Gotta hand it to you, kid. Comin' after me . . . after what happened to you. That took some real guts."

"Thanks."

I stretch, get to my feet. Groan.

I'm stiff as a board, but at least I'm breathin'.

"So you did it, right?" Freddy says. "You killed O'Connell, and all those guys up there. Stopped whatever it was they were up to, with the weapons they were buying from V.C. . . ."

His voice trails off as he sees I'm shakin' my head.

"Not exactly." I give him the short version—the very short version—of how I ended up on the side of Kawagebo. His eyes go wide anyway.

"A kid? What . . . I mean, that's great, but . . . well . . . we gotta get back up there. I guess."

"*I* gotta get back up there," I say, correcting him, already beginning to work out in my head how I'm gonna do that. Can't go in the front; they'll be watching that. Can't go through the hole in the tunnel, assuming it's still there, which it may or may not be. I'll have to check that out.

"I can help," Freddy says.

I shake my head. "I appreciate the offer, kid, believe me I do. And I appreciate you comin' to get me, but I gotta take it from here on my own."

"In case you hadn't noticed . . . I can take care of myself."

"Yeah. You did good back on the trail before . . . with the rifle."

He nods. "That's right. "

"And jumpin' out of the copter . . . even though you didn't know what was gonna happen . . ."

"Yeah." Freddy's smile is back now. "It's my instincts. I got good instincts. I—"

He stops talkin' all at once, because I've popped my claws and put 'em right up next to his throat.

"Good instincts, huh?"

His eyes go wide.

"You didn't see that comin', did ya?"

"Easy," he says, tryin' to back away, which he can't, 'cause my other hand is holdin' on to his arm. "What are you doing?"

"Provin' a point." I lean in close to him. "Listen, what you got ain't instinct, it's luck. You oughtta be dead right now, like Shailo. It's a miracle you're not."

He opens his mouth to argue.

"Don't. Don't speak. You got no training. You don't know how your power really works. Most of all, you have no idea what's up there. Who's up there. How quick they'd kill you if they thought for a second that you posed any kind of threat to them."

"They could try, you mean."

"Oh, they'd do more than try. The second they see you're still alive, after a thousand-foot drop, they'll pay special attention to you, I guarantee it."

Give the kid credit, he doesn't back down.

"Teach me, then," he says. "Show me how to stay alive. You owe me that much."

"I owe you?"

"I just saved your life, right?"

"It's debatable," I say, shakin' my head again.

But the wheels are turnin', even as I'm sayin' no.

A frontal assault on the lab ain't gonna be easy.

A distraction—like, say, a three-hundred-pound guy who can bounce—would certainly help.

"Please," Freddy says. "I'll do whatever you say."

I frown again. Let go of his arm, retract my claws.

"Maybe," I say.

He smiles. I take a deep breath.

This is a bad idea, I know it. Freddy's played way too many video games for my taste. A video-game kid. He thinks that's what he's gettin' to do now, play the sidekick role, and we'll go in, and the bad guys'll fall down just like they do on the video screen, no muss, no fuss. Easy as clickin' a button.

On the other hand, I tell myself . . .

He did do pretty well there, back on the trail. Moved pretty well, considerin' how hefty he is. Appearances aside—fat Freddy, sleek Mama—it seems like the apple didn't fall far from the tree at all.

It hits me then, like a ton of bricks.

Genetic variance. Brave New World. No more extreme cases.

I feel the blood drain from my face.

"Jesus," I say.

"What's the matter?" Freddy asks.

"Everything," I say, and turn and start headin' up the mountain.

"Wait a minute," Freddy says. "Where are you going? You can't—don't we need a plan or something?"

I ignore him and keep movin'. All I can think about is Ronnie and the kid. Gettin' 'em out of there, because if I'm right about what Project Shangri-La is, about what Wilson and the others are planning, they don't need those two alive anymore, either. In fact, the odds are they're already dead, that while I was snoozin' out there in the snow, Wilson's boys took care of the two of them. But I realize I can't think that way, I can't, and so I put the negative thoughts to the back of my mind, try and banish 'em, which is when I realize that my senses are howling like a banshee as I run. *Danger. Danger. Danger.*

Somethin' leaps down from the mountain, right into my path.

A white tiger.

Snow crunches above me, to my left, and then, a split-second later, to my right.

A half-dozen others appear.

"Experiment," the first tiger says. It's got a big scar runnin' down the side of its face. A scar I gave it.

It's one of the tigers from the ambush on the trail, when Shailo died.

The animal's face twists into something resembling a smile.

"Now we finish it."

18

BEST DEFENSE BEIN' A GOOD OFFENSE, I TAKE IT TO him.

Scream, pop my claws, and leap. The tigers weren't expecting any kind of offensive reaction from me; they take a split-second to move, by which point I've already cut the leader across the leg it raises to defend itself.

I do a somersault, come up in attack position on its other side.

The tigers—seven in all—form a half-circle facing me. The leader falls back.

The others step forward.

A shadow passes overhead, and the tigers look up.

A rock falls and lands on one of them. It howls.

Freddy bounces down next to me, smiles, and takes off again. Up into the air.

"Kid, stay away before you—" I stop my yell in mid-sentence, not only because he's already out of hearing range but because the tigers are preoccupied, watching him go, so I make my second move, goin' for the two tigers on the left edge of the circle, both claws out, two slashes, then I'm past them and in front of the leader again.

And it snarls, and the other tigers turn toward me . . .

And another rock comes down. No, make that a chunk of ice, small, relatively speaking, about the size of a fist, but it does the trick. One tiger howls and leaps out of the way into the middle of two others, and the three of them nearly tumble off the side of the mountain. I have to smile; nice work, Freddy. But then, out of the corner of my eye, I see another one of the animals off to my right, just lookin' up at the sky, lookin' at Freddy, tensing as it looks, preparing to leap and attack even as Freddy begins to come down from the sky himself.

I'm too far away. Positioned wrong to stop him.

Freddy's dead, unless . . .

I turn and charge the leader again, claws out, and it raises its good leg to defend itself, and I kick it aside, and it sprawls onto the ground . . .

And I plant my right hand, vault myself up in the air, and land on the tiger's back.

The leader snarls.

My claws are at its throat.

"Stop!" I yell, as Freddy hits the ground, but the

other tiger is already in the air, and it slams into Freddy, hits him square in the chest.

I look for blood to come pouring out of his jacket.

Instead, the tiger bounces off Freddy and goes hurtling off into the distance as if he was shot out of a cannon.

I'm surprised, but just for a second.

There's more to Freddy's power than I thought it first. Seems to have something to do with kinetic energy, and an ability to convert it to his own purposes.

Xavier's gonna have a field day training this kid.

If I can keep him alive that long.

Freddy smiles at me, yells, "Good instincts, see?" and takes off into the sky again.

The leader hisses beneath me. The other tigers growl and move forward.

I suddenly realize none of this is necessary.

"We're on the same side here," I say. "The people up in the lab there? They're my enemies—same as yours."

The tiger beneath me hisses and twists and tries to throw me off. Almost succeeds.

"You lie, experiment," it says. "You went in the helicopter—"

"'Cause you were chasing us, remember?"

Two of the tigers on my left move forward, a slow, careful step. I ignore them, because it's a distraction, of course. The real danger's gonna come from the tiger on the other side of the circle, to my extreme right, circling behind me, tensed to spring the second I'm distracted.

"Listen to me," I say. "They used me—the same way they used you. For the same reason. It's all part of their plan."

"Plan?" another of the tigers says. "What plan?"

"To make sure that we're the last of our kind," I say. "To make sure that nobody—nothing—like us ever walks the Earth again."

The circling tigers pause.

It seems as good a moment as any to climb off the leader's back. To stand in front of them and let them know I stand behind my words.

"We could fight each other," I say. "Or we could fight them."

The tigers look to their leader. It looks me in the eye, and I swear I can see it frown.

After a good ten seconds, it speaks again.

"Tell me more, experiment," it says.

And I do.

Five minutes on, we're a team.

Me, Freddy, and the seven white tigers. I think they're only marginally interested in stopping the experiment, stopping Project Shangri-La from happening. What they want is revenge for what's been done to them already. Revenge on Wilson, whom they've only heard of but never seen, revenge on the monkey man, whom they hold in particular contempt, and most of all, revenge on Osborne, whom they just want to eat . . . slowly.

I decide not to tell them he's dead already.

I learn the tigers have given each other names, ones, unfortunately, that only they can really pronounce. I manage a mangling of the leader's—Torzay. A female, who, after we reach our understanding, takes charge of leadin' us up the mountain, up a trail that I would've missed completely on my own, a trail that's easy climbing for the tigers, doable for me, using my claws as pitons, and one that would've killed Freddy a half-dozen times over if he didn't have the ability to bounce back from his mistakes, as it were.

The wind picks up again as we climb, whipping snow all around us. I can't help but think of Dorval. Of Wilson. And Ronnie.

There's a crevasse a thousand feet deep on our right, a rock wall close to sheer on our left. The trail narrows, forcing us to go single file. I stay on high alert; I'm still not entirely sure I trust the tigers, to tell you the truth. Maybe they're leadin' us into a trap; maybe they're just waiting for a more convenient time and place to attack again, waitin' for me to drop my guard. Or maybe they're just interested in eating Freddy. He's in front of me on the trail, two tigers before him, the rest behind me. His butt hangs out over the edge as he takes a tight corner on the trail; I have to smile. He'd make a good-size meal, at that; dinner for three or four of them, at least. Loin of mutant.

Freddy chooses that second to turn around. "What's so funny?" he asks.

I wipe the smile off my face and motion for him to press on.

He turns and almost runs right into the tiger in front of him.

Our forward motion has stopped entirely.

"What's goin' on?" I call out.

"The path is blocked," the tiger in front of us says.

I come around Freddy and him, following the curving trail. Torzay is stopped behind a boulder the size of a double-wide.

"This is new," she says.

I look at it, frown, and guess I know why.

A minute's scramble up the side of the mountain, and I have my guess confirmed.

There's a gaping hole in the cliff face next to me, shredded bits of metal on the ground all around.

This is where the explosion took place. Where I was blown out of the side of the tunnel. The hole is still there; the tunnel inside, I see, is dark. Nobody bothered to fix it.

I frown, as Torzay leaps up alongside me. The other tigers follows suit, and then, a second later, Freddy ping-pongs up with us, too. We push through the rubble and into the tunnel complex, into almost complete darkness. A row of emergency lights along the floor gives off an eerie, reddish glow. Along with the lack of light, there's an almost total absence of noise.

"Looks like nobody's home," Freddy says from right behind me.

I turn to respond, and almost jump right out of my skin.

The big tiger—Torzay—is standin' six inches away from me. The pupils of her eyes burn like little red-orange coals.

"I smell them," she growls. "I hear them."

"Smell who?" Freddy asks.

She ignores him and starts padding forward.

My nose crinkles up. I smell somethin', too. A trace of gas. I look up, squint into the darkness, and see the pipes above me, hanging at an awkward angle. Just like they looked before the explosion.

I curse again. This time, Freddy hears me.

"What?"

"They never fixed the hole, they never repaired the pipes . . ." I shake my head.

"They abandoned this part of the tunnel," Freddy says. "Closed it off, probably."

"Maybe," I say. "Or maybe they abandoned the entire lab."

"No. The tiger smells something, right?" He smiles. "Don't worry. We'll find 'em."

I frown. "I'm worried," I say, as shapes flow past me in the darkness. The other tigers, following Torzay down the tunnel. I catch up, Freddy a few steps behind.

"You smell what?" I ask Torzay. "Soldiers?"

"Something," she repeats, and quickens her pace.

I quicken mine to stay with her. Something. That covers a lot of possibilities. Rats. Soldiers. Government bureaucrats.

Ronnie.

Second set of cells by the lab, Osborne said before he died. That's where she and the kid were. It was about a five-minute ride by cart from there to where the explosion took place; I figure fifteen minutes to walk it.

Five minutes on, we reach a fork in the tunnel. Torzay pauses, raises her head for a second, then goes confidently left. I confidently follow.

Then a little buzzer starts goin' off inside my head. I stop in my tracks.

"What?" Freddy says, stoppin' with me.

I watch as the tigers disappear off in the darkness, down the corridor.

"This way," I say, turnin' right.

Ten feet on, we pass a steel door, barely visible in the darkness, and my senses start goin' off like gangbusters.

There's somethin' behind that door.

I pop my claws and yank it open.

It's a man.

I grab him by the collar and pull him out. He screams and holds up his hands to protect himself.

A split-second away from smackin' him across the face, I hold my punch.

He's clearly not one of Wilson's people.

This guy has to be seventy years old, at least; he weighs all of a hundred pounds, soaking wet.

He's wearin' some kind of olive cloth wrapped around his waist, like a toga. He's got scraggly white hair, hangin' down his back, hangin' down in front of his face. He's bruised on one side of that face already, scratched there, too. The poor guy looks terrified.

He also looks not entirely there. Maybe not even entirely human.

He's another test subject, I realize.

He cringes, backs up against the wall, and shuts his eyes.

"Hey," I say, motioning Freddy closer. "You got any food left?"

"Huh?"

"Food. You got any in your pack?"

"For him?"

"Yeah, for him. Come on, give me what you got."

Freddy digs through his pack, comes up with a couple last hunks of bread and a piece of cheese. He hands it to me. I hold it out to the old guy, who shakes his head and shrinks back farther.

"Come on, don't be afraid, take it." I move it closer to him. He shuts his eyes, as if I'm gonna hit him with it.

I sympathize—they probably put him through hell up here—but I don't have time for this.

"Here," I say, puttin' the food on the ground. "Enjoy."

I turn my back and head off down the tunnel. Freddy comes with me.

Fifty feet on, I turn around. The old guy hasn't moved a muscle.

"He better grab that food and get out of here," Freddy says. "Before the tigers find him."

"Yeah," I say, realizing that even if the old guy does manage to make it out without being eaten, he's got a few thousand feet of cliff to get down before he reaches Wubeng and civilization, such as it is. The poor bastard's never gonna make it.

Neither is Ronnie or the kid, though, unless we find 'em.

We reach another fork; this time, my senses don't tell me anything.

I point Freddy off to the left.

"Twenty minutes from now," I say. "Meet me back here, at this exact spot."

"I don't have a watch."

"Count," I tell him, and set off on my own.

Another few minutes, and I reach the lab doors. No missin' them, even in the semidarkness.

I walk up and try the handles. Locked. I hammer on 'em with both fists.

"Hey!" I shout. "Anybody home?"

There's no answer, but I swear I can hear noises inside. I hammer again. Still nothing.

"Hey!" I yell again. "Open—"

Something slams into me from behind, slams me

face-first into the steel. I feel my nose break; blood gushes.

Somethin' sharp cuts into my back. Claws.

I scream in pain and try to turn, and my skin touches fur.

A foul stench reaches my nostrils. An animal stench.

The tigers. Torzay. I knew they were just pretending to go along with us, I knew—

The thing hurls me through the air, and I hit the ground. I lie there stunned.

A man stands over me and growls.

No. Not a man.

A man with the head of a wolf. Just like back at the Ark. Only bigger. Much bigger.

He launches himself at me again. I manage to roll out of the way; he manages to avoid hitting the tunnel wall, and turns again.

I get to my knees. The blood in my nose is still flowing; the cuts in my side still burn.

I pop my claws.

His growl turns into an out-and-out roar. I stand and match it.

And from the darkness, other figures emerge. A couple more wolf guys. A tiger—not one I recognize from the trail. A monkey with bloodlust in its eyes.

Experiments, all of them. Abandoned. Roaming the tunnels. Looking for food.

I say a quick prayer for Freddy, and then a quicker

one for myself, as the animals start to advance. I back up, toward the lab doors.

Metal creaks behind me. They're in the lab, too, I realize, as I turn and see—

A gun pointing out the suddenly open lab door.

"Move!" a muffled voice yells, and I look up from the gun barrel and see a figure in what almost looks like a space suit. A split-second later, I realize the figure's talking to me, and so I do as I'm told. I move. I slide to the side, and from out of the barrel of the gun, which I suddenly see is not a gun barrel at all but rather something else entirely—

A jet of orange flame shoots out. The animals— the experiments—make various shrieking noises and shrink back.

The door swings open wider, and whoever it is in the suit reaches out a hand and grabs hold of my arm.

"In!" the same voice yells. "Quickly, quickly!"

I push through the entrance, past the person in the suit, and the door swings shut behind me.

"Good Lord," the figure says, slumping back against the door. "That was close."

"Yeah," I say, dusting myself off. "Thanks."

My nose has stopped bleeding. I reach around under my shirt and feel the cuts on my back. Feel them healing up.

I look around. The lights in the lab are still runnin' full strength. Don't know if there's a separate circuit on them or what, but the room—the chamber—is lit up bright as day, just like the last time I was here. Other than that, though . . .

Everything's different.

Half the equipment is gone. I look for, and don't see, the genetic accelerator.

The place was spotless before; now it's a pigsty, for lack of a better word. Medical supply boxes ripped open, plastic containers strewn everywhere, tables overflowing with computer printout, two computer terminals, green text blinking against black, pulled up one next to the other on two different-size carts, connected with a long gray cord coated with electrical tape.

The figure in front of me pulls off its helmet. Surprise. It's not a person.

It's the monkey man. Brinklow.

He wriggles out of the suit and smiles. He looks a mess, too.

It's the first time I've seen him without his lab coat on. He's got hair all over, like an ape, but less of it. Reminds me of this Russian general I took a sauna with once, in Stalingrad, only the Russian had red hair, and the monkey man's is black.

His legs are long and straight, not bow-legged the way a chimp's usually are. His arms are long, too, longer than mine, longer than a human's but not so long that with clothes on he'd look unnatural.

"I don't know about you," he says, turning his back on me and heading toward a long white table, "but after that, I could certainly use a nice strong cup of tea."

I blink. "A cup of tea?"

"Yes. Would you care for one?"

"Tea." I shake my head in disbelief and take a step toward him. The look on his face changes as he sees the look on mine.

"Is there a problem?" he asks, putting the kettle down and backing off a step.

"Several. Startin' with those little experiments you ran on me back in Vegas. You remember those, right?"

"Well, yes, but . . ."

He backs up into a table, knocks over a glass beaker. It falls to the floor and shatters.

"Mister Logan. Let's be reasonable. Those things out there would have killed you—eaten you—without a second thought. They're animals."

I smile and pop my claws.

"Aren't we all?" I say.

I move closer.

19

HE STEPS BACK.

"I performed those experiments under duress," Brinklow says. "I would never have done those kinds of things on my own. You understand? It was a matter of surviving. Survival."

I smile. "Sure. I understand."

I keep moving forward. He keeps moving back. His eyes keep darting to his right. I follow them and see the flame thrower he just used. Sneaky bastard.

I circle a little, moving to put myself between him and the weapon.

"Tell me where they are."

"I'm the only left here," he says, misinterpreting my question. "You can see that. Everyone else is gone. After all the work I did for them, they left me—"

"I'm not talkin' about the soldiers or the government guys. I'm talkin' about Ronnie—the girl. And the kid. Where are they?"

"The girl? Ah. The female. The one we used the accelerator on?"

"Used." I say the word quietly. I offer up a nasty smile. "Yeah. That's right. The one you used."

"They took her," he says.

My heart starts pounding faster. "Who took her?"

"Wilson—and the others."

"Where? Where'd they go?"

"I don't know."

"I don't believe that."

"It's the truth. I was never part of their plans, and after the experiment was successful . . . after they'd decided to leave, they tried to kill me."

"Did they now?"

"Yes, they did! They sent soldiers here to the lab." He nods toward a corner of the room; I glance over and see an overturned cart, near the generator. I see two pairs of uniformed legs sticking out from underneath it.

"They drew their weapons. They tried to make me come with them . . . it was horrible. Horrible. I had to defend myself."

"With your flame thrower there?" I ask, nodding toward the weapon, taking my eyes off him for a split-second as I do so.

That's a mistake.

He dives across the room and comes up with something that looks like a raygun.

"With this. I killed them with this," he says, smiling, tightening his finger around the weapon's trigger. "The same way I'm going to kill you, you ungrateful—"

I ain't what I once was, that's for sure.

But I'm still more than enough to handle whatever Brinklow's got without breaking a sweat.

He's on the word "ungrateful" when I reach him. Grab his wrist with one hand, and twist.

He screams and drops the weapon.

"I'm sorry!" he howls. "I'm sorry sorry sorry, but I was scared, I was afraid you were going to—"

I grab him by the collar and shake him. "Stop whining."

He makes a last pitiful noise under his breath, and then nods.

"That's better. Now . . . where did they go? Wilson and the others?"

"I told you—I don't know."

"You must have some idea."

"If I did, don't you think I'd tell you?"

I look him in the eye.

He just might be tellin' the truth, at that.

"Okay. The kid. Where's he?"

He shakes his head. "They must have taken him as well, I suppose."

I pull him a little closer. "You're not bein' very helpful here."

"That's all I know, I swear it is. I wish I could tell you more but—"

"Shut up."

He shuts up, and I think a second.

Where did Wilson go?

Knowing what's next on his agenda might be a good way to find out.

"What are they up to? What's the plan? Project Shangri-La?"

He hesitates for a second, then shakes his head. "I don't know that, either."

He's lying.

I grab him by the neck and pull him closer.

"Tell me. What are they up to?"

He starts shaking his head again.

"I really don't know, I—"

I backhand him across the face. He screeches in pain.

"I don't know!"

"I don't believe you."

He opens his mouth again to protest, and I put the claws right under his chin.

"Tell me about Shangri-La," I say. "What they're up to. The truth."

He sighs and nods.

"All right. You're right, I know something about it. It's just—Wilson and Osborne never permitted me to speak of it, they didn't want me to—"

"They're not here now, though—are they?"

"No. They're not."

"So talk."

"I will." He looks down at my hand on his arm. "You could stop squeezing so hard, you know. I'm really no threat."

I can't disagree with that.

I let him go.

"Thank you." He rubs the inside of his wrist and frowns. "And if you don't mind, one other thing?"

I glare. "What?"

He gives me a wan smile. "If I could get my tea . . ."

I wave a hand, and he goes gratefully to his cup. "You sure I can't get you any?" he asks.

I growl. "Don't press your luck."

I move the flame thrower well out of reach.

I shove everything off the nearest table and pull up two chairs next to each other.

"Sit," I say, pointing to one of them.

The monkey man nods hesitantly and does as he's told.

"Talk."

He takes a sip of his tea and begins. "The X-Gene. It's all about the X-Gene."

"The what?"

"The X-Gene. That's what Wilson calls it. The dividing line between mutant and human. That's his phrase."

I have to laugh. "X-Gene? You gotta be kiddin' me. X-Gene?"

"It's a misnomer, of course," he says. "There's no single X-Gene, any more than there's a single type of mutation. X simply refers to the aggregate level of variance from the genotypic norm, as established by—"

"Put it in English, why don't you?"

"Shangri-La is about ensuring that development occurs within accepted genetic boundaries."

"English," I say again.

"Eliminating mutation."

"Right." Minus the stupid name—X-Gene—it fits the general outlines of what I suspected was goin' on. "No mutation—no more mutants. How are they gonna do it?"

"I don't know the outlines of the whole project, of course," Brinklow says. "I'm just a small part of it. They never really gave me anything important to do. They never trusted me enough to—"

I slam my fist down on the table.

He drops his mug to the floor. It shatters into a hundred pieces.

"Tell me, dammit!"

He gulps and nods. "With the virus."

A little chill runs up and down my arms. "Virus. What virus?"

"The one we injected you with—back at the Ark."

His voice, all of a sudden, sounds small and far away.

They injected me with a virus.

I don't know why that should be a surprise. I don't

know why anything people do to each other should be a surprise to me anymore.

Osborne and Brinklow and Wilson, throwing Ronnie and me together like breeding stock.

The mob at Fort Mac, chasin' J.C. and Ronnie.

Magneto showin' me the numbers tattooed on his arm, the numbers from Auschwitz.

I hear a sudden growling noise and realize it's me.

I blink and see Brinklow staring right at me, a nervous smile on his face.

"Mister Logan?" he asks.

"A virus," I say. "You injected me with a virus?"

"I'm sorry, of course, I didn't—I was strictly under orders, otherwise I would never have—"

"What did you do to me?"

"Heh." Brinklow's still tryin' to smile. "Nothing permanent, if it's any consolation. Your healing factor, of course, prevented any alterations being permanent, which made it even more difficult to—"

"What. Did. You. Do. To. Me."

He nods quickly, head bobbing and down. Eager to please.

"Yes. Of course. We injected a virus into your system. One of the XM series Mister Wilson had brought with him from the Canadian laboratory. The virus, ah, works on the sex cells within the body. It's very clever, actually. It incorporates itself into an individual's DNA sequence and, as reproduction occurs, checks for deviations from the baseline sequence.

The X-ceptable sequence, as it were." Brinklow grins. "That's a pun."

I restrain myself from cutting him in two.

"You injected me. You injected Ronnie, too."

"Yes."

"To see what kind of kid we'd have. Mutant or human."

"Heh." Brinklow does his stupid monkey laugh again. "Yes. Exactly."

"And?"

He looks confused. "And what?"

"What was the result of your experiment?"

"Oh no, oh no. Not my experiment. I was only—"

My hand shoots out, almost of its own volition, and grabs him around the throat.

"Ack," he says, making a choking noise deep in his throat. "Ack."

"Stop making excuses, and tell me what you found out."

He nods again, head bobbing, all the while trying to pry my fingers off his neck. The little bastard is strong.

But it's only when I decide to loosen my grip that he's able to talk again.

"The child," he chokes out, coughing in between words. "Perfectly healthy. Human, with an X-factor of—"

"So it works. Your virus."

"Yes."

"And what's the next step?"

"Widespread transmission."

I shake my head. "How are they gonna do that?"

"The last thing we did—we made an airborne varia-
tion."

"An airborne virus."

"Yes."

"And how were they thinking about spreading it?"

"Well, I don't know. Honestly. That's another part
of the project I was never allowed to—"

"That information must be somewhere."

"I'm sure of that, but I doubt there's a way—"

I look around the room and instantly spot what I'm
after. A computer terminal.

I push back my chair and walk to it. Brinklow follows me.

"I'm afraid unless you have the right access codes,
you're not going to be able to get into the system,"
he says. "For one thing, the access codes. Besides
which—"

I sit down at the terminal, punch the keyboard, and
curse.

The screen's completely dark.

"They shut it down before they left. They shut
down the whole power grid. That's how all the experiments escaped, of course. I was able to work off an
emergency generator here, but—"

I stand. Brinklow shuts up.

"There's got to be a way to turn it back on."

"I'm not sure it's worth spending the time, frankly. No doubt, they wiped everything off the computer before they left. But," he adds hastily, seeing the look on my face, "it's worth a try, of course. We'd have to go to the command center."

"Good. Where's that?"

"Down, past the cells. Past all those animals out there."

He points toward the door. On cue, the banging starts up again. Louder than before.

"I, uh, I'm not so sure that I'm up for that particular journey. But I could wait here, and if you did find something . . ."

"You're a prince," I tell him.

"We could both wait," he says. "I have food."

"What's that supposed to mean?"

"We wait here. Fourteen more days. And then the problem goes away."

"I don't get it."

"Well. It's quite simple, really. Catastrophic cellular breakdown." He smiles then, an actual expression of pleasure. "A little something I came up with, after we had so many problems with the tigers. The first round of genetically accelerated experiments."

I'm about to tell him to put that into English when I realize I don't need to.

"They die."

"That's right," he says. "They die, and we can leave here safely. Go to the command center and see what information we can recover from the system. I'd be happy to assist."

He smiles again.

I look at him and realize the monsters out in the hall are nothing compared to the one standing in front of me.

"Is there a problem?" he asks.

I'm about to gut him when I realize that yes, in fact, there is a problem.

"What about the boy?"

"The boy."

"The child. My son. Is that catastrophic cellular breakdown thing going to happen to him?"

A shadow passes across his face for a second. He tries to cover it with another smile.

"No no no no no. We left that out of his protocol, we surely did."

I know by now when Brinklow's lying. And he's definitely lying about this.

"But something's the matter with him, isn't it?"

"Well." He avoids my gaze. "I don't know that for certain."

My head starts to pound. "Tell me," I say.

"Well, ah, Wilson, Mister Wilson, was very interested in ensuring that the level of X remained constant throughout the development process of the experiment, that there would be no question of any hidden genes being triggered by different phases in the organism's life cycle—"

"English," I say again, in a very soft voice. "English, please."

"The protocol called for the experiment—the subject—"

"My son."

"Yes, yes, of course, your son. The protocol called for him to be accelerated at several points through the day—"

"Accelerated. How?" I know the answer to that question even as I ask it. "Wyndham's machine."

"That's right."

"You used the accelerator on him."

Brinklow holds his hands up in front of him, palms facing me, and shakes his head frantically. "I didn't, I'm just saying that's how the experiment was designed, so they probably did do that, I just wasn't there so I can't—"

"What did it do?"

"Well." He tries the nervous smile again. "Accelerated him, I suppose."

My head is pounding even harder. "Accelerated."

He nods. "Yes."

"By that you mean . . ."

He doesn't have to answer, because I know the answer already, but he does anyway. "Aged."

Along with the pounding in my head comes a hammering in my heart. A sickening, sinking feeling in my stomach.

I ask another question that I already know the answer to.

"Aged how much?" I ask.

"Well. The accelerator is a very temperamental machine," he begins. "There are indications that . . ."

He keeps talking. I don't know about what, really. I can't pay attention. The pounding, which I realize is not only coming from my head but from elsewhere in the room. A harsh, metallic sound.

It's the experiments—the animals—outside the lab, pounding on the door. Louder and louder. They want in.

They want Brinklow.

I know just how they feel.

". . . all in all, I've been helpful, yes?" Brinklow is still talking. "Wouldn't you say, in terms of helping you discover what's happening here? You'll get me out, won't you?"

I look across the table at the little yes man—yes chimp is more correct to say, I guess—and I see the hundreds, thousands, of other yes men people like Wilson depend on to get their dirty work done, people who punch the clock, take their orders, and do what they're told, whatever they're told, and go home, and sleep soundly at night.

"Get you out?"

"Yes." Brinklow nods. "Out. Back down the mountain."

I smile.

"Sure. I'll get you out."

Brinklow's eyes light up.

I get up from the table. I push back my chair.

I turn away from him and toward the entrance.

Toward the pounding. Toward the animals—the experiments—that are all going to die in two weeks.

"Mister Logan?" Brinklow asks. "What are you doing?"

"Gettin' the door for you." I put my hand on one of the handles.

He screams and rushes toward me.

I open it before he can get there.

The animals—the experiments—rush in. I manage to fight my way past.

Brinklow doesn't fare so well.

He does a little more screaming before he falls silent.

The control room he told me about is down the tunnels farther—farther into the complex. I'm gonna get there, eventually.

But first, of course, there's someone else I have to see.

As I walk, I remember.

Ronnie's hospital room. The night before she escaped and headed for the Falls.

It's goin' on midnight. I'm standin' in the doorway, lettin' my eyes adjust to the darkness.

When they do, I see she's sitting up in bed, wide awake.

"You might as well come in," she says, and I do. I sit on the edge of the bed and hold her hand for a while, just like Heather had earlier in the day, when her bandages first came off.

The last surgery removed the most extreme of the bird-form features, made her look human again. Gave her back an approximation of her own face. With the help of some of our compadres south of the border—high-tech docs, high-tech nanobot healers borrowed from a group called SHIELD, though the technology turned out to come from old Mr. Fantastic himself, Reed Richards—she took less than a week to heal completely. We were all there for the unveiling, Heather sitting next to the bed, holding Ronnie's hand as the doc removed the bandages, me by the door, J.C. standing by the bed, Jimmy pacing back and forth across the room.

When they were done with the unwrapping, Jimmy stopped pacing and smiled. I smiled, too. "They did a great job," I said. "Yeah," Jimmy chimed in. Heather nodded. J.C. didn't say anything. Ronnie didn't react at all, either. Not then, not for the next ten minutes or so, while Jimmy went through the rehab plan he'd brought for her, showed her the jobs she was going to be doing for the Department over the next couple of weeks. She nodded and said "Yes, sir" in all the appropriate spots. J.C. picked it up from there. He talked about the research he'd been doing since getting Hobie booted off her case. The big news was, he'd been talking to Reed Richards about ways to regrow the neural pathways that had shorted out.

"There are techniques they use in cloning," he said to her. "Richards told me. Not just cellular regrowth but replicative experiential processes—reliving the key moments that formed certain structures—to ensure growth occurs in the exact same way. The trick, of course, would be to accelerate the growth process so it takes months rather than years, but there are people doing work like that now. We can do it," he said, and went on like that for a good while longer, Ronnie nodding and thanking him in all the right places, too, but I'd had enough after five minutes and made my good-byes, promising to return later after Ronnie had a chance to rest.

Now here I am.

With no idea what to say. Ronnie doesn't seem to know what to talk about, either.

We sit there, in silence, for a good five minutes, before she starts crying.

"What?"

"My face."

"They did a great job. I'm not kidding you, you can't tell—"

"It's like a mask," she says. "I look in the mirror, and I want to take it off."

"You'll get used to it."

"I don't want to. I want the old me back, Logan."

"I know. J.C.'s working on it. That whole replicative experience thing? He says—"

"I know what he says," she snaps, interrupting me, and then falls silent.

I wait. Clearly, there's more to come.

"I liked Rick Hobie," she says after a minute. "He explained everything to me."

"I heard J.C. explainin' stuff to you, too. Just this afternoon, in fact."

"He does explain. He tells me everything I want to know—sometimes more, in fact. But he leaves the bad out. He is always positive, always optimistic. He refuses to tell me there may be no hope."

"And that's a bad thing?"

She goes quiet a minute.

We're on ground now I don't really feel comfortable treading. Her relationship with J.C. It's obvious how he feels about her—it's been obvious to everybody from day one. What's not so clear is how she feels about him.

What's even murkier still is what she thinks about me.

And as for my own feelings . . .

"Hobie said the damage was too extensive. That there was little chance I would ever be able to transform again. Regain my powers."

I make a mental note to smack Hobie the next time I see him.

"Little chance is not the same as none," I say gently.

"I want to fly, Logan," she says, in a tone of voice I haven't ever heard from her before. A determined, angry, almost desperate tone of voice. "I need to fly."

I squeeze her hand again. "If I was a bettin' man, I'd say you will. I'd say you'll find a way. Have faith, Ronnie."

She squeezes back, and for some reason, I go on in that vein for a little bit, sounding more and more like a bad Rod McKuen poem with every word.

Suddenly, her hand's on my cheek.

"You're a good man, Logan."

I shake my head slowly. "Not really. But I have my moments."

She smiles. "Do you ever wonder what it might be like to be normal? To not be doing what we do every day?"

I find myself smiling, too. "No."

"I do sometimes."

"Not me. I don't think I could do normal."

"I think you could do whatever you set your mind to."

"You're talkin' about nine-to-five normal, that sort of thing?"

"Yes, that sort of thing. Nine to five, dinner at six, asleep at ten . . . that married-people sort of normal." Her smile, all at once, is gone. "That's how my parents were. I used to think I'd be that way someday, too."

"I don't know how my parents were."

"I'm sorry."

"Not your fault." I shrug. "Maybe someday I'll dig those memories out of my head, and—"

I stop talkin' because Ronnie's hand, all at once, is on the back of my neck.

She pulls my face gently down to hers. Our lips brush.

"I'll bet they were good parents," she says.

"What makes you say that?"

"Because of how you turned out."

I shake my head. "You don't know me. Don't know the kinds of things I've done."

"I know you." She smiles again. "I know somethin' else, too."

"Oh, yeah. What's that?"

She smiles again. "You'd make a good parent, too."

I find him a few hundred yards from where we left him. Really, it's a miracle he's still alive. That the tigers didn't run into him first and make a meal out of him. That the other animals have missed him so far.

That he could be so old and still breathin'.

Which he is, just barely.

I recognize the olive cloth he's wearing now, of course, now that I can put it in context. The way it's torn, the little stains I see on it, the way he hugs it to his chest . . .

I guess I know what happened to Ronnie now, too.

He sees me comin' and presses back up against the corridor wall.

"It's all right," I say. "Nobody's gonna hurt you. It's all right."

I move closer, and his eyes grow wider. He's terrified of what I'm gonna do.

I have no idea what I'm gonna do.

"You gotta be hungry, right?" I ask. "Gotta be a long time since you've eaten."

He makes a grunting noise. Could be he's agreein' with me, could be he's scared, could be he's havin' trouble breathin' . . . who knows what.

"My name's Logan," I say, holding out my hand to shake. "Lo-gan."

He looks up at me, down at my hand, and then back up again.

He looks confused.

"Shake. Like this." I reach for his hand, and he pulls it away. I let him, even though he's so old and feeble I could probably immobilize his hand with my pinky, but what's the sense in that? He doesn't want me to touch him, and that's understandable, given that his whole life—all, what, one week of it—the only time anyone ever touched him was to hurt him. To mess with his body, or his mind.

He coughs once, and then a second time, and then goes right into a full-fledged coughing fit, making a deep, hacking, ugly sound that just about brings him down to his knees.

He looks up at me, and tears fill his eyes.

"It hurts, doesn't it? The cough." I point to my chest and make a coughing noise myself.

He grunts in response. That's gotta mean yes, I tell myself. That's progress of some kind.

I get an idea how I can make more.

I reach behind me and pull the canteen Freddy gave me off my belt. I unscrew the cap and hold it out. He looks at me funny.

He has no idea what to do with it.

"Like this," I say. I hold the canteen up to my lips and mimic drinking.

He shakes his head. He still doesn't get it.

I hold out my palm and spill water into it, just a drop or two.

He smiles, and now I hold out the canteen again, and he takes it and holds it to his lips and drinks.

And right away, he starts coughing again.

"Easy," I tell him, putting a hand on his back and tapping gently. "Easy."

He starts when I put my hand on his back, and tries to move away.

"It's all right," I tell him. "It's okay."

He makes another grunting noise and, after a moment, starts drinking again.

"We'll get you some food," I say.

He looks puzzled.

"Food." I mimic scraping something up off a plate. "Something to eat."

He smiles.

"That's right." I smile, too. "Food."

And then he talks. "Food," he says. "Food."

His voice is surprisingly deep, muffled.

"That's right. We'll get some in a minute. Down that way." I point back down the tunnel, back the way I came.

He looks scared.

"It's all right," I say. "I'll take care of you. Logan. My name is Logan."

"Logan," he says, and smiles. And then he points to himself and says it again. "Logan."

Well. He's got a right to the name, too, I guess.

He puts down the canteen and sighs.

And I swear, right there, before my eyes . . .

I see him gettin' older. See the skin wrinkle up and discolor. See his hands start twitching involuntarily.

Wyndham's machine. Still workin', I suppose, even after his last exposure.

He sighs heavily, and the sigh turns into a groan of pain. He staggers and leans back against the tunnel wall, and slowly—slowly—sits down.

I sit down next to him and take his hand. I squeeze it; he squeezes back.

"Logan," he says.

I laugh out loud. "That's right. Logan. That's my name. That's your name, too."

He smiles and closes his eyes, and we sit there together in the tunnel.

Time passes.

After a while, I look up. Freddy's standing over me.

"Dude," he says. "What are you doing?"

I look over at my son, whose eyes are closed now, of course, whose hand is cold, and then I let go of his hand and stand up.

"You wouldn't believe me if I told you."

"It's a madhouse down there," he says, nodding back down the tunnel.

"Yeah. We have to go back anyway. There's a command station past where we first found the old guy. Computers. I need the information—"

Freddy's shakin' his head. "I've been there. It's trashed."

"You've been there."

"Yeah, the tunnel I went down took me right to it. Place is totally trashed."

"Okay," I say.

I bend low and pick up Logan, which is how I'm thinkin' of him now. How I'm gonna think about him from here on in.

"I'm gonna bury him, and then we need to go."

"Bury him. Dude, what for?" Freddy shakes his head. "Leave him for the tigers to eat, they'll—"

I turn, and even though I don't say anything . . .

The look on my face shuts Freddy up pretty good.

We make it outside, and I find a place on the summit where I can dig. Freddy stands back at first and then pitches in.

After a while, I explain why we're doin' this.

When we're done, we start down the mountain. On the way, I fill him in on what I found out from Brinklow. What Shangri-La is. What they intend to do.

"Doesn't sound like any sort of paradise to me," he says.

"Paradise," I repeat under my breath. And then I get it.

I don't know why I didn't see it before. Build a huge underground laboratory, and then abandon it entirely . . .

It wouldn't be the first time the government wasted money like that, true, but . . .

I smack him on the back. "You're a genius, kid."

"What?" Freddy asks.

"I don't know exactly how they're gonna do it," I tell him. "But I sure as hell know where."

20

WE GO BACK THE WAY WE CAME IN.

Wubeng, where we thank Biquan and the villagers. Zhongdian, Kunming, Hong Kong, where Freddy raids his bank account and uses a chunk of cash to get us two tickets to Vegas. I take most of what's left over to a seedy part of Macao I know from way back and get us fresh passports. Fake passports. My name is Jules Masterson, he's my sister's kid Frederick. We're going to Vegas for an import/export convention and a little R and R. I give the customs agent a smile when I tell him about the R and R; he smiles, too, knowin' just what a businessman in my position means by R and R.

I pass through the security gate without settin' it off, one of the few times I can think of when I'm glad not to have the adamantium in my body anymore. Used to be every security guard in the airport would come runnin' when I tried to board a plane. No way to go undercover back then. It's a lot easier now, obviously, though I'll still have to be on my toes when we land in the States. The name on the passport may be Masterson, but there's a fair share of law-enforcement agents who'll know my real name and face, especially considerin' the way I left the country.

On the plane ride over, Freddy peppers me with questions—about Xavier's school in Westchester, about some of the press I've gotten, about Vegas and what happened there before. I keep my answers as short as possible, givin' him just enough info about the Ark, about what happened at the casino and at UNLV, so that he gets the whole picture of what we're up against.

Soon enough, he runs out of steam and falls asleep, slumped against the window of the plane. I can't rest. Can't even close my eyes. I'm thinkin' about Ronnie, wonderin' how she got from Niagara Falls to Vegas. Wonderin' how Wilson got hold of her in the first place, wonderin' how long he had her and what sort of things he did to her while she was in his custody.

I'm tryin' not to think about how the coverall she was wearing got ripped, how Logan came to be wearin' it.

I'm also wonderin' about the virus they made. Wonderin' if I'm guessin' right about where they intend to deploy it, wonderin' how they'll go about gettin' it airborne and exactly when this is all goin' to take place.

Mostly, though, I'm thinkin' about the old man.

About Logan. Not so much how he died but how he lived. Actually, how he never got to live.

A week. He had a week from the time he opened his eyes till he lay down on the tunnel floor and died. Never even knew what hit him.

Kinda like Brinklow, at the end, when I opened the door to the lab.

Thinkin' about the monkey man, and the part he played in ushering my son in and out of this world, I feel a sudden twinge of regret.

I should've killed him myself, to drag the process out a little longer.

I won't make that mistake with Wilson, when I see him.

We land at McCarran and luck out at U.S. Customs, breezin' through the same way we breezed through Hong Kong. I park Freddy in one of the airport bars and visit the nearest pay phone.

I put in calls to Westchester, to New York, to some people I know here and there. Nobody's home, no matter where I try. Automated systems shunt me over to people who don't know me from a hole in the wall. I leave one message for Xavier, one for old Mr. Fantastic himself, and hang up the phone.

Puzzling. Downright worrisome.

I go back to the bar to pick up Freddy.

"Dude," he says. "Check this out."

He points to the row of TV screens behind the bar

he's sittin' at. They all show the same thing on-screen. Not football. Not baseball. Not soccer, basketball, tennis, golf . . .

They all show Super Heroes. Some of 'em I recognize—X-Men. Xavier. A furry blue guy—Hank McCoy. Captain America. Mr. Red, White, and Blue himself. Some of the other Avengers. Wanda. The Scarlet Witch. Magneto's daughter.

There's a line of text on one of the screens; "BREAKING NEWS—GENOSHA: MUTANT/HUMAN TENSION EXPLODES!"

Guess I know now why no one's home to answer my calls.

Seems like they got troubles of their own to handle.

Genosha's an island country, a place where humans used to keep mutants as slaves. Last time I checked in there, the situation seemed to be improving. Now, though . . .

Things have obviously gotten a lot worse.

Seems like everyone's reacting the same way to Magneto's assault and its aftermath. Whatever kind of good feelings there were between mutants and humans have evaporated. Whatever kind of truce there was between the two sides has broken down. Whatever kind of restraints Wilson and his compadres were operating under have broken down, too.

As far as they're concerned, it's all out-war now between human and mutant. And they intend to do whatever it takes to win.

What's happening here in Vegas just might be related to what's goin' on there. Somethin' to think about. Somethin' to keep in mind.

"They're killin' 'em all," I hear someone down at the end of the bar say. "The mutants."

"And good riddance, I say." That from a guy with a buzz cut a few stools down from Freddy, with a pint of beer in front of him. "Freaks."

Freddy tenses in his seat and starts to rise.

I put a hand on his shoulder. "Let's not make things worse," I whisper.

He doesn't take the hint. "Come on, man," he says, loud enough to cut through the din of conversation at the bar. "You heard what that idiot said. I—"

The guy with the buzz cut turns around and glares at Freddy.

Then he stands up.

He goes about six foot, about a hundred-ninety. He's wearin' a white T-shirt with a big black X on the front, with a red line drawn through it. I recognize the symbol; I recognize the shirt. I know what it says on the back without looking: "Friends of Humanity." That's an antimutant hate group, a bunch of nut jobs. If this guy is one of them, he's lookin' for a fight. Probably been in the bar all day, drinkin', lookin' for an excuse to start somethin'.

"You got a problem, fat boy?" he asks.

Freddy starts to get up off his chair, too. I put a hand on his shoulder to keep him in place.

"Ow," Freddy says, and turns and glares at me.

The buzz cut guy looks at me, too, and then he frowns. The same way Osborne frowned back on that trail in the DNR. As if he knows who I am but can't quite place me.

Time to clear out before he can.

"No," I say. "No problem. We're just leavin'."

I toss some of Freddy's cash onto the bar and pull him out into the main terminal.

Freddy yanks free as we exit. "That sonuva—"

"Focus, kid," I tell him. "We got more important things to worry about, remember?"

He glares at me and rubs his shoulder. He's still rubbin' it as we move through the terminal, past the baggage claim, following the signs to ground transportation. A sign along the way catches my attention. "Monorail Service coming to McCarran," it announces; it's got a picture of the tram, silhouetted in front of a smiling show girl.

The next sign along the wall catches my attention, too.

It's the poster I saw a few weeks back, the one for the "All-New Paradise Casino and Resort Hotel, Vegas's Newest, Most Spectacular Gaming Destination, Featuring Authentic Native Dancers, the Fabulous Hidden Waterfalls of Tibet," etc.

This sign is slightly different, though. There's a red banner with black text splashed across the bottom of it. "Grand Opening Gala," it says, and gives a date.

I read it, and the hair on the back of my neck stands up.

That date is tonight.

"Doesn't necessarily mean anything," Freddy says.

We're in a taxi, on our way from McCarran to the Paradise. The streets are jammed, worse than I've ever seen 'em before. Worse than New York City on New Year's Eve.

"Could be a coincidence," Freddy goes on. "I mean, for all you know, we're not even in the right hemisphere. Maybe what Wilson's planning has nothing to do with the casino, and even if it does—"

"It's tonight."

"How do you know, though? How can you be sure?"

I don't bother answering that. I know. My instincts. They may not be what they once were, but I've learned over the last couple weeks that I'm better off trustin' 'em than not. The crowds I see around us make me even more certain that whatever Wilson and his boys are planning, it's happening right here, right now.

It's just after ten, local time. The knot in my stomach grows tighter, as I wonder just how much longer we have to figure out what exactly we have to stop from happening.

We crawl down the Strip, stopping alongside limos packed with beautiful people, being stared at by tourists passing on the sidewalk who wish they were beautiful people themselves. Wish they were a little thinner, a little taller, a little younger, a little more . . . different.

The irony kills me.

What's the old Chinese saying? Be careful what you wish for. I wonder if some of these good people aren't gonna get exactly what they're prayin' for. A new you. I wonder that 'cause I wonder what Wilson's virus is gonna do to normal people. Government scientists don't exactly have a good track record in my book as far as correctly figuring out side effects of their experiments. Exhibit A bein' my memory loss. I would contact the local authorities, let 'em know what was goin' on, except I have a feelin' that the first thing they'd do is lock me up, throw away the key, and then build a brick wall around the prison.

This one, it looks like I gotta handle myself.

The radio's playin' some bad '80s music; it ends, and the news comes on.

Genosha's the lead story.

The cabby makes a noise of disapproval and shakes his head. "Terrible thing, what's goin' on down there," he says.

"Oh?"

"Yeah. People are people, that's what I say. Human, mutant—all the same to me." He's an African-American guy, skinny dude.

I smile and nudge Freddy in the ribs.

"What?" he asks.

"Listen to what the man said," I tell him, reading the cabby's name off his license: "Jubilee." One word. I smile.

"What Jubilee said," I tell Freddie.

"That's my name." The cabby half turns and smiles. "Jubilee. Don't wear it out."

"Jubilee," Freddie says. "Like from the X-Men."

"That's right." I smile, too. "Like the X-Men."

"X-Men?" The cabby's smile disappears. "Don't talk to me about X-Men. Those guys are criminals. Ask me, they oughtta lock 'em all up and throw away the key."

We pass the next few minutes in silence, Freddy lookin' out the window, me tappin' my feet on the floor impatiently. I look at the clock on the dashboard. Ten-fifteen.

We go another few hundred feet. I watch the clock the whole time.

Ten-eighteen.

"That's it," I say, opening my door. "We gotta walk."

"Hey!" Jubilee yells. "You can't just leave me here. We got—"

I toss him two twenties and take Freddy's arm. We walk the last couple of blocks to the Paradise; the walk only confirms my hunch—my fears. Most of the crowd is headed this way, too.

Like most of the other new casinos, the Paradise is off the Strip, rather than right on it. There's an access drive leading off the main road; the crowd flows in that direction, carryin' us with it. We pass two of those big spotlights they use at movie premieres, one on either side of the road. Folded back behind them, on either side of the drive, are two giant fake stone gates; there's a fake stone archway high overhead, with a big neon sign reading "Welcome to Paradise" attached.

We move on through with the crowd.

". . . David Lee and Sammy Hagar," some girl is saying. "Plus there's rumors about the Eagles."

"What I heard"—this from a tall, skinny guy standing next to her—"was Madonna. And the Stones."

"No way, dude!" the girl says.

Freddy turns to me. "Those are bands," he says. "Rock bands."

I glare at him.

"They play music," he offers helpfully. "There must be some kind of concert happening."

I glare at him. "How old do I look, Sherlock?" I shake my head. "I know who those guys are."

We move on down the drive. A few hundred yards ahead is the Paradise. It ain't just one building, of course, it's several. My eye goes immediately to the one in the center, a long, flat building, done up in the style of the Taj Mahal, only about eight hundred times tackier—neon trim, inset diamond and gold decorations the size of basketballs. Looming behind it is your standard thirty-story hotel tower; off to the right is a gray rock about four stories tall, with a neon-outlined cement ring a few hundred feet around at the bottom of it. I can't figure out what the rock is. To the left is a three-story stack of outdoor restaurants, complete with balcony dining and beautiful balcony diners; behind those restaurants, as we get closer, I can see a long indoor arcade of shops. A place for the rubes to spend whatever money they don't lose at the tables.

A half-naked girl in a Hawaiian outfit steps forward and smiles.

"Welcome to Paradise," she says, and puts a plastic lei around my neck. Then she hands me a flyer and moves on.

The flyer's on slick paper, full color; it starts with a personal note from someone named E. G. Biester, president and CEO of Coral Gate Entertainment Properties, welcoming me to the opening of their latest and greatest entertainment property, the Paradise. Blah blah blah, thank you for your business, enjoy the festivities, which are detailed underneath the note. There is indeed a concert, and it turns out the girl was right about the Eagles; they're scheduled to go on at eleven, and following them will be the big fireworks display, with a grand finale at midnight timed to go off at the same instant 64,000 gallons of water explode out of the desert in a show the likes of which has never been seen on this planet before, the fabulous Cascading Waterfalls of Tibet, which is what the big gray rock I couldn't identify before is going to turn into come the witching hour.

Freddy curses in Mandarin.

"What?"

"Take a look." He points to the flip side of his flyer; I turn mine over, too.

First thing I see is the picture.

A man in a purple uniform and a matching purple top hat; two women assistants in purple vests and sparkly purple shorts. And arranged in a row in front of those three . . .

Tigers.

Half a dozen white tigers, wearing purple bow ties of their own.

There's text to go along with the image. It identifies the man as Herman Heiling and the tigers as Herman Heiling's Famous Siberian Wonder Cats, the Eighth Wonder of the World.

They're performing hourly in the Paradise's Main Atrium, starting at seven P.M.

I curse and crumple the flyer to the ground.

Could be a coincidence.

Could be we're too late.

21

IT'S TEN THIRTY-FIVE WHEN WE READ THE FLYER.

It's ten forty-five when we reach the main atrium. It's in the middle of the shopping arcade, on the ground floor; there's a stage set up, with a half-circle of about a hundred folding chairs in front of it. There's a huge banner hung above the stage—more pictures of the white tigers, more pictures of Herman Heiling, his purple jumpsuit, and his girls in purple satin shorts.

The folding chairs are all occupied; the walkways on the ground floor arcade are packed full of people. So are the walkways a story up, and the story above that. Folks are leanin' out over the railings, lookin' down, in anticipation of the next show.

Fifteen minutes, give or take.

There's no one official-looking in sight.

"You think they did it already?" Freddy asks. "Released the virus?"

I shake my head. "I don't know."

I look around the mall. I see a lot of families with kids in tow. Some barely more than toddlers. Some in baby carriages.

I think about possible side effects from the virus, and I shiver inside.

The seats are set up so that there's an aisle in the middle between them. Freddy and I are standing at the back of that aisle, behind a few dozen other people. There's a curtain drawn across it, a mall security guard on either side. I figure the place to start is there.

"I need a distraction."

Freddy frowns. "What?"

"A distraction. I need you to get her attention." I point to the guard on the right, a Hispanic woman who looks about five feet tall and three feet wide. Looks like the prototypical mall security guard.

"She's kind of cute," Freddy says.

"Stay focused, kid. Okay?"

"Sure. What do I do?"

"Make a scene. Get her attention."

"How?"

"You figure that out. But do not use your powers, okay?"

"Okay."

"We don't want to make a scene here, let Wilson and his guys know that anything's up."

"Right." He frowns now. "So any ideas what I should do?"

"Figure something out, kid," I say, and leave him to it.

In the minute or two we've been standin' there, the space behind us has filled up, too. I push my way past the people behind me, out of the atrium, and back out into the mall. I walk along the outer ring of shops until I'm standin' just about parallel with the security guard, a concrete planter about four feet high between us.

Freddy's walkin' down the aisle between the seats right toward her.

He's saying something to her; they're only about ten yards away from me, but over the noise of the crowd, I can't hear a word of it.

She takes out her nightstick and starts tapping it in her palm.

Freddy smiles and keeps talking.

Her expression doesn't alter. She's all business.

Freddy looks a little perplexed.

I realize I'm going to have to create my own distraction here.

I look around to see what—and who—is available to work with.

I'm standing in front of a shop that sells tacky Vegas souvenirs; it's crammed full of kids. Out in front is a display with helium balloons in the shape of all the Disney cartoon characters. A lot of kids milling around, but I'd rather not mess with kids. Personality quirk of mine.

I look right and see a cosmetics shop, with a half-

dozen women in white lab coats out in front, handin'
out free samples.

Possible.

I look left and see one of those fancy coffee shops,
full of skinny guys in black turtlenecks and skinnier
girls. In front of the coffee shop is a group of three
women who don't fit; they're wearing purple satin
shorts and matching purple satin jackets with white
writing on the back.

Herman Heiling's Siberian Tigers.

I smile and edge closer.

One of the girls—a redhead—glances at her watch
and frowns.

"Oh, my gosh, look at the time."

She drains the last of her coffee and pitches the cup
into a nearby trash can. The other two do the same. All
three head off down the arcade at as close to a trot as
they can manage.

I try to give Freddy the high sign, but he's in the
middle of an argument with the security guard and
isn't looking. So be it. He'll catch up later.

Or not.

I follow along behind the girls. They go fifty feet
and hang a right, off the main arcade down an unmarked corridor. I give 'em a few seconds' headstart,
then follow, just in time to see a door at the end of the
corridor marked "Authorized Personnel Only" slam
shut behind 'em.

I try the knob. Locked.

I glance back over my shoulder; people are flowin' down the corridor in the direction I just came from, hurryin' to get to the stage. To see the show. None of 'em so much as glances down the little corridor as they pass it.

I pop the middle claw on my right hand and pry the door open quietly—or as quietly as I can, anyway—and step on through.

Déjà vu.

I'm in a concrete tunnel. Dim, lit with an overhead fluorescent light. Steam pipe above me, electrical conduit along the wall. Reminds me of the tunnels up at Kawagebo. Back in the Ark. The tunnel I escaped through last time I was here, when the Paradise was just a construction site. For all I know, I'm in exactly the same place.

Voices sound off to my right. I go that way; the corridor bends and goes on past a steel door. I stop in front of it.

I smell something. Takes me a second to place it, but by then, I'm already turnin' the handle.

This door's open. I push through, and the smell hits me even more strongly.

Tigers.

I'm at the back of a low-ceilinged room. People are scurrying around, most of 'em dressed in purple. Herman Heiling's people.

The tiger smell comes from the cages right in front of me, a half-dozen of 'em along the far wall, filled with a half-dozen pacing animals.

Heiling himself is in the front of the room, clapping his hands.

"People!" he booms. He's a big, beefy guy, with red hair and a red handlebar mustache. "People, please. Come forward. I have something to say before the next show."

He's Dutch, with an accent to match and a Germanic cadence to his command that makes everyone hup to and turn their attention to him.

Gives me a chance to slide along the back wall toward the cages while he talks.

". . . keep the animals on the stage after this show," Heilling is saying. "I know that will involve extra difficulties, extra effort, and I want you all to know . . ."

I reach the nearest cage and kneel down next to it.

The tiger inside is cleaning its paws, lookin' in Heiling's direction.

I make a low hissing sound. The tiger raises its head and starts to turn my way.

". . . don't understand why," one of the girls is saying. "It just takes a few minutes to bring them through the other tunnel. We ought to be able to share—"

"The fireworks display, as I've said, takes precedence. It is part of my agreement with the casino," Heiling says. "And that is that."

The tiger sees me. I look into its eyes. It looks back and opens its mouth.

It doesn't talk.

It roars.

A bona fide, one-hundred-percent tiger roar. An actual animal noise, no hidden meanings or attempts at communication here.

These are tigers, no more, no less.

Hearing that roar, it's like a little bell going off in my head. Like a spell being broken.

These tigers have nothing to do with what Wilson's planning. Their presence here is a coincidence, no more, no less.

I'm wasting time.

"You there! Hey! Yes, you!"

I look up to see Heiling himself striding toward me, a frown on his face.

"Who are you? What are you doing here, bothering my animals?"

"Sorry," I say, straightening up. "I'm from animal control."

"Animal control?" He frowns. "I don't understand. What sort of animal control? Are you from the city, or the casino, or—"

"Both," I say. "Neither."

I'm backin' away from him as I talk, backin' toward the door I came in through. I reach out behind me, my hand touches the knob—

And the door swings open.

Two guys walk into the room. I step to the side just in time to avoid gettin' run over.

They're both in black jumpsuits. Very familiar black

jumpsuits. They're big guys. Muscular guys. Military guys. With military haircuts to match.

One steps to the left of the doorway. One steps to the right, almost knockin' me over in the process. He gives me a dirty look and then turns to face front again, hands clasped behind his back, at attention.

A third guy walks through the door.

He's got a military haircut, too. I catch a glimpse of a goatee as he walks past; it's not much more than stubble, reddish-blond, shading to gray.

I do my best to keep my mouth from fallin' open.

I don't have to see the new guy's face to know he's older than the two who preceded him, that he's higher up the chain of command than they are.

I don't have to hear his voice to know who he is.

"Mister Heiling," the newcomer says. "It's ten fifty-five. You have five minutes till we shut the lower-level tunnels. If you want to use them to move your animals, better do it now."

"We do, of course," Heiling says, snapping to attention. "We will. Thank you."

"Five minutes," the man says again. "After that, you'll have to parade 'em down the main corridor."

He turns to go. I catch a quick glimpse of his face, head-on, as I slide farther back against the wall and toward the soldier next to me, so that he can't see mine.

It's Osborne, all right.

He marches out the door, and his men follow.

• • •

Of all the impossible things I've seen over the last few weeks—the talkin' tiger, the monkey scientist, Ronnie climbin' off that cart at Kawagebo . . .

Osborne's dead; he has to be dead. He died in that explosion in the tunnel complex. I saw his body burn; there's no way he could have survived, and even if he had, by some miracle, he'd have burns all over. Horrific burns.

But he looks as good as new, exactly the way he did on the trail at the DNR. Except for the scar on his face, the scar I gave him when I escaped from the Ark.

The scar that had healed by the time I saw him up near Wubeng.

How is that possible?

The answer, of course, is that it's not. It's not him.

I think about some other things I've seen these last couple of weeks—the genetic accelerator first and foremost among them—as well as a few things out of the past, and this time, it ain't just a little bell goes off in the back of my head, it's a damn Chinese gong, two feet across.

Bam.

Heiling claps his hands. "You heard them, everyone. No time to waste. Let's get moving. Quickly now, quickly."

He turns toward the tiger cages, having forgotten about me entirely. I see now those cages are on wheels. Heiling's people pop out the chucks holdin' 'em in place and start wheeling the cages toward the door. I oblige by holding it open; Heiling himself is the last one through.

He shoots me a dirty look as he goes by.

I refocus and shoot him a smile. "Animals look under control," I tell him. He frowns again.

I follow him out the door and down the corridor. I'm at the end of a mini-convoy of cages and people, heading in the opposite direction from the way I came in, away from the mall, deeper into the bowels of the building complex.

Right in front of me, pushing not a cage but a trunk full of what I can only assume are props for the show, are the three girls from the coffee shop.

"Faster," Heiling says. "Let's move, please."

He claps again. I can see the three girls exchange dirty looks. I think I know how they feel; if I worked for Heiling, and he kept clapping like that . . .

We round another corner, and I have to stop myself from screeching to a halt entirely.

The tunnel dead-ends in front of a service elevator as big as a decent-size living room. Heiling's tigers, and their cages, and all his people are crowding into it, accompanied by occasional animal growls and human exclamations—"Watch it," "Watch where you're goin'," that sort of thing.

Half a dozen of the jumpsuits and Osborne himself flank the doors, watching them load up.

Osborne's only half payin' attention; he's talkin' on a cell phone as he observes the elevator filling up.

In about two seconds, I'm going to pass right in front of him.

The three girls in purple shorts and the trunk they're pushing are right in front of me. I bow low, slide past Osborne, and squeeze in between the redhead and the blonde to lend a hand.

The blonde glares. The redhead smiles.

"Hey, thanks, mister."

"Don't mention it," I say, in as quiet a voice as I can manage.

We pass within three feet of Osborne; he's still talkin' on a cell phone. To Wilson? I strain to hear.

". . . under a lot of pressure. All the valves. J-14 popped two times this last hour . . ."

The redhead leans in closer.

"You look awful familiar," she says. "Are you, like, famous or something?"

The rest of what Osborne is saying flies away into thin air. I look at the girl, tryin' not to be irritated.

"I'm in the papers from time to time," I say, as we wheel the trunk in as far as it can go.

Her eyes widen as she stands up. "You know anybody in Hollywood?" she asks. "Because really I'm an actress, I'm just doing this tiger thing until . . ." She looks down at me and frowns. "You all right?"

"Fine."

"Then how come you're not getting up?"

I smile and don't answer.

Not until the elevator doors close, at least, and Osborne's out of sight.

Which is when I stand up and see that he's come into the elevator with us.

Osborne and his people are at the front of the elevator, near the control panel, facing the doors. Facing away from us.

"You all right, mister?" the girl asks, even louder.

I take the redhead by the arm and position her so that she's standin' right in front of me.

"Fine now," I say.

She smiles. I smile back.

We continue our conversation about the difficulty of getting a good casting agent.

It goes on till the elevator door opens, and Osborne and his men step off. The redhead and I and the other two girls step around to the other side of the trunk and push it out into the corridor. Heiling and his people are moving off to the right. My guess is there's another elevator in that direction, one that pops up right underneath the stage, that they'll bring the animals in that way.

I stay low again, push the cart until I hear the sound of the elevator doors closing behind me, of machinery startin' up again. I straighten and risk a glance around.

Osborne is nowhere in sight.

"So, anyway," the girl is saying, "I almost had that

part, but they said I was too tall. Can you believe it? Too tall?"

"You are tall," I say. "But don't let it get you down. I got a thing for tall redheads."

She smiles.

I give the trunk a final push, give her a final good-bye, and watch them disappear down the corridor.

I walk back toward the elevator. Two of Osborne's men are guarding it.

"Wrong way, short stuff," one of 'em says.

I smile. "That's a good one. Short stuff. I never heard that before."

"Get lost. Go play with your tigers."

"What are you, security?"

"None of your business what we are. Now, move."

"Really? You don't even know what my business is."

The second guy steps forward. "Hey. You look familiar to me. This guy look familiar to you, Bobby?"

The first guard takes a closer look at me and frowns. "I don't know. Maybe."

I shrug. "I get that a lot—in the business I'm in."

"And what business is that?" the first guy asks.

"You could call it animal control."

"Yeah, well, ain't no animals to control in this direction, buddy. So move along."

"I'm not so sure about that."

The two guards both frown.

"What's that supposed to mean?"

I smile.

Heiling's people are long out of sight. So are Osborne and the rest of his guys. There's nobody around but me and these two bozos.

"Animal control," I say, stepping forward. "Let me give you a demonstration."

Ten seconds later, give or take a heartbeat or two, I've shown Osborne's guys what I mean. The two of them lie side-by-side in front of the elevator, dead to the world. At least for the next little while.

I rip the jumpsuit off one guy—the shorter of the two—and put it on.

I rip the jumpsuit off the other and slice the cloth into long strips that I use to make a couple of gags and a makeshift set of ropes. I tie the two guys back to back and drag 'em into a little utility closet I find down the hall. Gut the locking mechanism and slam it shut behind me.

The two guys had earpieces, and headset mics, too. I slip both on, one in each ear. Right away, I hear a voice, crackly, almost inaudible at first. Then getting louder.

It's a computer-generated voice.

". . . minus forty-one fourteen and counting. T minus forty-one thirteen and counting. T minus . . ."

A little jolt of adrenaline shoots through my veins.

Forty-one minutes till T. I can guess what that means.

Time is shorter than I thought.

I take the big elevator down a level, to the bottom level. Luck's with me; no one's in it, no one's in the hall when I emerge. I got my choice of directions to take: straight ahead, left, or right. I choose left—moving deeper into the Paradise complex. Toward the hotel, and the casino, and the concert, and the waterfall, and the fireworks. Multiple targets of opportunity.

". . . T minus forty oh-ten and counting . . . T minus forty oh-eight . . ."

The tunnels twist and turn, intersect and curve; it's like a little maze down here. I wonder how people keep track of where they're going, and I look up and see letters stenciled on the wall. M-7. A little farther on, M-8.

The letter-number combination rings a bell in my head. As it does, the computerized voice in my ear gives way to another.

"Station check, one." It's Osborne's voice.

"One, roger," comes the response.

"Station three, check."

"Three, roger."

"Five . . ."

As I hear him in my ear, I hear him in my head, on the trail at the DNR. Back in the tunnels at Kawagebo. Tellin' me I look familiar; tellin' me to lie down on the floor of the cart.

Tellin' me to call him O'Connell.

". . . fourteen?"

"Fourteen, roger."

"Fifteen, check in."

I think about Osborne and Wilson, and Ronnie and my son. About the experiments at the Ark and at Kawagebo. How they used Wyndham's genetic accelerator, what other sorts of technology they might have had access to, and for how long.

How it is that he's here, when he died up on the mountain.

I'm so busy listenin' to his voice and thinkin' about his nine lives that I don't hear the footsteps until it's too late.

I turn a corner, and comin' at me head on—comin' fast, at a march that's almost like a jog—are four more guys in black jumpsuits. The lead one looks at me and frowns.

"Who the hell are you?" he asks, coming to a sudden halt.

I'm just about to pop my claws and go at him when I get a better idea.

"Malfunction in J-14," I say, echoing Osborne's words back in the big elevator.

He frowns. "Malfunction."

"That's right." I nod. "The valves. J-14."

He sighs and shakes his head. "Those damn valves. All right. Better come with us, then, give 'em the details."

He turns to his left and heads down another corridor. His guys follow. So do I.

Forty feet on, the tunnel dead-ends in a set of solid steel doors. "Utility," says the sign above 'em. The guy knocks twice, and the doors both swing open. Two more jumpsuits, two more guns. We're waved through. I close ranks with the guy right in front of me, stay as close to him as I can to avoid being noticed.

As we walk in, the temperature goes up ten degrees, and the noise level goes up fifty decibels. The ceiling inside goes up fifty feet; pipes of all different thicknesses run up from the floor and disappear high above. There's gantrys and walkways everywhere I look; machines, too, water boilers, central air units, turbines—

I see Wilson.

He's standing next to a pipe as thick as his arm, alongside a couple of guys in regular military uniform—a couple of different military uniforms, in fact. One U.S., one Canadian. The U.S. guy has a phone to his ear; Wilson and the Canadian officer watch him talk.

"Hey!"

I turn and see the leader of the guys I came in with lookin' over his shoulder at me, frowning.

"Come on, let's go."

I nod, and then he and the others start movin' off toward the other end of the room. I go with them for a little bit, then slide back behind one of the big pipes.

As I watch, the American officer puts his phone away. He nods at the other two.

All three smile.

Wilson turns off to his right and motions toward two jumpsuits standing nearby. They nod and move, and it's only then I can see they've been standing in front of a dolly, one loaded up with a big metal suitcase about the size of a coffin. The suitcase is dark blue; it's got black letters stenciled across the side. I can see only the first couple of them, but that's all I need.

XM.

The virus.

I'm ten yards away. I count a dozen soldiers between me and the suitcase. Another thirty yards to the door. Too far to grab it and go, before I get shot. I need to get closer.

I move out from behind one pipe, head for another—

And somebody jabs a metal rod in my side.

I look up and see the guy I came in with frowning at me. It's his gun, of course, pressing into my gut.

"This is him," he says.

He's lookin' at me, but he's talkin' to the guy behind him, the guy who's now starin' right at me, a look of shock mixed with amusement on his face.

It's Osborne.

"Unbelievable," he says.

Endgame, I think.

22

"YOU'RE DEAD," HE SAYS.

"I could say the same about you."

He smiles and shakes his head.

A drop of water falls on my arm.

I glance quickly up and see, runnin' between the big thick pipes that stretch from floor to ceiling, a tangle of others—thinner, horizontal pipes that connect the thick ones, maybe fifteen feet off the ground.

I also see, along the near side of the thick pipe I just stepped out from behind, a series of rungs, spaced a few feet apart, climbin' all the way to the ceiling.

I lower my gaze to meet Osborne's again.

"Wilson!" he yells, and somehow, even over the din of the machines, his voice carries, and Wilson turns and sees me.

He doesn't smile. He's not even the slightest bit amused by the situation.

He says something to the two military guys and starts walking toward us.

"How did you get here—never mind, don't answer that." He looks up at Osborne. "Is everything all right? On schedule? Did he—"

"I don't think he got a chance to do anything. We'll do a complete system check now, of course."

"Get on it." He turns to me then. "Brinklow couldn't keep his mouth shut, could he? Told you where we were."

"I figured that out for myself. Brinklow helped, though, I'll give him that much."

We lock eyes for a second.

Wilson looks to Osborne and opens his mouth, and even before any sound comes out, I know exactly what he's goin' to say.

Kill him.

No sense waitin' around for that to happen.

I slap the gun in my side away and jump. Straight up into the air.

I ain't Magneto's boy Toad, but I do all right. I reach a rung on the side of the pipe maybe ten feet up, high enough that the guys holding weapons on me can't just squeeze the trigger; they have to raise their guns and retarget, and, of course, by that point, I'm movin' again, usin' my feet to push off the big pipe and up toward the thinner ones, the horizontal ones. I reach out my hands and grab hold, swing myself up and over on top. Luck is with me; not only do the pipes hold my weight, but Wilson is screaming, "Hold your fire! Hold your fire!" Why, I don't know, but I ain't gonna look a gift horse in the mouth. So, I crouch down and start runnin' along the pipes. They sway and rattle as I go, and I reach another one of the big thick ones and grab hold of those rungs, figurin' I'll climb again—

And a guy pops up on a walkway next to me.

I got no idea where he came from; he clubs me with his gun once, sends me staggering, and tries it again, and this time, I dodge, grab his wrist as it goes past, and send him on his way, down to the ground. He goes with a little yell. I hop onto the metal walkway he just vacated, bullets suddenly pinging around me. I dive forward and roll up onto my feet and keep moving, through a half-open metal door with a big wheel in the center, just like the kind you find on cargo ships.

I slam it shut behind me and spin the wheel.

It's suddenly very quiet again. I take a deep breath.

Out of the frying pan, for the moment, but just for the moment, because I hear the countdown in my head again.

". . . minus thirty-two forty . . . T minus thirty-two thirty-nine . . ."

I don't have many moments left to waste, I realize. About half an hour, all told, before they do whatever it is they're gonna do to spread the virus.

Pipes, I think. *Hold your fire,* Wilson said. *The valves on J-14.*

I look up.

This is corridor J.

I'm tryin' to put it together when two guards walk out into the corridor right in front of me.

They're as surprised as I am. They're carryin' their weapons down at their sides; before they can raise 'em, I pop my claws. Guard one goes down; guard two backs up, outta my range, but I pivot off one foot and use my momentum to deliver a quick spin kick to the chest that slams him into the tunnel wall. He goes down, too.

I take a look at the room they just came out of. There's some kind of gauge on the wall opposite me, maybe a control panel of some kind, with a bunch of LEDs on it. There's four columns of those LEDs, green and orange and red. One column—the column all the way to my left—is all green, all the way to the top, maybe twenty lights; the other three are half green, half orange, a couple of reds.

As I watch, one of the orange lights changes to green.

I hear metal clang behind me.

I go back out in the corridor and see the wheel in the center of the door slowly turning.

I turn to run. As I do, the door slams open behind me. Bullets ping along the hall.

The tunnel splits, branching right and left. I go left and then left again, quickly, footsteps sounding behind me.

I go another twenty feet, and the corridor dead-ends

again. No branching corridor this time, just a ladder straight in front of me. I look up.

It goes on and on, up into the darkness.

I fly up it, quick as I can, climbin' hand over hand, usin' my feet when I can, not worryin' about when I can't, 'cause I'm a sittin' duck here. Gotta hope another corridor intersects this tube higher up, because if not—

". . . twenty-nine twelve . . . T minus twenty-nine ten . . ."

I hear voices; I look down and see faces. A couple of rifle barrels stickin' up, pointin' right at me.

Bullets ping at my feet as I turn and reach across to the other side of the tube and grab hold of a cable. Electrical cable. Rip it out, the lights go. No. Bad idea; bullets don't need light to find their targets.

I let go of the cable and grab hold of a pipe next to it. It's cool to the touch, water condensed on its surface, water thrummin' inside it. Water under a lot of pressure.

Ah.

I yank as hard as I can; metal groans.

I yank again, and the pipe breaks at a joint; water spurts up right in my face.

I grab the lower half of the pipe and twist, bending it around so that the water spurts down the tunnel, toward my pursuit.

I hear a lot of cursing behind me.

I smile and start climbing again. Up, and up, and

up. I'm counting rungs as I go; forty-eight, forty-nine, fifty.

". . . twenty-eight oh-six . . . twenty-eight oh-four . . . twenty-eight . . ."

A few bullets fly again. Still no intersecting corridor.

I reach across and grab the electric cable, and this time, I rip.

Sparks fly. The lights go out.

I hear more cursing. Shouts of "Hold your fire, hold your fire!" Osborne's boys are in the crawlspace, too; they can't fire willy-nilly anymore.

A second later, lights flicker in the darkness. Dim lights, emergency lights, is my guess, barely enough to see by, certainly not enough to fire accurately in.

I start climbing again. Ninety. A hundred. I'm higher up than I could get inside the shopping arcade, I realize. Best guess, I'm in the hotel tower now. Probably four or five stories up.

The voice in my ear crackles and turns to static.

Ten feet above me, the access tunnel ends.

I look to my right, and there's a passageway—another corridor. I turn and start down it. This one's narrower than the others, darker, different smells. Stencils on the wall identify this as tunnel J.

This is where they had that valve problem.

I go fifty feet straight on and end up at another one of those metal doors, with a metal wheel in the center. I spin the wheel; the door pops open—

Light flashes in my eyes.

Wind blows in my face.

I'm four stories up, lookin' out at the Vegas skyline. Lookin' at neon, and open space, and the stars.

I look down and see a solid gray wall of rock, sloping down to a solid mass of people, a crowd gathered beneath me for a display unlike anything ever seen before in human history. Or so the hype machine would have them believe, anyway.

The Hidden Waterfalls of Tibet.

Sixty-four thousand gallons of water, shooting out of the side of this rock, shooting out of pipes just like the one I ruined a few minutes ago.

Which is, of course, how they're gonna spread the virus.

A mist, a spray. It'll reach the people directly underneath us; it'll blow halfway across the city . . .

And the tourists who leave here will take it back home with them when they go.

"Logan!"

I turn and see Osborne fifty feet away from me, walking slowly down the passageway in my direction, gun drawn, two of his guys right behind him.

I look down again and see the crowd below me milling around the entrance to the Paradise. There's even more people than before, if that's possible. Doesn't even look as if there's room to breathe down there. People linin' up for the concert, for the casino, the fireworks, the waterfall, and the Brave New World to follow, which, of course, they don't know a thing about. And they never will.

A cop in the crowd catches my eye. Movin' through that crowd like a knife through butter. No, not a cop. The uniform is the wrong color. A security guard. Sort of a wide, fat security guard.

Right alongside that cop, a wider, fatter guy.

My mind races.

"End of the line, Logan." Osborne's ten feet away now. He slaps a new clip in his gun. "Unless you can fly."

I take a deep breath.

"We'll see," I say, and turn around, and jump.

23

FREE-FALLIN'. WITHOUT A NET.

I wonder, for a second, if this is what Ronnie felt like when she changed. When she was in the air. Doubtful, I decide. She had control.

I plummet like a stone.

"Hey, kid!" I scream out loud as the ground rushes up toward me. "Freddy!"

A bunch of people look up; some of 'em start screaming as well. Less coherent things.

I got a split-second of wonderin' what it would feel like to hit, wonderin' if Wilson was right about how powerful my healing factor is. Hopin' I don't get the chance to find out.

Hopin' my eyesight is as good as I think it is.

Then somethin' slams into my gut, and I literally go flying back up through the air, back the way I came, back past Osborne, who wears a look of complete and utter confusion.

I look down and see Freddy jumpin' up toward me.

We slam together again; this time, he grabs on. I grab on, too.

He's screamin'. So am I, I realize, as we pass Osborne a second time.

I look over at Freddy and smile.

He looks seasick.

"Good instincts!" I yell.

He manages a smile.

We shoot back down, past Osborne. This time, he sees Freddy and looks even more confused.

Freddy sees him and frowns. "You said he was dead!"

"Long story!"

We bounce a couple more times before finally coming to rest on level ground and letting go of each other. I shake my head to clear away the cobwebs.

Freddy puts his hands on his knees and gasps for air.

The security guard is the first one to reach him. She puts a hand on his back, concern all over her face.

"Frederick," she says. "You all right?"

He nods and coughs and looks up at her and then at me, and he smiles.

"Frederick?" I say.

He blushes.

"That was unbelievable." The security guard's nametag says "Valdez" on it. "You saved this guy's life. You're like a Super Hero."

He straightens up, smiles at her and then at me. "Not yet."

"Not ever, if we don't move quick." I stop a second then, because the little voice in my head is back. The computer-generated voice.

The countdown.

"T minus twenty-two eleven . . . T minus twenty-two eight . . ."

"You all right?" Freddy asks.

I snap back to the here and now.

"I'm fine. It's the waterfall." I nod toward the big rock. "That's how they're gonna do it."

"Do what?" the woman asks.

"The waterfall." Freddy nods. "Right. Of course."

I turn to the woman. "You gotta clear these people out of here—all of them."

"Are you crazy? Why? What's goin' on?" She turns to Freddy.

"Long story," he says.

She folds her arms across her chest. "I got time."

"No, you don't. We got a little more than twenty minutes." I turn to Freddy. "I gotta get back up there."

"What?"

"Back up there." I point back at the rock. "Can you do it?"

"Uh . . . I hate to break it to you, dude, but those guys want to kill you."

"The feeling's mutual. Can you do it?"

Freddy looks at me, looks up at the rock, and shrugs. "I guess. I mean, I have to get some kinetic energy goin', I need some way to—"

"Hey, mutie!"

I turn and see a big guy with a goatee and a long ponytail walkin' toward us. Correction. Walkin' toward Freddy. Clenchin' his hands into fists. Lookin' for trouble. Guy looks like a Hell's Angels refugee, like a sixties leftover, except, of course, for the "Friends of Humanity" shirt he's wearin'.

There's another guy comin' behind him, could be his twin. Bigot number two has the same clothes, the same ponytail . . .

No, check that. Bigot number two is a girl.

I'm about to pop my claws and move the riffraff aside when I realize they're just what we're lookin' for.

"Kinetic energy," I say, lookin' at Freddie.

"Yeah."

"I got an idea."

Bigot number one steps in between us. "Hey, mutie, didn't you hear me before?"

"I heard you," Freddy says.

"Good. Now, hear this." The guy pokes his finger at Freddy's chest. "You're not wanted here."

"Hey, ugly."

I tap Bigot number one on the shoulder. Takes him a second to realize someone's talkin' to him. Takes him another second to refocus his attention and turn around.

"You want somethin', short stuff?" he asks.

"Short stuff." Bigot number two—his girl, I assume—laughs. "That's a good one."

I smile. "Yeah, I want somethin'. Kinetic energy."

He frowns.

"I'll spell it for you." I grab his right arm with both of mine, lean back, and start swingin' him around me in a circle.

"Hey!" he yells. "What the—"

"K," I say, beginning to spin him. "I. N. E."

His girl starts toward us. I step sideways and slam him into her. She goes flyin'.

"You're a dead man!" he yells.

"T," I say. "I. C."

He yells somethin' else. I can't make heads or tails of it. I just keep whippin' him around, turnin' faster and faster.

Freddy's smilin'.

"Tell me when," I yell.

The security guard—Valdez—is frowning. "Take it easy, man, this is—"

"Now!" Freddy yells, and I take a couple of steps forward and swing bigot number one right into him, as if I'm swingin' a bat. They come together with a bone-shattering crunch. Freddy takes off into the sky, like a rocket comin' off the launchin' pad.

The bigot's out cold; he drops to the ground.

Freddy's power's a lot like Juggernaut's, I realize. With a little Rogue mixed in. He absorbs kinetic energy, yes, but it also seems he absorbs other kinds of energy, too. This guy looks completely drained.

We'll leave figurin' out exactly what's goin' on for another day, though.

High overhead, Freddy slams into the rock wall and bounces off, twisting his body in midair so he's now falling straight toward us.

"Incoming!" he yells.

I'm not quite sure what to do, so I just stand there, and the next thing I know, something slams into the ground next to me, a hand grabs me, and I grab, too, and hold on. Then me and Freddy are flying again, up past the door I came out of, up the sheer face of the rock, past a couple more of those same kinds of metal doors, past a bunch of pipes where the water's goin' to flow out of in a few minutes, past some artificial rocks and artificial plants, and then we clear the face of the rock, and we're lookin' down at the top of it.

It's a lot smaller up top than at the bottom.

It's a square spot about ten feet around on either edge.

"Drop me!" I yell, and Freddy frowns but does as he's told. As I fall, he's yellin' somethin' about cops, and I give him a thumbs up, whatever, I got more pressing things to worry about, as I land on top of the rock and roll once, twice, and grab hold with my hands, but they slide off the rock. It's damp, and it's not really rock, of course, it's cement, and I skitter right to the edge, one leg slides over, and the other follows, and the rest of me's about to go, too, and right then, I realize I'm an idiot.

I pop my claws and dig 'em in, and I stop falling.

I drag myself back up onto the roof and stand.

I see right away why I was about to fall: the whole top of the rock's on a slant. No surprise there; the water needs a place to fall from. It also needs a place to come out of. I turn and see that, four pipes about a foot thick, peerin' out over the edge of the roof.

I take a couple of quick steps in that direction; lean out over those pipes. They're attached with big, thick metal brackets to the back of the structure; the whole back of the rock, in fact, is coated with pipes. They branch off at all different heights, in all different directions. There's at least a couple dozen of 'em. I had in mind rippin' out a half-dozen, figurin' that might gum up the works, but I can see I'm gonna have to back-track to the source itself.

I look down and see a way to do that, too. A ladder, fastened right alongside the pipes. Good thing I don't have a fear of heights.

I take a step over the edge and pause for a second.

I hear something. Machinery. Close by.

I look up, and a ski mobile appears over the roof of the hotel. A second follows, and then a third and a fourth. Of course, they can't be ski mobiles, not five hundred feet off the ground. What they are is little jet-propelled scooters.

They hover in the air for a second, silhouetted against the neon haze, and head straight toward me.

There's one guy on each of 'em. A guy in a black jumpsuit.

As they close, they start shooting. Guns built into the throttles of the scooters. Nice equipment, if you can afford it, and black ops can afford just about anything.

I'm dead if I don't move, so I go the only way I can, over the back edge of the rock, headfirst, reaching out for the ladder as I fall. I miss with my hands; the claws dig into the cement and slow me down. Skin peels off the backs of my forearms, off the backs of my wrists.

I grab a rung, and I flip end over end, my butt slamming into the cement with a crack that tells me I broke a bone.

I can't hold on.

I keep fallin'.

I reach out again, this time with both hands, and slap at one rung with my right and the next with my left, and then again with my right, and this time I grab metal and hold on.

The impact nearly rips my arm off. Makes me cry out in pain.

I hang there a second, tryin' to get my bearings. Tryin' to let my healin' factor do its thing.

I get to the count of three before a spotlight cuts

through the dull neon haze around me. I blink, and behind that spotlight, the outline of a scooter appears.

A split-second later, three other spotlights target me, too.

Here they come again.

I hug the rock. They come diving down in formation, two at a time, firing quick, short bursts. The scooter on my left comes so close I can see the grin on the driver's face. So close I can see his little blond goatee.

Osborne.

He shoots past, breakin' off the attack. I wonder why they're takin' it easy on me, and then I remember. The pipes. One thing in my favor, at least. They don't want to do anything to jeopardize the virus's release.

There's about twenty feet of clearance between the back of the rock and the hotel behind it. I see they've arranged the windows so nobody gets a clear view of the plumbing behind the fabulous hidden waterfalls. Which means nobody has a clear view of what's happenin' now.

". . . minus eighteen oh-four . . . T minus . . ."

The scooters come at me again, changin' their angle of attack, comin' right at me, instead of down from above.

That's a mistake.

They'll have to use the clearance space behind the rock to pass, which means they have to attack one at a time. One on one . . . those kinds of odds I can handle, even without a flying machine.

I push away from the ladder, get as close to the pipes as I can. As close to the rock face as I can, too.

And here comes Osborne.

Bullets rip up the concrete next to me. I dig in next to the pipe and calculate. Distances, speed, strength . . .

A bullet skins the back of my right hand. I cry out in pain. It feels as if someone took a potato peeler to my flesh.

Osborne rockets past, still grinnin'.

I focus on scooter number two, already comin' at me. The guy on it's not flyin' as fast as Osborne, not shootin' as accurately as him either. Huggin' the back wall of the hotel, keepin' his distance from me and the rock and the pipes.

No chance, I decide as he flies past.

Scooter number three's a different story altogether.

He comes in strong. Faster than Osborne even, which makes the timing tricky, but his aim's terrible, so that gives me my chance. I stay balanced on the ladder; I stay focused on the scooter, not the guy.

It passes, and I jump.

My timing's good, and my aim's good enough. I planned to knock the guy out of his seat; instead, I land right on that seat, a big, thick, wide cushion right behind him. Slams the wind out of me, slams the whole scooter sideways. The guy's got all he can do to keep it from crashing into the hotel. We accelerate up and out from behind the building. I jab my claws into that seat and hang on for dear life.

I hear a huge crash behind me.

I turn my head in time to see an explosion, scooter number four behind us bouncing off the back of the big rock and bursting into flames, red and orange against the dull gray of the big tower.

That's what you get for tailgating, I think, and then somethin' hard as a rock catches me at the base of the neck—the driver's elbow, I realize—and I see stars. At the same instant, the scooter pitches hard right, and I lose my grip with one hand.

And all of a sudden, I'm danglin' out in space, five hundred feet off the ground.

I glance up and see the guy drivin' the scooter lookin' over his shoulder at me. Smilin'. He starts to lean right again.

I never fall for the same trick twice.

As the scooter pitches, I swing with it and then quickly back, like a pendulum.

I use the momentum to lunge up at the driver with my free hand and grab hold of his collar.

His face changes.

I yank hard, and he comes off the scooter and goes tumblin' past me, screamin' as he falls.

The scooter goes into a dive. I manage to pull myself up into the seat and grab the controls. Not hard to get the hang of it; it is kind of like a ski mobile. Or a motorcycle. Brake, throttle, clutch, gearshift, a little black lever mounted on the left handlebar that turns out to control the gun . . .

And now I got a scooter of my own.

Just in time.

Here come Osborne and his comrade-in-arms. He's on my right, scooter number two on the left. They're comin' in pincer formation, at a sharp enough angle that I can only concentrate on one of 'em at a time.

I focus my fire on Osborne; based on past performance, he's the only one who can hit the broad side of a barn. Even while I'm emptying my guns at him, though, I'm throttling hard toward the guy in scooter number two. As I suspected, he's not smart enough—trained well enough—to take advantage of the free shot I'm givin' him. He fires in short bursts, tryin' to aim every bullet. Which ain't gonna work at all, 'cause I keep the scooter pitchin' from side to side as I come, varying the target I present to him and his guns.

My little acrobatics don't fool Osborne, though. He stays with me, moves with me, matching me shot for shot, move for move. Movin' closer.

My plan was to break off and take down scooter number two as Osborne flew past. That's not gonna work now; gonna have to improvise.

I lean to my left, hard, and slam the throttle to full power, goin' into a steep sideways dive, a crazy angle dive, forty-five degrees, maybe even steeper. It takes me right across scooter number two's flight path and then right under him.

I get a split-second look at his face as I shoot toward him. He's just a kid. Terrified. For a second, I feel sorry for him.

Then I think about what happened on the mountain, and the second passes.

I bank hard, come up behind him, and give him both barrels.

Exit scooter number two, in a ball of fire that the people down on the ground probably think is the start of the big fireworks show.

I realize the countdown in my head is gone. Somewhere along the way here, I've lost the earpiece I picked up from those guys in the elevator. I got a pretty good internal clock, though. A pretty good sense of time.

I might have ten minutes left to stop Wilson. Maybe.

But first, of course . . .

Osborne.

The spotlight from his machine finds me just as the guy on scooter number two buys it. He squeezes off a couple of rounds and misses. I bank right, and he flies past.

We circle around again and come straight at each other.

I lean into the machine like Steve McQueen on a Harley. I picture him doin' the same.

We're en route to a midair head-on collision. Unless one of us blinks.

A game of chicken. It's a perfect way to end things between us.

Except, of course, I can't do it.

Mutually assisted suicide might work for him but not for me. There's still the little matter of the virus to deal with.

I gotta do what it is I do best: survive.

We're two hundred feet apart. A hundred. Fifty.

I see the whites of his eyes.

At the last second, I jog left, stick out my right arm to clothesline him.

He, unfortunately, does exactly the same thing.

Our hands slap together as we fly past.

We come around again.

I've got the Paradise hotel tower and the rock behind me; he's got the Vegas Strip behind him, the sky lit up by a dozen different shades of red and orange and yellow neon billboards that glint off the metal sidewalls of his scooter.

I got an idea.

He comes straight for me again, guns blazing, and I make a show of doin' the same, as if we're gonna repeat our little dance of a few seconds ago.

Except, as my scooter jets forward, my guns sputter and then stop firing entirely. As if I've run out of ammo.

I break off my approach and dive; Osborne follows me down.

I swoop left, and then right, and he sticks to me like glue.

I can't lose him. I can't even maintain the separation between us; he moves closer with each maneuver I try. I flatten out and climb again. I get a glimpse of the crowd as I shoot past; the little plaza is no less full of people, but a lot of 'em are cops now. Movin' people back from the rock, away from the debris fallin' down from on high. I wonder, for a second, if the police presence means they'll postpone the fireworks and the waterfall display, and then I realize it doesn't matter what they do officially, Wilson'll make sure the falls flow on schedule, even if no one's expecting them to. I still have to handle him.

If I can get out of this alive.

Osborne's bullets ping off the back of my machine. I risk a glance back and see he's gained even more ground. He's twenty feet behind me, comin' as fast as he can, which is just a tad faster than I can fly. He's had more training on these machines, of course; it looks as if he's just a flat-out better pilot. I'm sure that's what he's thinking. He's probably right.

It's not what's gonna decide things between us, though.

We're zoomin' full speed toward the rock. I cut hard left, and then right, into the narrow passage between the rock and the hotel. I brake hard; he goes flying past. Not a big deal, of course, because he knows I got no bullets left.

Of course, what I know is that I haven't actually been squeezin' the trigger for about five minutes now, that I only pretended to run out of ammo to make him careless. And careless is what he just was.

And careless is goin' to cost him.

I take careful aim and fire. My target isn't Osborne, it's the engine pushin' him forward.

The bullets hit. His scooter wobbles, just a little, but in such a tight space, a little wobble is plenty dangerous.

He strains to hold the machine under control; he can't.

It glances off the back of the rock and then starts spinning. Osborne raises his arms in front of his face.

Fat lotta good that does him.

The machine slams head-on into the hotel wall; he slams into it, too. The scooter explodes. Osborne . . .

Bad things happen to him, too, though I don't see exactly what.

I use my imagination to fill in the blanks.

It's finished between us now, just like it was back on Kawagebo.

Which means, of course, that it might not be finished at all.

Osborne's ability to rise from the dead isn't my main concern right now, though. The virus is. By my internal clock, it's T minus ten minutes or so, tops.

I take the scooter down the back of the rock, keepin' the headlights focused on the ladder. A couple hundred feet down, I spot what I'm lookin' for, another one of those metal doors with the metal wheel on it. A way back into the rock.

I set the scooter to hover and step off onto the ladder. I spin the wheel, open the door, and step inside.

I pull the door shut behind me and turn around.

There's a gun sticking in my face.

There's a cop on the other end of it.

"Gotcha," he says.

24

THERE'S A SECOND COP BEHIND HIM, HOLDIN' A gun on me as well.

"Come on, buddy. Hands up," the first one says.

I raise 'em, 'cause what else can I do? Last thing I want is to go up against the law again. I got one big black mark on my record here already.

But I'll do it if I have to. This guy's health and my reputation don't even take a close second to what's about to happen.

"Don't even think it," the cop says, somehow readin' my mind, or maybe my body language.

But I am thinkin' about it. In fact, I know exactly how I'm goin' to get that gun out of his hands and get on my way, and I'm about to demonstrate the results of my thinking to him when I hear footsteps. More than one set of 'em, on the run, heading this way.

I tense, ready to revise my thinkin' to accommodate the newcomers.

Freddy and Valdez come whippin' around the corner.

"Logan," Freddy says.

"Valdez," the cop with the gun says.

"What are you doin'?" Valdez asks. "He's with us."

The cop frowns. "He's got the black jumpsuit."

"Borrowed goods," I reply. "Not my size, if you notice."

I make a show of pinchin' the loose material around my gut.

The cop lowers his weapon.

I turn to Freddy. "Fill me in. What's happening? Make it quick."

He gives me the thirty-second rundown.

Valdez indeed called the cops. She's an ex-cop herself, turns out. They listened, especially when Osborne's little aerial show started up above the rock. They've closed off the access drive to the Paradise. They've closed off the plaza in front of the hidden waterfalls, too.

But the show itself is still happening.

Fireworks at midnight exactly, followed by the inaugural valve-turning ceremony at the waterfalls. Nobody seems quite sure how to stop it.

The cops, it seems, aren't even sure it should be stopped.

"So, let me get this straight," the guy who had the

gun on me is saying. "There's, like, DNA in your body, but DNA is what made your body?"

I ignore him.

"Valve-turning ceremony," Freddy says. "What if they can't turn the valves? There's gotta be a shut-off some place in the building here—"

Osborne's words come back to me then. A problem with the valves. Corridor J-14.

The little room with the green LEDs on the wall.

"I know where it is," I say. "Let's go."

"Wait a minute," Valdez says. "Shuttin' off the valves—don't we need more of a plan than that?"

I stop and think for a second.

Summers was always big on plans, on makin' sure we knew just what everybody on the team was gonna do before we went into action. Scriptin' out every eventuality and then executing.

Not my forte.

"More of a plan?" I shake my head. "We find 'em. We stop 'em. What else is there?"

Freddy and Valdez look at each other, then back at me, and both nod.

"All right," they say.

"All right," the cops say.

I smile.

We move.

One hundred twenty-six seconds on—Valdez has a serious wristwatch, with a timer—we're back in the subbasement. Up ahead is corridor J. We're in the branching tunnel I turned down to reach the access-way.

I'm in the lead, followed by Valdez, then Freddy, then the two cops, who are named Kennedy and Blood. Young guys, foot patrol guys, a little bit nervous, maybe just a little bit trigger-happy, which is why I put 'em on the back.

I hear voices ahead.

I put a finger to my lips and walk a fraction slower, a fraction higher up on my toes.

I reach the intersection and peer around the corner.

I curse under my breath.

There's a dozen guys, at least, armed and alert, stationed in the corridor in front of the little room with the green LEDs. The only plus in the situation I can see is that they're all bunched up around the entrance. Through a grenade in the middle of 'em, we'd get every single one. Except, of course, we don't have a grenade.

Which is when it hits me—what we do have to throw.

I turn around and smile at Freddy.

"What?" he whispers.

I open my mouth to explain what I want him to do and then realize that lengthy explanations aren't necessary.

"Make like a bowling ball," I tell him.

"Huh?"

I grab his arm.

I swing him like I swung bigot number one a few minutes back, only there's a lot less room in the corridor than there was in the plaza, so I have to hold him not by the wrists but by the upper arms, and even then, I just barely miss clippin' his feet on the corridor wall in the first circuit I make.

I see the cops lookin' at me as if I've lost my mind.

Valdez looks worried.

Freddy's wide-eyed.

"Dude," he manages. "I hope you know what you're doin'."

"So do I," I say, and take a step forward, and let go.

My aim, once again, is not the greatest.

First thing that happens, Freddy slams into the ceiling. Bounces off that and hits the floor, screaming the whole time. It sounds more like a scream of panic than like something planned, but it freezes the jumpsuits at the end of the corridor anyway, at least for a second, which is long enough for him to bounce off the floor and then the ceiling again, picking up speed, and now he's movin' too fast for them to do anything about anyway.

One guy sees what's about to happen and tries to step back. He trips over the guy behind him and falls, and that starts all of 'em stumbling.

And then Freddy hits, and the stumbling turns into outright tumbling, jumpsuits floppin' on top of one another, and half the guys had their backs turned, don't even know what hit 'em.

And no one's payin' the slightest bit of attention to me, runnin' full steam down the corridor right toward 'em.

That's just fine. I do the hitting I need to do to clear my path, and then I'm in the room.

Wilson's not there, but two guys in lab coats are.

One's standin' over by the LEDs on the wall, the four columns, which are all now completely green. There's a wall panel folded out underneath them, revealing four big buttons, also lit up in green.

And underneath those buttons, standin' up on the floor, there's four metal canisters, about the size of fire extinguishers. Blue, with white writing on the side.

XM-35.

Thin metal tubing connects valves on the top of the canisters to little valves in the wall.

"T minus one oh six." The other guy with the lab coat on is wearing a headset mic. Talkin' into it. "One oh . . ." His voice trails off as he sees me.

I pop my claws and walk up to the guy next to the LED readouts.

"You can't stop it." He sneers.

I poke my claws a half-inch into his shoulder. He screams.

I pull 'em out and jab right between his legs, cutting cloth, not skin.

"You stop it, then," I say. "I'll count three. One. Two—"

He punches the four buttons underneath the LED columns. They turn orange.

"Seal the canisters," I tell him.

He does.

"Good work." I crack him across the jaw, and he goes down.

The other lab coat makes a break for the door. Valdez meets him halfway across the room and gives him a love tap of her own.

He goes down, too. I pick up the headset.

"T minus forever," I say, and snap it in two.

We go out into the hall.

The cops have the situation under control. My guess, they moved in with weapons drawn and radios live. Nobody likes shooting at law enforcement, especially when the situation appears to be goin' south.

I push past the jumpsuits and on down the corridor.

There's still a little bit of unfinished business to attend to.

I enter the big room from above, from up on the gangway, and there's Wilson.

He's at the far end of the room, runnin' for the exit, holdin' tight to somethin'. Another one of the XM canisters.

He's ten feet from the door when I drop down from the gangway in front of him.

"Danny boy," I say, takin' a step forward. "The pipes, the pipes are callin'."

He drops the canister, draws a gun, and fires.

Give the guy credit, he might be a desk jockey, but he's got the cojones for fieldwork, too. Back in the day, I suspect, he even did his share. Now, though . . .

He's old. He's fat. And he's slow.

I already got hold of his wrist by the time he squeezes the trigger. The bullet flies up in the air and richochets around harmlessly.

I twist his arm up behind him and march him forward.

"One million," he says. "Into a Swiss bank account we'll set up for you, you'll be the only one with a password—"

I twist harder and push him out the door in front of me, out into the tunnel.

"Two million. Cash. Small bills, untraceable—"

"Shut up, or I break it." I yank the arm higher, to show him I mean business.

He doesn't say another word, not when we get onto the elevator, not when we get off. Not until I march him out of the tunnels and into the Paradise's little shopping mall. Then his curiosity gets the better of his caution.

"Where are you taking me?" he asks.

"Wait and see."

He decides he doesn't want to.

"Help!" he shouts. "Help! Police!"

Despite the fact that it's after midnight, despite the cops swarming around the front of the building, the mall is still full of would-be shoppers. The kids are gone now, of course, but there's plenty of grown-ups still loose in playland, and the stores—all of them—are still open, too. Now more than ever, it seems to me, Vegas never sleeps.

Wilson's still shouting for the cops. Two big guys come out of a Sports Authority store and move to cut me off.

"Hey, buddy," one says. "What's the problem here?"

I pop the claws on my free hand and give 'em my nastiest smile.

"No problem," I say. "None at all."

The guys back off; we keep movin'.

Wilson keeps screamin', till I flick away the hair from the front of his face with one of my claws.

"Next time, it's a scar," I say.

He shuts up.

We move down the main corridor, toward the atrium. Toward the banner hanging above the stage there and the crowd gathered around to see the show.

Toward the tigers.

They're in the middle of their act, Herman and his animal friends. He's got one of the bigger ones out; it's pacing around the stage, followin' him around. One of the girls with purple shorts is on the stage, too. My old friend the redhead.

Whatever they're doin', the audience is really enjoying it. Oohing and ahing. I hate to interrupt the show when it's going so well, I really do.

But I made myself a promise.

I force my way forward through the crowd, pushin' Wilson in front of me.

He spots the tigers and starts to struggle.

"Listen," he says. "You're making a big mistake. If anything happens to me—"

I yank his arm so hard I hear somethin' tear inside.

He screams.

People notice us for the first time; a murmur makes its way through the crowd.

Heiling stops his spiel and frowns.

I push through the last of the crowd and up onto the stage.

The redhead moves to cut me off.

"Sir," she says, "you can't be up . . . hey. You're the animal control guy."

"That's right," I say, pushing past her. I see where I want to go now. The back of the stage. The tiger cages.

Wilson sees them, too.

"Oh, no," he says. "Please."

Heiling steps in front of me.

"You again." He keeps his voice low, but even without the volume, he manages to sound plenty angry. "You cannot be up here now. I am in the middle of a performance. You will have to—"

I push him aside, too. I push aside the two assistants who take his place, two big muscle-bound guys in purple tights.

And then I'm at the cages, and Wilson's on his knees, gasping, crying.

I push his head forward, right up against the bars. My plan is a simple one.

Put him in the cage with the tiger, let the tiger chow down. Poetic justice, I think.

I reach for the latch that holds the cage door shut.

The tiger inside moves forward and looks up at me quizzically.

I meet its gaze.

There's nothing there at all.

I'm expectin' to see intelligence. I'm expectin' to see hunger, cruelty, like I saw in the eyes of Torzay and those other tigers up on the mountain. Instead, all I see is a blank stare.

It's an animal. No more, no less. And I, unfortunately . . .

"You can't do this," Wilson says. "You can't."

I sigh.

Unfortunately, he's right.

When I exit the mall, the arrests are in full swing. Black jumpsuits bein' hauled away by blue uniforms. A police copter's landing in the middle of the plaza. A button-down guy in a suit and tie is the second one out of the chopper. All eyes go to him right away; I go to him, too, figuring he's gotta be somebody pretty high up to merit all that attention. I hand over Wilson into his care, make sure he knows to round up all five canisters of the XM stuff, and step back out of the way to let them do their job.

I spot Freddy and Valdez talkin' to a couple of guys in bad suits; detectives, no doubt, tryin' to get a feel for what just went on. No need to interrupt that scene.

I feel a tug on my sleeve and turn.

I'm starin' at two teenage kids, one boy, one girl.

They're wearing X-Men T-shirts.

"Wolverine," the boy says. "You did it, man. You stopped 'em."

I smile.

The boy wants me to write in his autograph book. I sign him a nice note.

The girl wants me to write across her chest. I defer on that one.

They leave, and I turn to go myself . . .

And a gust of wind blows through the plaza. Blows a flyer through the air straight toward me.

I grab it as it passes. It's one I haven't seen before; not Heiling's, just a shill for the fireworks display and, of course, the waterfall. "YOU'VE NEVER SEEN THE LIKE BEFORE" the headline shouts.

And I hope I never will.

The wind blows again, and I realize, all at once, it's not a natural wind. It's comin' from directly above me.

I look up and see a helicopter.

This one is different from the police chopper that came in before—bigger, more heavily armored. More

obvious weaponry. Way louder engines, which all at
once go whisper-quiet as it lands in the middle of the
plaza in front of the waterfall.

A half-dozen soldiers pour out, but these guys aren't
U.S. Army, they ain't special ops, they ain't Marines;
they don't belong to any nationality, in fact. I recognize
their uniforms right away.

These guys are SHIELD troops. SHIELD, as in
Supreme Headquarters International Intelligence
Law-Enforcement Division. Accent on the International; they ain't answerable to any single government,
certainly not the U.S. one, though, as it happens, the
head honcho is as American as they come.

He hops out now, right behind his guys, catches sight
of me, and unleashes a string of curse words that would
make a sea captain look down and shuffle his feet.

I can't help but smile.

"Nick Fury. About time you got here."

Fury's still cursin', but behind his anger, I can see a
smile tryin' to break through, too.

"Logan, what the hell have you done now?" he
shouts out as he heads toward me, chompin' on the
cigar as he comes.

He stops five feet short of me, hands on hips, and
waits for an answer.

"You wouldn't happen to have another one of those,
wouldja?" I ask, nodding toward the cigar.

He pulls one out of his pocket and tosses it to me.
"Talk," he says.

"Relax. It's done." I take a light from him and a puff on the cigar.

"What? What's done? Tell me, so I can tell the governor, who can explain it to the National Guard, who can—"

I interrupt and give him the five-minute version. As I talk, I see the SHIELD troops takin' Wilson onto the copter. The dolly with the metal suitcase—and, I presume, the five canisters—follows.

I finish my story. When I'm done, Fury shakes his head.

"Wilson," he says. "Never heard of him. And that general with him, the American one?"

"That name I never got."

"Yeah. You probably never will, too." He shakes his head. "I think you're right. Sounds like black ops to me."

"Heads oughtta roll for this."

"They should. But they won't. They never do."

He sees the look on my face, then, and frowns. "What?"

"I got a personal interest this time."

"You don't say. Well, then . . ."

He pulls something—a device about the size and shape of a pack of cards—out of his back pocket and starts punchin' all sorts of keys on it.

"What's that?"

"My new favorite gizmo. Give me a minute here."

I give him two. It's a good cigar.

At last, he stops punchin' keys and looks up.

"General Leland Crane."

"Who?"

He holds up the device so I can see the front of it, which is a little TV screen. There's a guy's picture on it.

"That's him, all right."

"He's based in D.C. Assigned to—"

"Let me guess. The Bureau of Mutant Affairs."

"Bingo."

"So this is their work?"

"Looks like it. Though it apparently originated with one of your guys."

"What?"

"The genesis for the project is out of Canada. Someone from CIC approached Washington with the basic idea."

"Someone from Canada? You mean Wilson."

"No. Not Wilson."

"Then who?"

"You oughtta know," he says, and then he says the name, but even before he speaks, I realize he's right.

I do know.

I guess part of me's known all along.

25

TEN YEARS AGO.

A cold, wet fall day in Fort MacMurray, Alberta. I'm squeezed into a suit that belongs to a friend of Jimmy Hudson's, standin' behind Jimmy and Heather in a line of mourners, waitin' to pay our respects to Ronnie's parents. Her adoptive parents, a man and a woman who look to be cut out of the same timber that built the white-frame church behind us. Hard folks, sinew and bone, but from what I remember Ronnie tellin' me about them . . .

They loved her.

No matter what she was, what she did, they loved her.

Jimmy and Heather shuffle forward. Heather introduces herself to them, Jimmy hangin' back, and I realize it's gonna be my turn next, and I've never been good at this stuff, no matter how many times I gotta

do it, which is gettin' to be too many, and so I start
lookin' around, not like I'm gonna turn and bolt, but
just so I don't have to think about what I'm doin' here
too hard . . .

And my eye falls on a little rise a few hundred
yards down the road the church is on—the entrance
to the cemetery, I know, because we passed it on the
drive in.

There's somebody standin' there, lookin' back at me.

From this distance, I can't make out his face, but I
know who it is anyway.

J.C.

We were all wondering where he was during the
service; we saw an older man toward the back of the
church who looked a lot like him, could've been his father, I suppose—J.C. grew up here, too, after all—but
we had no way of knowing, so nobody said anything.

I slip out of the line and make my way up the hill.

I stand beside him for a minute. He doesn't say a
word. Doesn't even move or acknowledge my presence in any way.

"You all right?" I ask.

Nothing.

"We were worried about you. Heather tried the
apartment—"

"I was at the lab," he says. "I had work to do."

"Work?"

"Yes. Very important work. I should be there now,
in fact."

"Yeah, well . . . it's good you came. Her parents . . . I'm sure they'll appreciate it."

"Her parents." He practically spits the words out. I get a sudden inkling of why he didn't come to the church.

I wait for him to say more, but he doesn't.

I clear my throat. "I guess I'm gonna go back. We can talk later, if you want."

He doesn't react. Doesn't move at all.

I turn away and start heading back down the hill.

"Logan!"

I turn back, and for the first time, J.C. looks up at me.

His eyes are bloodshot. He's got deep, dark circles under both of 'em. He looks as if he hasn't slept in days.

He looks like a crazy person.

"She's not dead, you know."

I don't quite know how to take that.

"Yeah," I say finally. "I guess you're right. As long as we remember her, she's not dead."

He smiles then, a crazy person's smile.

"That's not what I mean at all," he says.

This time, I take it slow. No stealin' motorcycles, no dodgin' border cops, no rush whatsoever.

I pick up my own bike at the base of Tickapoo Mountain, on the northern edge of the DNR, right where I left it a couple of months back. Fury's straightened out the mess with the local cops and the Army so that I can travel without fear of bein' stopped.

He's also promised not to rat me out to Xavier and the others back in Westchester.

"It's not like I talk to 'em a lot anyway," he tells me, in a way that makes me think there's somethin' else goin' on between him and them, some other reason he might not be all that anxious to fill 'em in on my whereabouts and what sorts of things I've been up to. I'm almost curious enough to press him for answers, but then I decide that'd be openin' up a whole 'nother can of worms, and I got my own can that needs closin', so to speak, before I tackle any others.

A week after the scene at the Paradise, I pull into Fort Mac. Take the loop around town and out into the woods. Park my bike at the head of the trail and walk on in.

There's a guy standin' in front of the house, arms folded across his chest.

Big guy. Biceps like bowlin' balls stickin' out from his shirt. Probably goes about 250 pounds. His hair is blond and longish in the back, reddish-blond, shading to gray.

"That's far enough," he says. "Wolverine."

I look him in the eye. "You know who I am, then."

"That's right."

"So, what am I supposed to call you?"

"Osborne'll do fine."

"Not O'Connell?"

"Nope." He shakes his head.

"Not Joubert—"

"I'm Osborne," he says. "The real deal. The template."

Template's a good word for him, all right. I can see a little bit of the others—Osborne from the Ark, O'Connell from Kawagebo—in him. Shadows, cast by the original.

Clones, to use the scientifically accurate term.

"So, how does it feel to have so many others like you floatin' around in the world?"

He grins. "Profitable."

"Yeah. I bet. Now, if you don't mind . . . I got business with your boss."

I take another step forward.

He does, too. We stand chest to chest.

"Actually," he says, "I do mind."

"I was hopin' you'd say that."

I pop my claws.

He takes a step forward and, with one hand, rolls up the sleeve over his opposite wrist.

He's wearing a metal bracelet, with what looks like three different-color jewels set into the band. He presses the middle one, and all at once, energy crackles all around him. Looks like electricity.

Shades of Maxwell Dillon.

"Amazing what money can buy these days," he says.

I smile and step forward, too.

"Let's check the workmanship, shall we?"

We're about to get it on when the front door swings open. J.C. steps out.

"That won't be necessary," he says.

"You told me to keep him out," Osborne says.

"I changed my mind. He can come in. As long as he promises to behave."

I shake my head. "I'm not promisin' you anything."

J.C. shrugs. "All right, then. Both of you."

He turns his back and heads inside.

Osborne powers down.

I retract my claws and step to the door.

Osborne holds it open for me. "After you," he says.

Inside, we turn right. We go through the door that was closed before and into part of the house I haven't seen. Into a living room with a long brown leather couch, two brown leather chairs, a long, low glass coffee table.

Looks as if people actually live in this part of the house. I wonder who, for a second.

And I smell the air. That same perfume I smelled last time I was here.

"Have a seat," J.C. says, heading toward a set of wooden cabinets along the wall. "Something to drink?"

He pulls out an ice bucket, drops a couple of cubes into a glass. Holds it out to me, waitin' for my reply.

"You let Wilson drink from that glass, too?" I ask. His face darkens.

"'Cause if that's the case, I pass."

J.C. shrugs and pours amber liquid from a cut glass bottle.

"One thing you should know about Wilson and me," he says, takin' a sip from that glass. "We were business partners. That's all. We're not partners any longer."

"Yeah. He's in jail."

"Where he belongs. He's a thief."

"Is that right?"

"That's right. He stole my work."

"Define *work* for me."

J.C. smiles. "My protocol for replicative experiential processes."

"Jesus." I shake my head. "Can't you guys talk English once in a while?"

Osborne's standing behind the couch. He laughs and crosses behind J.C. to pour himself a drink.

"You know what I'm talking about," J.C. says.

"Why don't you fill in all the blanks? Just to make sure I get the picture."

"All right." J.C. swirls the ice in his drink. He walks to the far wall of the room and touches a panel there.

The wall turns from a mottled tan paint to transparent glass, giving us a view of the forest beyond.

"After Niagara, Wilson developed an interest in my work. He financed it. He provided me money and certain raw materials I might otherwise have had trouble acquiring."

J.C. glances over at Osborne, and it suddenly occurs to me how what should have been a fifteen-year prison sentence lasted only twenty-four months.

"Like Osborne here?"

"Osborne came later," J.C. says. "After I was comfortable with the basic protocol."

"After he played around with the chimps for a while," Osborne supplies. "And the tigers."

"And this is in Vegas?" I ask.

"Tibet," J.C. says. "Wilson felt a more remote location would serve us better."

"And provide him deniability, if anything went wrong," I add.

J.C. nods. "As the experiments continued, others became interested as well. Washington, for example. The Americans purchased a stake in my work and provided the key to the next breakthrough. A machine that enabled me to accelerate the replicative process."

"The genetic accelerator."

"That's right." J.C. smiles. "You've always been smarter than you looked, Logan."

"So, what happened? Why the split between you and Wilson?"

"Our interests were never entirely congruent. Replicating cell structure was always my primary focus. In order to form a complete understanding of how those structures evolved, though, I needed to develop a comprehensive understanding of evolution itself."

I nod. I'm beginning to get the picture. "And they were more interested in that."

J.C. nods. "In how to stop it. Particularly after Avalon."

He falls silent and stares out the back window.

"They wanted me to continue my work along lines I wasn't comfortable with. When I refused . . . they continued without me. Stole my work and—"

"That's not what Nick Fury says."

He looks up at me. "What?"

"Fury says the idea originated with you."

"He's lying."

"Is that so?"

"That's so. They stole my work, Logan," he repeats. "Along with one of my assistants—"

"Brinklow."

He nods. "Brinklow, yes. They took him, and they took some of my test subjects, and . . ." He shrugs. "Well. You know the rest."

"I get the picture," I say. "Almost."

"Oh? What part don't you understand?"

He turns his back on me as he asks the question, turns casually to the window. As if he has no idea what I'm about to say.

"The part about Ronnie," I say. "Tell me about that."

He takes a sip of his drink and stands quietly.

I start countin' in my head then, one, two, three, on the way to ten, which is when I'm gonna pick up Osborne and beat J.C. over the head with him.

When I reach six, he speaks.

"Four days after she jumped, I found the body," J.C. says quietly. "She was . . ."

I wait another five. "She was what?"

He sighs heavily. "There was nothing I could do."

"Of course there was nothing you could do. She was dead."

"No, I mean . . . I couldn't . . . I had grown certain cellular structures that I'd thought about implanting, but the tissue decay . . . it was no use. I had to begin at the beginning, an undifferentiated sex cell, and so—"

"That's when you went to Wilson. He didn't go to you, did he? You went to him." I can picture that scene in my head. Wilson, dismissive at first, then his beady little eyes lighting up as he realizes the implications of what J.C.'s telling him. The potential applications of the protocol. Not just cloning but actual duplication. Find someone valuable—a one-of-a-kind soldier, say, or a Super Hero, or a politician—and make another. An identical twin, with the same personality, knowledge, and capabilities.

J.C. doesn't bother denyin' it.

"Wilson gave me what I needed. Money. A place to work, the equipment . . . a way for Ronnie to live again."

I shake my head. "The woman I met wasn't Ronnie."

"Admitttedly." J.C. nods. "There were some flaws in the early replicative process."

I frown. "Were?"

"Were." He nods and then turns toward a door at the far end of the room.

"Cherie?" he calls out.

The door opens.

A woman steps hesitantly into the room.

Long dark hair. Pale ivory skin. Deep blue eyes.

She sees me, and a smile as bright as the noonday sun lights up her face.

"Logan. My God, Logan."

She runs to me, and before I can do anything, say anything, she's got her arms wrapped around me tight and is squeezing for all she's worth.

"I never thought I'd see you again," she says.

I don't know what to say.

"Is something the matter?" She turns to J.C. "I'm sorry—did I do something wrong?"

Everything she is—everything they are together—is in that question. Her voice, her manner, their relationship . . .

Replicative experiential processes, my ass.

"Everything is fine, *cherie,*" J.C. says. "Please leave us for a moment."

She nods and turns to me again. "Logan. I will see you soon. We will talk again, yes? As we did at Burns Lake?" Her eyes twinkle as she speaks.

I wanna throw up. "Yeah," I say. "Talk."

She leaves the room, the scent of her perfume—that same perfume I smelled the first time I was here—lingering behind her.

"Is it so bad?" J.C. asks. "What I did?"

I turn and look at him. "That's not Ronnie," I say. "Any more than the woman at the Ark was Ronnie. Any more than the next clone off your assembly line is gonna be Ronnie. Get it through your head, Jean-Claude. She's gone. Ten years gone."

He shakes his head. "If you spent ten minutes with her," he says, "you'd see what I see. I know you would."

I look him in the eye, and as I do, it's as if I step back in time for a minute, as if we're in the control room at the Athabasca Sands Power Plant, me and Jimmy and Ronnie and J.C., and he's that kid, that little genius who's angry at the whole world for callin' him a freak, who wants to put up a wall between him and everybody else and knock down anyone who tries to climb over it.

It was my responsibility then to get him out from behind that wall.

It's no less my responsibility now.

"Come with me," I say. "Come back to Montreal. Let's go see Jimmy and Heather. Let's get out in the real world, for God's sake. Let's live."

For a second, I think I'm reachin' him.

Then he looks behind me and nods, and I feel a hand on my shoulder.

Osborne's hand. "Time to go, short stuff."

I follow him to the door before turnin' around one last time.

"I'm gonna talk to Hudson," I say. "I'm gonna talk to Fury. I'm gonna make sure that every piece of scientific equipment you need you don't get. Every raw material you ask for gets shot down. I'm gonna make sure that what you're doin' here stops. That you stop."

J.C. doesn't bat an eye. "You can try," he says.

"I'll do more than try," I tell him.

And having said my piece on that subject, there's nothin' left to say.

I get back on my bike and head off to do some livin' of my own.

Acknowledgments

The X-gang, from 429 High: JK, MOB, the Hawk, EGB3, old Smitty. The new gang, from the unmarked house on State Street: Maddy-girl, monkey-boy, pointy dogs A&B, Der Schmocker.

The gang at Marvel, the gang at Pocket.

Ross and Phil, for the inspiration. Stan and Jack, Chris and John, ditto.

And Margaret. For your patience and feedback . . . and patience . . .

—Dave Stern
November 2007

PHILADELPHIA FCU
1400 ARCH STREET
PHILADELPHIA   PA

CARD: XXXXXXXXXXXX6711

DATE   TIME   TERM
05/19/08 10:41   825070

RECEIPT NUMBER   3011
 WITHDRAWAL
FROM CHECKING

AUTHORIZED AMT $80.00

TERMINAL FEE $1.50
NET AMOUNT $81.50

ACCT. BAL $345.06

PFCU
PHILADELPHIA
FEDERAL CREDIT UNION
pfcu.com | better. honest.®

Not sure what to read next?

Visit Pocket Books online at
www.simonsays.com

**Reading suggestions for
you and your reading group
New release news
Author appearances
Online chats with your favorite writers
Special offers
Order books online
And much, much more!**

urgent   5-19
TAXES

- loan   1000
- Acc   700
- Lunny   300
  MP   2000
          ─────────
           4000

Court   20.0
P A   10.0
P A   10.0
u $ I   10.0
Foksen   500
CAR   500 -
─────────────────────
Audit - 4th Floor